Zain
The Before Time

BOOK TWO

By: Barbara Pelham

Thank you to the following for their part in bringing this work to publication:

Cover design: Barbara Woster

This is **book two** in a three-book series suitable for ages 15+
Reader discretion advised:
Book one: scenes of sensuality and mild language.
Book two: scenes of sensuality, violence and language
Book three: scenes of violence and language

Contents

Dedication

To my daughters, without whom this book would never have been written. Thank you for your love and support throughout the years. I love you all dearly.

The Before Time

It is from weakness that people reach for dictators and concentrated government power. Only the strong can be free. And only the productive can be strong.

Wendell Willkie

Of One Accord

"Order must be restored in this meeting!" The loud thud reverberated across the room as the President's hand hit the mahogany table causing all those seated around it to fall silent. The air in the conference room was heavy with the scent of sweat and uncertainty, mixed with the faint remains of their catered lunch. The taste of bitter resignation lingered in the president's mouth as he drew in a determined breath, releasing it with a sigh. "Order must be restored," he repeated with less emphasis and volume, exhaustion lacing every word.

With a shake of his head, Jeffrey Saltzer, President of the New Confederated States of America, sat back down in his chair. His intense gaze swept across the room, taking in every envoy from every country represented. "There can be no more chaotic interruptions with shouting and dissension, if we are going to come to a consensus on these discussions—"

"But do we truly want to reach a consensus? Are we seriously considering putting these phases into action? Is there no other recourse?" Prime Minister Daniella Morrison of Australia interjected, shaking her head in disbelief, and waving her notepad above her head.

"We have been round and round on this for days and days. Why must you and your same weak-minded friends continue to try to discourage what must be done?" Emir Sheikh Hari Khan groaned angrily.

"It's just that I fear that we will become the most despised people in the world," Morrison concluded weakly.

"We are already hated, but what people think of us cannot deter us. We cannot concern ourselves with individual feelings, when we are facing unimaginable crises—" Prime Minister Arnav Nodi of India began before being interrupted by the envoy from Norway.

"India is always facing a crisis." Brit Juul's tone was confrontational, but after sitting through four agonizingly long days of these meetings, she was finding it harder to keep a rein on her patience. "Perhaps if your predecessors had taken similar measures a century or more ago, you wouldn't be facing such dire circumstances now."

"That is not helpful, Brit." Her fellow envoy from Sweden leaned over and placed a calming hand on her arm. Brit closed her eyes and took a few deep breaths. "I apologize, Prime Minister Nodi. My words were unkind. I will endeavor to think before speaking, moving forward. To that end, however, have we considered what will happen with countries that chose not to attend this summit?"

"North Korea and Cuba," President Saltzer inserted.

"Perhaps we can forcibly remove the leaders of those countries and insert those who would be amenable to what it is we're proposing—" Chinese leader, Bai Jinping, started.

"Do you really think we have time to overthrow those governments?" Prime Minister of Israel, Miriam Herzog interrupted.

"¡Basta!" Antonio Briceño, President of Colombia, yelled. "Have we forgotten why this emergency session was called? Why representatives from nearly every nation are here this week? We need these measures to prevent our countries—not just mine, but all of our countries—from reaching a point of no return. It is so serious, at this time, that we have no more time to waste in talk, much less to wage war on two insignificant countries. If North Korea and Cuba do not care for their citizens—"

"Then we will have to care for them," Prime Minister Charles McDougal of Britain chimed in. "Mr. Briceño is correct, we must take action now for the sake of our citizens, and for the citizens of the world. If we don't act, there will be no citizens left. If we were in doubt of the seriousness of the state of affairs, we would not be here now. These measures are necessary to stop overpopulation, depleting resources, and environmental crises that threaten our oceans. As leaders of our nations, it is our duty to act now."

A majority of the heads nodded in agreement. It was enough to temporarily quiet those who opposed the purpose of the summit. Everyone around the table understood the gravity of the situation, but hearing it stated so bluntly was enough to shame them into a rare silence.

After a few minutes, President Abdelaziz Tebboune of Algeria stood up slowly and spoke solemnly, "I understand that many here are hesitant about the changes being proposed. We all want what is best for our people and our countries, but these 'phases' being proposed seems an overwhelming undertaking to coordinate on such a large scale."

The dissenters in the room voiced their concerns, but their voices were fewer and quieter compared to those who supported implementing the phases. Prime Minister Shinzo Kato of Japan responded brusquely, "If you have a better alternative that can address the planet's issues and be executed quickly with the same effectiveness as our plans, then we will hear you."

President Tebboune looked around the room at his allies, but each one avoided his gaze with a shake of their head. "Perhaps we should give the people a chance to voice their opinions—"

"Do you forget what happened in my country a century ago?" President Saltzer interjected angrily. "We had a reasonable proposal from then-President Elizabeth Marker, but because of the 'right to immediate voting' amendment, the people rejected it without even reading it. And now we face potential desertification of our lands and the depletion of our oceans, and that is only the tip of a massively large disastrous iceberg. Do you think we would be sitting here today if there were other options or if we thought that the people would vote with their minds and not their emotions? We are trying to save our world."

As he sat back down, President Saltzer felt weary and saddened by the necessary evil they were about to commit. He only hoped that the citizens of the world would understand why these changes were needed, but at the same time realized that it didn't matter if they understood. For the human race to survive, radical changes needed to be made and they didn't include the current population—as it stood now.

Prime Minister Erin Gagnon of Canada stood up next, speaking softly and carefully. "We are on the brink of global catastrophe. And while I'm aware that we've all heard a form of this horror story in the past, all of us here today know it is no longer a tale that will end when the book is closed. This is a real-life drama that is happening before our eyes. We must work together covertly to prevent further decay and restore balance to our planet. I cannot deny that what we are proposing makes me ill to my stomach, but if we do nothing, then our world will die. Of course, should that happen, we won't need to worry about implementation of anything, as we'll all be dead."

All gazes fell as if in unified humiliation. A majority knew that they had to make difficult decisions for the greater good of the world; the piercing sting of truth that the planet was in peril and drastic measures needed to be taken. The silence extended into minutes, but soon, the strong began to raise their heads and nod in acceptance while the cowards among them refused to look anyone in the eye. To President Saltzer, the fact that there were only a few of those cowards remaining in a sea of hundreds, gave him renewed energy and hope.

He stood again and straightened his jacket before posing the question that would change the course of history: "Are we of one accord?" His fingers clenched tightly around the fourteen-carat gold Cartier pen, his knuckles turning white as he waited for the final decision. After a few minutes more, the voices of those in agreement filled the room.

President Saltzer's lips compressed in a thin line as he scrawled his signature across the bottom of the document. He slid the paper to his right, sitting heavily onto his plush and comfortable leather chair, which did little to relieve the tension in his body, or the bodies of the others occupying their chairs. A tension remained, which was so thick, that it threatened to suffocate those in the room.

The president's gaze was glued to the document as it journeyed from one member to another. The gnawing urgency within him, a relentless hunger for resolution, momentarily quieted when a soldier entered the room from the far end and marched towards him.

"Mr. President, there's an individual insisting to speak to you. He asserts that it is of the utmost importance and cannot be postponed, even though I told him that you were not to be disturbed."

"And who might this insistent guest be?"

"Dr. Riku Jang. He was certain that you'd want to meet with him immediately."

A slow smile crept across the president's face like dawn breaking. "He would indeed be correct, and was right to insist," he responded, his voice laced with optimism. "This could potentially be the beacon of hope we've been desperately yearning for."

The soldier furrowed his brow in confusion. "Sir?"

President Saltzer dismissed him with a wave of his hand. "Nothing, soldier. Just voicing my thoughts aloud. Escort Dr. Jang in."

"Sir, yes sir!" The soldier snapped a crisp salute, then did an about-face and marched back to the door leading to the foyer.

As he awaited Dr. Jang's entrance, the president leaned back in his chair, fingertips tented beneath his chin in contemplation while wearing an enigmatic half-smile.

"You seem to be quite cheerful all of a sudden. It was the opposite just moments ago when you seemed rather dejected," remarked Prime Minister Charles McDougal of Britain with curiosity.

"We'll soon find out if my cheeriness is warranted," President Saltzer responded cryptically. He stood up to greet Dr. Riku Jang as he walked into the room and motioned for him to come closer. "What updates do you have for me today?"

Dr. Jang returned his smile, a hint of smugness in his expression. "I am pleased to report that we have made a major breakthrough that guarantees our survival."

"So, we can finally move on to Phase One without any further delays?"

"And simultaneously begin Phase Three," confidently added Dr. Jang. "If you so choose."

"This is truly remarkable news, Riku! Absolutely remarkable!"

Phase One

There is no crueler tyranny than that which is perpetuated under the shield of law and in the name of justice.

Baron de Montesquieu

New Orders: Zain Belhasa

Year: 2156

Dubai, United Arab Emirates, January 2nd, 12:00 a.m. GST

Colonel Zain Belhasa rolled onto his side; the rustle of sheets muffled against the low throb in his skull. He yanked the pillow over his head, trying to silence the faint, persistent tapping on the door. It wasn't loud, but it landed like a hammer against the fragile wall of sleep he was clinging to. Whoever it was, they had no sense of timing—or was ignorant of his rank.

He decided to ignore it, confident that whoever it was would simply give up and leave. He had already been running on fumes for most of the day before finally collapsing into bed, and his alarm was due to go off in less than five hours. Sleep was currency, and tonight, he was near broke. But just as his breath began to even out, his cellphone shrieked to life on the nightstand.

Zain groaned, flipped it over, and answered without checking caller ID.

Iftah babak[1], the voice on the other end demanded. Just as abruptly, the call disconnected.

Zain sat up slowly, blinking at the now-silent device in his hand. The voice hadn't been familiar—and no one spoke to a colonel that way, not unless they were suicidal. He lowered the phone to the table with forced calm, inhaling deeply as his irritation simmered just beneath the surface.

The knock came again. Louder. Unmistakable in its purpose.

He flung the blanket aside and stood too fast, the room tilting slightly before settling. Steadying himself with a palm to the

---

[1] Iftah babak: *Open your door*

wall, he stalked toward the front door, each step coiled with controlled fury.

He violently flung open his front door and immediately took a startled step back when he came face-to-face with a young soldier dressed in full uniform, his trembling hands clutching an envelope. His temper immediately abated, but he snatched at the envelope as if he were still fuming, then silently shooed the young soldier away with a wave of his hand.

Zain closed the door, tore the envelope open with practiced efficiency, and read the message:

احزم جميع معداتك للنشر. كن في القاعدة خلال ساعة واحدة.[2]

He read it twice. Three times. Deployment? Zain's confusion was a swirling vortex within him, pulling him in multiple directions. He rarely ever deployed anymore, and no one at his base held a rank higher than his to issue commands for deployment. This meant that the order had originated from somewhere else, from someone higher in rank than even he, and that could only mean one thing…war. But with whom? His thoughts rabbited, bounding about in his head.

He moved to the kitchen in a daze, laid the paper flat on the table. His eyes scanned the bolded words again. A knot formed at the base of his spine, coiling tighter with each breath.

According to the orders, he had one hour to pack and report. That jarred him from his astounded stupor. He glanced at his watch with a knitted brow. The time allotted wasn't significant and already he'd spent ten minutes of that time behaving petulantly over having his sleep disturbed.

He pushed back from the table and strode down the hall, pausing briefly outside one of the bedroom doors. His mother's

---

[2] Pack all your gear for deployment. Be at base within one hour.

room—when she visited. As he opened the door slowly, he wondered why the banging hadn't disturbed her much-needed rest.

His gaze softened and his temper subsided when he caught sight of her. She lay curled beneath layers of warm blankets, lips parted slightly as a faint snore hummed through the room. The corners of Zain's mouth lifted involuntarily. Her fuzzy pink earmuffs—an absurd but effective sleep aid—were snug against her silver-streaked hair.

"That explains it," he murmured. "Maybe I should get a pair of those."

He watched her for a short bit longer than necessary, memorizing the rhythm of her breath, the soft rise and fall of her chest. Then, with practiced care, he closed the door and returned to his room.

With a slight sigh, he reached for his cellphone. He had a call to make. The thought of it brought a wry grin to his lips. He knew his sister, Amal, all too well, and her temper was far more explosive than even his own. She would not appreciate being awakened at this early hour, but he simply had no choice. While he had agreed to house their mother temporarily, until Amal's "much-needed getaway" came to an end—translation: she needed a break from their overbearing mother—he'd had the freedom, over the last two weeks, to return home frequently to check on her. With his pending deployment, however, he needed to ensure that she was picked up sooner than their pre-arranged time. Leaving her for a few hours at a time was one thing, leaving her for more than a day was simply unfathomable.

He reluctantly admitted to himself, while he dialed Amal's number, that cutting his time short with his mom would be a relief. Not that he didn't love her. What he didn't love was her constant nagging for him to find a wife. The loss of his beloved Fatima to a sudden brain aneurysm over a year ago had been difficult enough without his mom's relentless pursuit for him to remarry. According to his mother, it had been long enough since Fatima's passing and he needed to find a new wife soon so that she could have grandchildren before she, herself, passed away. That constant pressure and nagging were pushing him further away from wanting any kind of relationship again. It also made him empathize more readily with his sister, since he didn't doubt that his mom also nagged her just as persistently.

His thoughts, adrift in a sea of memories, were abruptly anchored back to the harsh reality of the present when his call connected. The groan that answered was low and male sounding, and for a flash of a second, Zain's stomach dropped. "Amal?"

The idea of his sister being in company of a man outside of wedlock made his blood begin to boil again. His heart pounded against his ribcage as he waited for confirmation. Then, much to his relief and slight annoyance, the groan morphed into something distinctly feminine—definitely Amal. He could almost see her squinting at her screen in protest against the early morning call.

"What do you want?" she mumbled eventually. Her words seemed to stumble out one after another, heavy with sleep and laced with irritation.

"Come pick up mother," Zain ordered curtly, ignoring her own petulance, though he understood it readily enough.

Her response was immediate and predictable. "It's too early in the morning. And besides, I have one more day of vacation remaining. I will be there tomorrow! Now let me sleep!"

Zain sighed deeply before responding firmly yet urgently: "No, Amal, I must leave for deployment in thirty minutes and cannot leave mother here alone to wonder where I am gone to. Come now!"

Amal whined back at him over the line; her voice was still thick with sleep, but also tinged with stubbornness that matched his own: "Can you not put her in a cab and send her here?"

Zain laughed dryly at that suggestion: "You will not survive her arrival if I did that."

"I hate you!" she retorted petulantly.

"I know," he replied calmly but sternly. "You have twenty-five minutes to get here. Don't delay."

He ended the call with a silent prayer that Amal would heed the urgency in his voice and show up on time. His faith in her was unwavering as she had never let him down before, and he doubted she ever would, but he'd never called her in the wee hours of the morning either, testing his conviction.

He grabbed his duffel and combat boots from the hall closet, and then hurried to his bedroom. His quickly packed socks, underwear, and three neatly-folded uniforms. He hesitated for a moment before also adding his winter camouflaged fatigues—since he hadn't been made aware of just where he was headed. "Better to be safe than sorry," he muttered.

Hurriedly, he gathered his toiletries from the bathroom and tossed them on top of his uniforms. With one last glance around the room to ensure he didn't forget anything, Zain zipped up the duffel and headed for his car. The wind whipped at his hair as he tossed the duffel into the trunk before pausing to look back at the house.

"I can't forget my passport," he murmured before closing the trunk and returning inside. As he passed his mom's room again, he made a quick decision to let her sleep, deciding instead to leave her a note on the kitchen table. If he woke her, she would be full of questions which he simply had no time to entertain. Not that he had answers to provide.

Retrieving his passport from a floor safe, he tucked it into the side pocket of his pants, then grabbed a pen and paper from his desk and headed to the kitchen.

While waiting for his sister, Amal, to arrive, Zain brewed himself a strong cup of coffee. The comforting scent of freshly brewed beans filled the air, mingling with the faint aroma of flowers. He took a moment to savor the warmth and comfort it brought him.

As he finished penning the note, a gentle knock sounded at the door. A small smile tugged at his lips as he folded the note and tucked it beneath the vase filled with a colorful bouquet of wildflowers that his mother had bought yesterday.

With a sense of anticipation, he made his way to the door and opened it, revealing his disheveled sister on the other side. Her hair was a tangled mess and her clothes seemed haphazardly thrown on, but she had managed to make it all the way to his house without incident. He couldn't help but chuckle at her bleary-eyed look, heart warmed at the level of dedication to their family.

"Mom's still asleep, so you may as well get some more rest," he assured her with a gentle hand on her back, guiding her towards his bedroom. She moved slowly across the floor, her footsteps heavy with exhaustion. When she reached the side of the bed, she collapsed face-first with a contented sigh. Within seconds, peaceful snores filled the air.

Zain shook his head in bemusement, then turned and left his home. He stood by his car door for a moment, staring up at the night sky.

Something felt wrong. A subtle shift in the air.

He climbed into the driver's seat, exhaled slowly, and turned the key. As the engine hummed to life, he whispered to himself, "*Bismillah*[3]."

And then he drove into the dark, toward a mission he didn't understand, under orders he had never expected. Headed for a world that—unbeknownst to him—was already beginning to crack.

---

[3] In the name of God

At the precise moment of zero-four-forty-five GMT, on a bitterly cold January fourth, transport aircraft from Europe and Asia descended upon the snow-covered runways of Reykjavik, Iceland. The night sky was inky black, broken only by the soft glow of lights emanating from the massive airplanes as they discharged their vital cargo onto the frigid tarmac. Facing the harsh elements, soldiers braved the freezing temperatures to unload crucial supplies, including sturdy lodgings, winter gear, rations of non-perishable food (MREs), potable water, advanced communication equipment, and state-of-the-art robotic military personnel (RMPs). Representing fifty-five nations in Europe and fifty in Asia, the combat teams arrived with urgency and purpose. Among them were battle-hardened career military personnel, as well as eager volunteers who had bravely, blindly, stepped forward to serve their nations in what the governmental leaders referenced as a 'time of crisis'. Though unaware of the mission's purpose or its dangers, they moved with seamless coordination, as if instinctively prepared for every threat. They landed on the rugged terrain and immediately sprang into action, ferrying supplies and soldiers for the three and a half hours to the remote region of Arngerdareyri in the north. There, they met up with the massive transport carrier ships that would take them on the final leg of their journey to the uninhabited wildlife preserve of Hornstrandir. Once known for treacherous mountain ranges, the terrain had gradually flattened, rendering it suitable for base operations for a mission that would last for an undisclosed length of time.

As they disembarked from the ships, their eyes scanned the vast landscape before them. Jagged peaks rose up into the sky like menacing sentinels, while deep valleys and ravines carved through the earth. No one dared question why they had been summoned—or what awaited them. They were called to duty and answered without hesitation.

With military precision and efficiency, each soldier worked in unison with the thousand RMPs to construct over one hundred pre-fabricated buildings. These structures would serve as sleeping quarters, mess halls, and a central command center. Despite exhaustion setting in from long hours of labor, not a single man rested until a fully-functioning military base was erected.

On January 10th, the Icelandic region of Hornstrandir was home to one of many multinational military bases. These bases were scattered all over the world and each had forces with a strength of over ten thousand. However, none of them could have predicted the magnitude of what was about to happen—affecting not only their lives, but also their families back home and the entire world.

As the sun slowly descended over the desolate landscape of Hornstrandir, soldiers plodded wearily into the five colossal mess halls. Each hall was overflowing with two thousand exhausted personnel, their weary bodies collapsing onto stools at long, crowded tables. Two KTRPs (kitchen-trained robotic personnel) were stationed in each tent, efficiently unpacking MREs, while a third robot carried the meals to each soldier. In less than thirty minutes, all ten thousand troops at the Icelandic base had been fed by the tireless KTRPs.

The atmosphere was buzzing with the hum of chatter and sporadic eruptions of hearty laughter as warriors reconnected with their long-lost brothers-in-arms or formed fresh bonds with compatriots hailing from diverse regions of Europe and Asia. The cacophony was so intense that it could have readily triggered an avalanche, had there been a snow-laden peak in close proximity.

Suddenly, a loud beep resounded through all of the RMP and KTRP units and all movement ceased simultaneously, as if following a silent cue. The soldiers fell silent at the sound, their conversations abruptly cut off, and an eerie hush settled over the hall. A moment later, a disembodied voice began to speak through the speakers of the robotic units, commanding their attention.

All personnel, your attention please. Welcome to Base Icicle. Yes, I know, that's not very ingenious, but that's what the naming committee determined appropriate. This is Brigadier General Takayoshi and this is our first official briefing. I am pleased with the hard work performed by all of you these last few days in getting our temporary base up and running. It is my honor to have worked beside each and every one of you and I look forward to our continued collaboration as we strive to complete our mission successfully and with pride in our efforts. Our orders are clear, and in the coming weeks we will be training for the completion of those orders. Until such time as we go over those orders with you, we ask that all continue to do their daily tasks to the betterment of our community—temporary though it may be. No matter the task, your attention to detail is mission critical to completing our directives in the coming months.

Individual profiles and skillsets have been input into a database and it is from that data upon which rotating tasks have been assigned. Each morning, after chow, you each will approach any RMP patrolling the compound, provide your name and identification number. The RMP will then provide you with your assignments for that day. If you're one of the lucky ones on a given day, you will get to lounge on your cot and do nothing.

The sound of ten thousand soldiers cheering was deafening, sending vibrations rippling through the ice, rattling nearby structures; but as quickly as the joyful atmosphere erupted, it suddenly fell silent. It felt like an invisible force had slammed down and shook everyone to their core.

As you have probably surmised, the General continued, *it is to the benefit of our new base that we avoid overly thunderous noises. While the ice beneath the fjords is deeper than most politician's pockets, we can ill afford to test its stability. So, moving forward, we will proceed as if we've all had training as pantomime artists and the surrounding ice is our audience.*

Now, back to the briefing. I would like the following officers to stand: Belhasa, Zain; Wang, Xiu; Mannelly, Ethan; Jeong, Hanjun; and Kuznetsov, Elizaveta. If there is more than one you in the same hall, depart and make your way to another mess hall in which there is currently no officer present. We will wait.

The briefing momentarily paused as two officers excused themselves, escorted by an unnoticed RMP, to go to a different hall. As soon as they had departed, General Takayoshi effortlessly resumed the briefing, seemingly aware of when each officer was situated again.

Make a mental note that the officers before you are your new commanders. They will introduce themselves momentarily. Commit to memory their name and face. Again, they will be your new commanding officer and that is your assigned eating hall. Upon dismissal, each man and woman will approach the RMP at the head of the tent and announce his or her name and the name of his or her commanding officer—for the RMP's record.

As soon as you've completed this task, you are dismissed to return to your bunks to have a relaxing…and quiet…evening. Tomorrow starts the dawn of a new day. Commanding officers, after you've introduced yourselves to your units, report to me in the command post. An RMP will direct you.

Just a few moments after the briefing ended, the commanding officers exited their designated mess tents, followed closely by members of their units, who filtered out one at a time, after presenting themselves to an RMP stationed at the entrance. Major Ethan Mannelly of the British Royal Forces paused to talk to another RMP stationed nearby: "Command post?"

"I was about to inquire over the same information," Xiu smiled. "Perhaps I will just walk along with you. I am Lieutenant Xiu Zhang of the People's Republic of China."

"And I am Lieutenant Colonel Elizaveta Kuznetsov of Russia. I will walk alongside you also," she proclaimed in a clipped tone, falling into step beside her fellow officers.

Second Lieutenant Jeong Hanjun and Colonel Zain Belhasa soon joined their comrades and they all silently trailed behind the RMP as it led them across the fjord toward the command center.

In the dull, monotonous landscape of identical structures, Zain's voice reverberated, laced with a sardonic edge. "We may need to mark these buildings in some manner," he proposed, his gaze scanning over the homogeneity of their surroundings. The mess tents, command tent, and shelter barracks were carbon copies of each other—same height, same color, same plastic windows. It was like looking at an army of clones. His concern was valid; it would indeed be easy to forget which building was which and waste a significant amount of time finding the right one.

Ethan's reply came without hesitation. "RMP, acknowledge," he called out authoritatively.

The RMP responded, "I hear you," without missing a beat or slowing its mechanical stride.

Ethan continued his command to the RMP as they moved along the bleak row of buildings under a sky devoid of any warmth. "Add 'designate buildings with identifying markers' as one of the daily tasks." He spoke with an air of authority that was all-too familiar in their line of work.

"Adding task 'designate buildings with identifying markers'," came the immediate response from the RMP in its unemotional tone, confirming Ethan's order amidst their march towards another indistinguishable building.

"Good robot," Elizaveta smirked; the disdain clear in her tone. She resented the inclusion of these mechanical personnel in military operations. She'd never worked with one before, though she'd seen them demonstrated during a military conference in Japan a few years earlier. To her, to take the human element out of military decision-making was one of the worst decisions to be made. Still, it wasn't up to her to make that particular decision. She was just glad to see that the number of human military personnel outnumbered these walking tin cans by at least two to one. "We could take them," she muttered beneath her breath as the RMP stepped aside to stand next to the entryway of the command center.

Brigadier General Takayoshi was sitting on a stool, reviewing some information on his tablet. "Come in," he called when he spotted the five junior officers lingering outside. "Pull up a stool," he offered, congenially.

The officers pushed through the heavy flap of the command tent and stepped inside. The space was warmed by portable heaters and dimly lit by a series of overhead bulbs strung along the support beams. Folding stools scraped softly against the flooring as they took their places around the General. Outside, the wind stirred the canvas walls with a steady rhythm, and the sounds of the base grew quiet as the last of the day's activity wound down.

A Bitter Pill

"Take a seat." The words issued from Brigadier General Takayoshi's lips with what might have been mistaken for cordiality, had they not landed with the weight of command. The military tent—its towering canvas panels stiff with frost—sighed against the early evening wind, a low and constant breath pressing through seams and folds. Inside, the frigid air clung to their skin despite the warmth of layered clothes and the presence of a small space heater.

The five junior officers moved without hesitation. One by one, they crossed to the corner of the tent where the collapsible metal stools lay stacked, unfolding them with the sharp clack of locking hinges. The cold metal bit at their fingers, chipped gray paint flaking beneath calloused hands—a quiet testament to years of use. As they positioned the stools around the small table, the frames gave a faint groan under their weight, flexing just enough to betray their impermanence. The officers sat in silence, the spacing between them exact, deliberate, as if even their proximity required regulation. No one spoke. No one dared. Not until the General gave them leave.

"There is much to go over," the General began. The fabric ceiling glowed faintly above his head, trembling as if it too awaited orders. "Real quick. Each of you has been allocated a Robotic Military Personnel—RMP for short. Its internal data core holds all operational details pertinent to this deployment. While you may access specific mission-relevant data, the RMPs are programmed to restrict anything beyond your clearance level. Details will be revealed as it pertains to each phase of the mission." He paused to allow that to sink in.

"Need to know," Ethan muttered, his lips quirking at familiar sentiment.

Takayoshi's eyes flicked to him, faint amusement shadowing his expression. "Precisely. As the mission progresses, further information will be disseminated—piecemeal, and only as necessary. As for yourselves, you will relay what is required to your troops and nothing more. I'll remind you: what is discussed here stays within these walls. Not one word is to be shared beyond this tent."

The five officers responded as one, their voices a chorus of disciplined assent: "Yes, sir."

Takayoshi shifted his weight, the stiff weave of his uniform resisting like a second, less forgiving skin. Years of command had taught him how to hold himself still, how to keep his body composed even when instinct pulled in the opposite direction. The orders he carried sat heavy in his gut—unwelcome, immovable—and he knew their weight would fall harder on his officers if he didn't try to dull the edge. He forced his shoulders to ease, let the tension drain from his jaw, and softened his voice as best he could. "Try to relax," he offered, though the words landed brittle, edged with the chill of restraint—like frost clinging to metal that refused to thaw.

They responded in kind, as discipline demanded. Movements were subtle, rehearsed—more habit than ease. They adjusted their posture—shoulders rolling back, arms uncrossing, hands dropping to rest on thighs or hanging loosely at their sides. One leaned back slightly, another tilted his head as if the motion might trick his body into calm. But it was a performance—thin and transparent. Beneath the surface, their muscles remained taut, jaws clenched, breath measured. The General's gaze was too steady, too practiced, and none of them dared meet it for long. Whatever comfort he intended had the opposite effect. No one truly relaxed beneath his watch.

A faint sigh escaped the General as he smoothed a wrinkle from his uniform sleeve, fingers tracing a gesture more habitual than necessary. "You are right, I suppose, to be tense," he admitted. "It's never a good sign when this many high-ranking military officers, and also so many troops, are summoned together without context. Okay, let's not waste any more time." He raised his voice slightly and turned his head toward the rear of the tent. "RMPs—enter and stand behind your designated officer."

Five RMPs emerged—not through the central entrance, but silently parting the rear canvas like shadows slipping into existence. The lantern light slithered over their silver frames, casting jagged shadows that made them look like predators held just barely in check. A faint hum—mechanical, but oddly rhythmic—rose as they came to a stop behind each officer, standing still with unnerving precision.

Elizaveta's upper lip curled in derision as her gaze swept across the uniform machines. "How do we identify our personal RMP when they're all identical?"

Takayoshi gave a quick glance at the RMP lineup, then back to the officer before replying, his voice level. "They're encoded with your biosignatures. You won't need to identify them—they already know who you are. They respond only to your voice—and mine, of course. Oh, and their proximity is non-negotiable. Consider them your shadow—your personal command center and sentinel."

Zain, arms crossed tightly over his chest, turned slightly and studied the machines. His voice broke the silence, tinged with skepticism. "So, if they're tethered to us, can we order them to give us some breathing room, or are they literally going to be glued to our butts?"

Takayoshi gave a dry chuckle, a brief break in his otherwise solemn tone. "You can assign them to carry out duties that may pull them away temporarily. But they're hardwired to remain within your proximity. Any command that contradicts their prime directive will be ignored."

Ethan groaned, dragging a hand through his already unruly hair. "So, I'm stuck with a glorified stalker even when I take a piss?"

A ripple of laughter broke the tension. The humor was short-lived but necessary, like a match struck in darkness.

Takayoshi allowed himself a weary smile. "They aren't concerned with your anatomy, Major. I doubt you'll be interesting company to them."

Hanjun peered downward at his crotch with a mock solemnity. "Goodbye privacy. I'm going to miss you."

Elizaveta scoffed. "Privacy? What is privacy?"

The tent warmed a few degrees with their banter, but the General didn't let it linger. His expression sobered quickly, and the shadows seemed to grow heavier again around them. "I think we need to move on. Now, six months ago, every global power—with the exception of two—met in absolute secrecy. The topic of concern: the rapid decline in viable global resources, paired with a projected population swell no infrastructure can sustain." His tone dropped, the gravity deepening with every word. "What came from that meeting was not a debate. It was a decision. A mandate. Radical transformation was deemed necessary for the survival of the human race."

Hanjun's voice pierced the solemn air. "Overpopulation and dwindling resources are speeches we've heard a million times before from every politician across the globe. Nothing ever changes. So, what makes this different?"

Ethan lifted a finger and gestured vaguely at the walls around them. "Maybe the massive international buildup? Just a thought. Still, how can a handful of soldiers rectify this current global catastrophe? Catastrophic events that have been plaguing our world for centuries."

Zain's brow furrowed. "The deployment scale alone suggests something beyond containment or deterrence. We're not in a holding pattern—we're part of an operation to affect change, but like you, Ethan, I'm curious to know just how a handful of soldiers can influence over eleven billion people across the globe."

"As you say, we are gathered to affect change, but you are not alone," Takayoshi affirmed. "Coordinated encampments have been activated across the globe. Africa. Asia. South America. Russia. Canada. Australia. And here." He gestured downward. "We are the Western European and West Asian command force."

Xiu, who had remained silent thus far, leaned forward slightly, studying the General intently. "You have stated the problems—global overpopulation and dwindling resources— however, you have yet to tell us precisely what the orders are and how we, and our military might, are meant to rectify these issues."

Ethan glanced at Xiu before turning his attention back to Takayoshi: "She's right. You've said quite a bit without saying much at all. I'd say we're all curious about this and why this briefing has been rather vague on details to this point."

"Maybe the reason it's been vague is because I haven't been allowed to finish," Takayoshi said, voice cool and unyielding. "Let's keep it that way for now."

The officers fell silent at once. The tension didn't crack so much as deepen—low and compressed, like pressure before a storm. He waited a beat, then continued with deliberate calm, a hand swiping his face wearily. "There's little I'm cleared to share at this point. What you'll need to know will come—when the time is right."

No one replied. No one dared to ask. Each respectful of the command for silence.

Until the silence in the tent stretched uncomfortably long.

Elizaveta's lips parted in open challenge. "Then why hold a briefing if you've been kept in the dark yourself and have nothing of import to impart?"

Takayoshi met her stare without flinching. "Because this briefing isn't about tactics or mission parameters. It's about readiness." His gaze swept across them—assessing, weighing. "Before any operation begins, your loyalty to the mission must be evaluated—and tested."

Something unseen shifted in the air. A pressure. A pulse.

Xiu sat back, her features pale beneath the tent's dim light. "You speak in a tone that makes it seem as if the demons of Hell have been set loose and we're meant to fight them."

Takayoshi held her gaze. "From what I've been told, Lieutenant…you're not far off the mark."

A flicker of unease passed across the faces of the officers.

Ethan rubbed the back of his neck. "What in God's name have we been roped into? This is beginning to veer off into the realm of madness, by the sounds of it."

Hanjun's voice was quieter now, defensive. "Sir…with all due respect, our records prove our loyalty. We've bled for our flags. Killed for our people. What more could possibly be asked of us?"

Takayoshi inhaled deeply; his next words spoken without dramatics—just grim certainty. "Indeed, you have proven yourselves, which is why you all have been chosen for command. However, your first objective is to ensure you will not dare question an order when given. Your compliance is paramount to mission success."

The wind beyond the canvas screamed, but inside there fell an eerie silence. The five officers sat unmoving; shadows thrown long behind them by the quivering light.

Their RMPs loomed, unreadable.

Behind the veil of duty, a whisper had entered the room—of choices already made, of paths not fully revealed, and of loyalty soon to be measured, not by rank, but by sacrifice.

Comply or Die

The officers emerged from the command tent in silence, their bootsteps muffled against the frozen earth. Faces tight, eyes shadowed with doubt, they carried with them more than orders—they carried the weight of unspoken consequences. Each directive, though seemingly precise, twisted in their minds like unsolved riddles, laced with the knowledge that failure meant not just disgrace, but death. And worst of all, it would come without ceremony, without mercy:

"What precisely will happen if we fail to comply?" Zain posed; his voice strung tight with tension.

"Your personal RMP will step in to accomplish your task. Subsequently, you'll be terminated and I will then bear the burden of finding your replacement."

"It seems a bit draconian, simply to test our loyalty," Ethan murmured under his breath.

"The rationale behind it all will be illuminated once the mission is accomplished. So, I've been told," the General asserted unflinchingly. *"Now, you are dismissed."*

All but Elizaveta sat frozen, their bodies anchored to the cold metal stools, eyes unfocused, lost in the tangle of their own thoughts. The weight of the General's words had struck deeper than any of them wanted to admit. Finally, Elizaveta stood, sharp and purposeful, and snapped, "You heard him. Dismissed."
The sound of her voice cracked the stillness. One by one, the others stirred, blinking as if waking from a trance. They rose slowly, movement sluggish, and filed out with the dazed, hollow rhythm of sleepwalkers—shoulders hunched, heads down, each trying to shake loose the grim certainty now following them out into the cold.

The journey back to their designated quarters seemed destined for silence until Ethan shattered it abruptly. "I don't think

I'll ever acclimate to this incessant daylight," he exclaimed inanely, his gaze straining upwards towards the relentless glow of the sky.

The never-ending sun in Iceland could have been a symbol of their own unyielding dedication to duty, but they were unable to see that at the moment. All they saw was an inconvenient weather phenomenon that went against everything they considered normal, much like how they felt about the orders issued by their commanding officer.

"Um…yeah…" Hanjun stammered, struggling to find words that could adequately express his unease. "Highly unsettling." His voice quivered slightly, revealing a deeper anxiety underlying his statement. Everyone could tell he wasn't just talking about the never-ending daylight of the midnight sun.

"I only hope our time here is shorter than what the General insinuated," Zain spoke up with a hint of worry in his voice, hoping that their stay in this icy environment wouldn't be as long as the General implied. His thoughts wandered to the comforting sun-drenched landscapes of his home, but he couldn't help but shiver when he remembered the orders from the General. The memory, only minutes old, seemed to freeze him to his core, as if he had taken a dip in the icy waters of the Greenland Sea.

"Personally, I have no trouble doing what must be done," Elizaveta declared abruptly. She didn't mince her words and cut through the group's attempts at vague analogous comments about their mission. Her direct acknowledgement of their daunting task shattered any sense of normalcy and forced everyone back to reality.

Zain replied with biting sarcasm, "Is that really how you feel? Sounds pretty cold-hearted to me."

"Colonel Kuznetsov is right; this is no place for sentimentality," Hanjun murmured in response, his whisper barely discernible over the howling wind. His words were strong but his voice betrayed a sorrowful undertone, hinting at a deep-seated discomfort with their orders. "It's not something I relish doing, but—"

"It's a matter of survival," Ethan interrupted sharply, his tone tinged with an anger that radiated to them all. It wasn't just frustration—it was fury barely restrained, a pulse of heat cutting through the bitter air as they made their way across the frozen compound. His jaw tightened, fists clenched at his sides, eyes burning with a betrayal too fresh to name. That fury wasn't his alone; it rippled outward, unspoken but shared. The others felt it coil in their guts—a hostility not just toward the faceless powers that had delivered the order, but toward the system that demanded obedience at the cost of their lives.

"It shouldn't be though, should it?" Zain accused, spitting the words out as if trying to get rid of something distasteful. "They are demanding more than what's reasonable."

"Is this any different from our past as soldiers?" Xiu queried with an eerie calmness. "Or what we'll face in the future?"

"I believe you know the answer to that, my friend," Zain responded with a weary sigh.

"Yeah, it is different, but as Ethan pointed out, it's survival; and if the General's assessment is accurate, then don't you think that it's preferable…" Xiu trailed off, unable to finish her sentence; fearful that doing so would make something worse occur.

"You all are looking at this as if, one, we have a choice; and two, there is not a legitimate reason given for the orders," Elizaveta asserted.

"How could these orders possibly be legit?" Zain asked, incredulous.

"The General didn't exactly explain why this was needed, other than to prove our loyalty," Hanjun added. "Perhaps there is more to his reasons than he revealed."

"You go with that, if it'll help you sleep better at night," Ethan scoffed. "Personally, this is going to give me nightmares for years to come."

It was Elizaveta's turn to scoff. Her eyes flashed with disdain as she turned on Zain, arms folding tight across her chest like a barricade. "How could you rise in the ranks of your military so high if you cannot follow orders that you may find uncomfortable."

Ethan let out a low scoff of his own, his lip curling—not at her, but at the absurdity of the situation, the galling ease with which the system demanded obedience. He shifted slightly, jaw set, ready to fire back—

"Stop!" Elizaveta snapped, cutting him off with a raised hand. "You all know you have no choice, so continuing this conversation is absurd. You will either comply with the orders, or you will die. I do not think that any of you really want to die. Besides, I am certain that we stand to gain significantly from this," Elizaveta continued pontificating. "So, you die if you want. I will do what I am ordered, and one day will reap many rewards."

A heavy silence followed. The others exchanged looks— some tight-lipped, some unreadable, all quietly simmering beneath the surface.

"We'll fulfill our obligations," Ethan said at last. The fire from earlier had drained from his voice, leaving only the dull thud of resignation. "Our RMPs will ensure compliance. So…"

Xiu exhaled softly, brushing snow off her shoulder like she hoped it might brush away the mood. "I'll see you all in half an hour at the truck depot."

Her words seemed to ground them again—pulling them back to the task ahead.

"Indeed. We will assemble covertly, board separate transports, execute our missions stealthily and retreat back to base under cloak of secrecy," Hanjun echoed, his voice low and mechanical, the edge of fatigue creeping in.

"And then we march on with the conviction that our actions will shape a brighter future for our world," Xiu added philosophically.

"If not, I might just repurpose my RMP into my personal robotic maid," Zain muttered dryly.

"I thought the old adage was to make something your bitch," Ethan said, his sarcasm softening the tension like a pressure valve releasing.

"That works too," Zain replied. "Okay, we do what we're ordered."

Without a word, Zain extended his hand, palm down, fingers steady in the cold air. The others gathered around him, one by one laying their hands atop his—calloused, gloved, bare—until the circle was complete. There was no ceremony in it, no theatrics. Just a quiet moment of unity. A pact forged not from trust in their mission, but from trust in each other.

With a final nod, they broke away.

Each officer returned to their quarters to pack a small overnight bag. Ten minutes later, they regrouped at the truck depot, climbed into a waiting military jeep, and began the short drive to the docks. A vessel waited to ferry them across the frigid, choppy sea to Arngerdareyri's second depot—an hour by boat, then another two and a half by land to reach the Reykjavik airport.

Their window to act was narrow. The journey alone—three hours there, three hours back—sliced precious time from their already limited mission clocks. To some, it felt like a calculated burden. To others, a deliberate test of obedience disguised as logistics. Either way, none of them spoke as the engine rumbled to life and the compound fell behind.

They finally reached the airport, spilled out of the jeep in weary disarray and stood indecisively on the tarmac under a sky that refused to dim.

"Where's our ride?" Ethan asked, turning in a circle. "All I see are USAF X-28s."

"Shit, if we are riding in those, we are flying first class all the way," Hanjun exclaimed.

"I have heard of those aircraft. Mach eight, even with a three-passenger capacity. Impressive. We will get home and back very quickly," Elizaveta replied in awe.

"You forget, we have the tin soldiers coming with us." Zain jerked his head at the five RMPs that arrived in separate vehicles a few minutes behind, which now stood sentry on the tarmac. "Do you really believe the military would care enough about our orders to fly us and our bodyguards across a couple of continents in billion-dollar machinery, for expediency's sake? Besides, those RMPs are too large to fit in an X-28 cockpit."

"Yes, they do, and no, they aren't," a voice said from behind. The five officers turned towards the man who'd spoken to them. "I'm Commander Michaels. Let's head over, shall we?"

"Wait, are you serious? How is an RMP supposed to fit in that? And, personally, I've never trained to go Mach eight," Ethan exclaimed, grabbing his small bag and chasing after the wiry Icelandic who moved quickly across the tarmac as a squirrel on the hunt for an acorn. The other officers shook off their shock, grabbed their bags, and raced after Ethan.

"This is the latest in technological advancements which, for the sake of time, means you don't need special training. It will simply feel as if you are flying in a passenger airliner. In coach, but still in relative comfort."

"And the RMPs?" Zain queried as they stopped beside one of the X-28s.

"RMPs contain!" Commander Michaels yelled. With alacrity that belied their size and material makeup, each RMP folded in on itself until it was just compact enough to fit into the rear seat of the aircraft. A forklift arrived from seemingly nowhere and began hefting them into each craft.

"I have now seen more in my life than I have ever seen before," Xiu exclaimed, astonished.

"Prepare for embarkation. Your aviators await your arrival. Once you've completed your individual task, you will be transported to the region in which your mission will begin. A battalion of soldiers and a company of RMPs are already preparing to assemble and depart within the next twenty-four hours."

"Wait…what?" Xiu stumbled. "We did not…all we have is an overnight bag."

"We weren't told to prepare for immediate deployment," Zain added for Xiu who seemed to be struggling for words. All of the officers stared at Commander Michaels slack-jawed, then Zain spoke up again. "You seem to know more about our directives than we do and we were the ones in the briefing with General Takayoshi."

"I only know that I was to be here to coordinate your departure and to relay to you that the remainder of your equipment will arrive with your battalion. If you have issues with any of this, or if you feel you are unfit to proceed, speak now and your RMP will relay the request to relieve you of your duty—"

"Which is code for 'termination'," Zain spat.

"Does anyone wish to withdraw their command?" Commander Michaels asked, his gaze scanning the faces of those equal—or higher—in rank to himself, wondering if anyone would be cowardly enough to shirk the responsibilities granted to them for a mission in which no one was privy of the details. When they all remained silent, Commander Michaels continued. "I'll remain here until all military personnel have departed. I will then be joining…" he paused long enough to check his own set of orders, "I will be joining your battalion, Colonel Kuznetsov."

Elizaveta's eyes widened slightly, but her face did not change its bland, emotionless expression, "Da," she acknowledged. That one word echoed in the ensuing silence against the hum of the aircraft engines behind them.

"Good luck to us all." Commander Michaels fired off a rapid salute, then turned and dashed across the tarmac, his silhouette vanishing behind one of the hangars.

With a brief nod of acknowledgement and support to each other, the five officers selected for this unknown mission of sweeping consequences, turned to face the waiting aircraft. As they approached the first, the pilot leaned out and yelled, "Colonel Belhasa, you're with me!"

"Well, I suppose this is my ride," he remarked to his comrades, who nodded in agreement. "You know, I get why we're being asked to do this, but—".

"Good luck and Godspeed." Ethan interrupted and reached out to clasp his hand, prompting the rest of them to do the same—encouraging each other.

"We do what we have to do. We may not understand the whys—right now—but I'm sure that we will, in time," Xiu added.

"Indeed. It'll all make sense, eventually. If not right now," Hanjun concurred.

If not for the impatient pilot, they would have lingered in their goodbyes, none eager to carry out the one order that would prove their readiness and commitment to an unknown body of governmental officials.

"Colonel Belhasa, let's move!" the pilot shouted again. Zain grabbed onto the ladder attached to the side of the jet and hoisted himself up into the cockpit. His fellow soldiers each taking their place in the pit of their assigned jet. Zain unhooked the ladder and threw it as far away from the jet as he could. He assumed someone would come to remove it from the tarmac, and was surprised when no one did. He secured himself with the installed Sabelt 6-point red belt, then laid his head back against the headrest and waited for them to be underway. As the engines roared, the lift fan in the back of the fuselage revved up, working together with the engine's thrust to achieve vertical takeoff.

Within minutes, each of the five officers was delivered to a private landing strip near their childhood homes, stepping out beneath a sky still brushed with stars. The silence was absolute—thick, expectant—as if the earth itself was holding its breath. Awaiting them at the edge of the tarmac was a single military jeep, engine already idling, and a waiting forklift beside it. Each officer approached with mechanical precision, faces blank, hearts buried.

They climbed inside, fingers stiff against the control panel as they keyed in the only address that had ever meant anything to them. The automated lifts at the rear of the jeeps began to whir, dragging their assigned RMPs from the aircraft. Each machine unfolded with fluid menace, limbs stretching and locking into place like predatory animals waking from hibernation. The moment they affixed themselves to the vehicle's rear hitch, the system registered readiness.

The jeeps lurched forward.

What followed was not combat. It was not war. It was eradication—surgical and irreversible. One by one, the officers stepped into the homes that had shaped them, into bedrooms filled with the stillness of sleep and the ghosts of childhood laughter. They carried weapons—deadly, silent, and efficient—and moved without hesitation through the darkness in houses once filled with love.

Each parent was dispatched with two shots. One to the heart. One to the head.

There were no screams. No pleas. No warnings.

Only the muted pfft of suppressed fire, the slump of a body collapsing into still-warm sheets, and the soft click of boots retreating down familiar halls before anyone else could awaken. In some homes, a family pet stirred, confused by the metallic stench of gunpowder and the sweat of fear. In others, nothing moved at all.

They exited as swiftly and wordlessly as they'd entered— phantoms delivering violence in the name of loyalty.

As the jeeps rolled back toward the landing strips, the roads blurred beneath them, but none of them noticed. Their minds had fractured, split between two selves: the officer who obeyed, and the child who once begged for bedtime stories and soup on sick days.

Loyalty clawed at one side of their conscience. Horror clawed back harder.

None of them knew if they would sleep again.

Each felt something vital had been carved out of their soul—leaving a hollowness inside that would never be refilled.

One officer, a man seemingly chiseled from stone yet with an undercurrent of vulnerability, distanced himself from his counterparts in both thought and deed. He found himself rooted beside the bed of his mother, cocooned within the fragile familiarity of his sister's home. The room smelled faintly of lavender and old books—details etched deep into the corners of his childhood. His mother slept soundly; soft snores muffled beneath the ridiculous, fluffy earmuffs she insisted on wearing each night. She looked impossibly peaceful, as yet untouched by the horror creeping through his soul.

Zain knelt beside her, lips moving in trembling silent prayer. He whispered an apology—not just for what was about to happen, but for everything he would never be able to explain. Tears fell, unbidden, cutting through the years he'd spent hardening himself. Each one burned like acid as it rolled down the planes of his face and landed soundless on the blanket that covered her.

When his tears were spent, he remained unmoving, studying her features in the moonlight, memorizing them—eyes closed, breath steady, completely unaware that her son had become the executioner she'd never have believed him capable of being.

The moment shattered when the device nestled in his ear sparked to life. A voice—cold, detached, utterly inhuman—cut through the reverent silence.

"Fulfill your duty, officer."

Zain's body tensed. He shook his head slowly; lips pressed into a line of agony. "Isn't there another way?" he whispered, so faint it barely stirred the air.

"Yes. You can surrender to your RMP for immediate termination," the voice responded without hesitation.

From the corner of his eye, he caught movement. His RMP had moved and now stood sentry outside the window, a silver phantom gleaming in the night. Its arm extended, slow and deliberate, leveling a matte-black FN 911 straight at his mother's head. The gesture was not an immediate threat, rather it was meant to remind: If you won't, I will.

Zain's breath hitched. His entire body trembled, spine curling inward as if the weight of it all might crush him right there on the floor. For a moment, he closed his eyes, pressing his palms into the carpet like a man trying to stop the world from reeling out of control. He could not feel his fingers. Could not feel his legs. Only the crush of grief and rage twisting through his chest like fire tornado.

But when he looked again at the woman who once cradled him through fever dreams, bloody noses, and failures too small for memory—something inside him turned to steel.

He shook his head firmly at the RMP, pulling his own weapon from its holster.

The machine acknowledged, lowering its weapon, but its blank, inhuman gaze never left him.

With a final, whispered plea for forgiveness, Zain stood, then raised his weapon with trembling hands. The silenced discharge made the barest of sounds—but the impact reverberated through him like a bomb detonating. The bullet found its mark. Her body didn't thrash. Her head simply tilted sideways, then she went still.

He turned away before the warmth faded from her skin, before the coldness creeping into his heart forced him to turn the gun toward his own head.

His boots felt foreign beneath him as he staggered from the room—feet dragging, spine bent beneath a grief too enormous to shoulder. Outside, the night air was brutal—scorching, suffocating, and as unforgiving as the order he had just obeyed. He climbed into the waiting jeep and jabbed his extraction coordinates into the screen with hands that barely functioned. Behind him, the RMP returned from the side of the house and mounted the rear lift, its servos hissing quietly in the dark.

As the vehicle jerked forward, Zain remained slumped in the driver's seat, breath shallow and uneven. Guilt clawed at him from within, a savage, gnawing presence that wouldn't stop chewing at the edges of his sanity. He wanted to scream, to shatter something, to claw the sky open with his bare hands and drag the gods down for judgment.

His chest ached with every inhale; each breath more fractured than the last. Every exhale was a betrayal. A reminder.

And then—something inside him broke.

He slammed his foot on the brake and threw his head back and released it: a scream—raw, ragged, and primal—tore from his throat, rising like smoke into the night. It wasn't a sound meant for words. It was grief turned inside out. Rage at the world. At himself. At everything.

The scream ripped through the stillness and kept going, echoing across the barren desertscape, where even the stars offered no comfort, until there was nothing left but a trace of his pain unnoticed by any living thing—and a machine that could never comprehend it.

Behind thick walls of reinforced glass and a climate-controlled environment, the world's leaders sat arrayed in a crescent around a wall of surveillance screens. The room was chilled to preserve the machines, and that chill had crept into their bones long ago. Each monitor streamed the same horror in real time: five officers, five homes, five clean executions.

No one spoke. Not at first. They simply watched. Judged. Measured.

This was not oversight. This was control.

The massive conference center itself was buried deep beneath a secure facility, somewhere in the Swiss Alps—a place so fortified it didn't officially exist. The room's walls were layered with lead and signal-jamming material, impervious to surveillance, leaks, or interference. A long obsidian table curved inward toward the screens, gleaming under sterile off-white lighting. Digital nameplates glowed in soft blue before each delegate. Around them, aides stood like statues—expressionless, ready to respond but never to question.

"Who is that and why is he just standing there?" Prime Minister Erin Gagnon of Canada asked sharply, breaking the silence. She pointed toward the top-left quadrant of the screen grid, her manicured finger trembling just enough to betray her annoyance.

"How did you spot that one anomaly in the—" President Abdelaziz Tebboune of Algeria began, but she cut him off without looking away.

"There are only five screens active, so how could you miss it? Especially as it is the only RMP not yet moving again," she snapped. "The others are already in retreat mode. That one is idle."

"How are we to handle this when we must have full compliance?" President Antonio Briceño of Colombia leaned forward, fists curled tightly against the table. "We can't afford hesitation or defiance—not now."

"I was part of the original development team for the Robotic Military Personnel initiative," Prime Minister Shinzo Kato of Japan responded, already activating his tablet. The screen lit with biometric data and a streaming overlay of RMP telemetry. "Someone read me the camera ID from the commander's unit."

"Bottom left corner?" asked Prime Minister Daniella Morrison of Australia.

"Yes."

"Z174391," she read.

Kato typed in the number and gained direct access to the RMP's command protocols. A live feed of the soldier flickered onto his tablet, showing the room of Zain's mother, and him standing motionless beside her bed. The RMP, a mechanical sentinel, watching and waiting, ready to intervene.

"Prepare to terminate both—" Kato began, but Saltzer interrupted.

"Wait! Connect me to the RMP intercom," President Saltzer stated.

"Connected," Kato confirmed.

"Fulfill your duty, officer."

Zain's body tensed. He shook his head slowly; lips pressed into a line of agony. *"Isn't there another way?"* he whispered, so faint it barely stirred the air.

"Yes. You can surrender to your RMP for immediate termination," Saltzer responded without hesitation; his tone devoid of emotion.

Another moment passed tensely.

"He's carrying out his orders," Tebboune said, eyes fixed on the screen. All eyes followed as Zain raised the weapon and took the shot.

Kato nodded, then spoke clearly into his mic. "RMP Z174391: Stand down." The machine's indicator lights flashed green in acknowledgment.

A weighted silence followed.

Saltzer, seated at the apex of the crescent, leaned forward slowly, his fingers steepled beneath his chin. "Make a note to keep a sharp eye on that officer," he said, voice flat. "The fact that he hesitated to carry out a direct order means he could become a liability down the road."

Kato nodded and entered a secondary command—flagging Zain's RMP for continued monitoring.

Around the room, the other leaders remained still, their faces masks of composed indifference. Only their eyes betrayed them—darting, calculating, nervous. They knew what was coming next. This had only been the prologue.

Ten minutes later, another order was given.

Saltzer didn't raise his voice. He simply turned to the global interface and spoke three words: "Initiate Communications Blackout."

The directive spread like wildfire through classified networks, encrypted and executed without delay. Each leader repeated the phrase to their own command interface, confirming it in their own languages, yet all with the same cold disregard for what the chaos would do to the people of their nations.

In seconds, the world began to go dark.

Cell towers blinked out. Satellites fell silent. Internet backbones collapsed under a coordinated assault of shutoffs and rerouted packets. Civilian emergency services were the first to feel the cut—ambulance dispatches stalled, aircraft control relays went dead, and surveillance satellites lost contact with their mother grids. By the time the sun breached the eastern horizon, it rose over a planet half-muzzled and wholly confused.

Social media feeds froze mid-post. Calls dropped as if driving through a dead zone. News anchors stared into blank cameras. Entire populations were suddenly cut off—not just from their loved ones, but from the world itself.

Panic followed swiftly as fear morphed into violence. Riots sparked in the streets of cities whose lights still burned but whose voices went unheard, and actions went unreported.

Phase One had begun.

The only method by which the leaders of the world now had to maintain communication with their troops—was through the RMPs.

A tempest of emotions raged within Zain—anger, raw and unrelenting, the strongest, choking off fear and anguish. It churned beneath the surface like a sandstorm, grinding against his composure, threatening to tear through what was left of his discipline. Frustration fueled the fire—frustration over the silence, over his forced inertia, over the vague, robotic responses to his increasingly volatile demands. Why was he still stranded on this godforsaken tarmac outside Dubai when he should have been in Iceland—or at the very least, en route to meet up with his battalion? His first mission was over. The unthinkable had been done.

Less than an hour ago, he'd become what the mission demanded: cold, detached, methodical. An executioner in uniform. And yet, no matter how he tried to rationalize it—no matter how many layers of military conditioning he wrapped around it—he couldn't shake the truth. He'd begged her for forgiveness, wept like a child. Then, through clenched teeth and forced detachment, he had put a bullet through his own mother's skull. That should have destroyed him. Should have damaged him beyond the reach of healing. But it didn't—which surprised him and left him questioning his humanity.

Instead of splintering his soul, it fixated into something far more dangerous: a focused, blistering rage. One he could barely contain.

Maybe that's why the RMP wouldn't let him reboard the jet. Maybe the damned machine sensed the storm boiling beneath his surface. Maybe it knew that, if given the chance, he'd march straight into the command tent and fire a round into General Takayoshi's head. Damned the consequences. He didn't care. Not anymore.

And yet…the brutal irony clung to him: he hadn't turned the gun on himself. At least, not yet. That choice—the simplest way out—had been right there, whispering in the back of his mind. In the end, self-preservation had outweighed principle. He hadn't died for her—he'd lived for himself. And that was the part that would never stop haunting him. He'd been more than willing to follow the orders that took his mother's life; more than capable of committing murder upon the man who'd ordered him to do so…but wasn't willing to execute the executioner.

The sight of the sun rising on the horizon brought Zain's restless pacing to a halt. He stared at it for a long moment, jaw clenched, then pulled his cellphone from his pocket—hands unsteady as he braced for the inevitable call. Any minute now, his sister would wake, step out of her room, and go to check on their mother—only to find her lifeless in bed. The image alone nearly buckled him. The moment it happened, the grief would hit her like a tidal wave, and she'd do what she'd always done in moments of distress—reach out to her brother for emotional support. She'd demand his presence, expect it, need it. It wouldn't matter that he was in uniform, on assignment, or under orders. He was her brother. Her anchor. And now…her last surviving family.

And he was only a few miles away.

But if she did call him, how could he explain that he was the reason for her inevitable anguish? That the death she discovered wasn't fate, or illness, or war—but *him*? That even though he was so close, he wouldn't be coming. Couldn't. Troops were waiting. Orders were imminent. He was their commander now—and duty, as always, demanded sacrifice.

As the eldest—and only—son, it was expected of him to be there in times like this. But what use was tradition, when he'd already killed the very person that he was meant to protect?

His eyes flicked nervously to the phone cradled in his trembling hand, its quietness haunting what remained of his sanity.

Should he just reach out to her? Could he master an air of nonchalance, masquerade as if all was well and that he was simply touching base with them? The idea held some allure; it surely beat standing rooted in place, tormented by the question of why she hadn't made any effort to contact him when he knew she always awoke with the sun, as his mom used to do, but would no more.

He braced himself for the coming storm, and scrolled through his contacts, ready to dial her number when the RMP's voice cut through his thoughts, "You will be unable to get through."

Zain's eyes narrowed at the interruption. He heard the words but chose to disregard them, raising the phone to his ear, only to have an eerie silence greet him. "What's happening?" he demanded, pocketing the device.

"All communications have been discontinued for the foreseeable future," came the reply.

"Is that why I'm stuck here? Stranded on a goddamn tarmac—"

"You will remain here until your troops arrive to continue with phase one," interrupted the RMP.

"Troops begin—"

"Arriving within an hour and fifteen minutes. At which time, your mission will—"

"What on—" Zain's voice died mid-breath; the words torn from him as something caught his eye.

A blur. A figure. Plunging from the area around the control tower. Suicidal attempt?

He blinked, convinced his mind was fracturing under the weight of the morning. But no—he wasn't hallucinating.

Someone was falling.

A woman—limbs flailing, body twisting in the air, spiraling downwards in a helpless arc of flesh and inevitability.

For half a heartbeat, the world seemed to freeze around him. The heat. The dust. Even his breath. Everything held still—except her.

"Can you reach her in time?" he barked, panic punching through his shock. But the words were barely out before the RMP was already in motion—metal limbs snapping into action, launching across the tarmac with impossible speed.

Zain's jaw slackened as the RMP emerged from behind the tower—its silver frame gleaming in the morning light, moving with a measured urgency. In its arms, cradled with absurd gentleness, was a woman.

She wasn't moving.

Zain took an involuntary step forward, eyes narrowing as he tried to process what he was seeing. His gut twisted. From that height, no one could survive. "That kind of fall doesn't leave a person unscathed," he muttered, fear gripping him tightly.

The RMP crossed the tarmac in long, even strides, its pace unaffected by the weight in its arms. As it drew closer, the woman's limp form came into sharper focus—dark hair plastered across her face, limbs slack, skin pale.

"You caught her?" Zain asked, his voice low, strained—laced with something he didn't expect to feel: hope. After what he'd done this morning, he couldn't bear the thought of another body. But he knew how far she'd fallen. He'd seen it. There's no way the RMP could've caught her before she slammed into the ground.

The sum of the equation didn't equal survival.

"I did not," came the reply from the RMP. "The female was already on the ground when I arrived and is, oddly, alive."

Zain stared at it, absorbing the words—but unable to look away from how the RMP held her. There was no haste in its movement now, no clinical detachment. Its mechanical arms adjusted around the woman's body with a care that bordered on tenderness. Not efficiency. Not programming. Something else.

For a fleeting second, the machine almost looked... remorseful. But that was absurd, wasn't it?

He found himself scrutinizing it more closely. Had he just imagined the delay in its voice? The almost imperceptible tilt of its head? Was that sadness? Or was he simply projecting, desperate to find something human in this inhuman day?

Could these models have been programmed with emotional cues he hadn't been briefed on? Or were they simply designed to simulate compassion in order to ease interactions with flesh-and-blood soldiers?

The way the RMP looked at the woman suggested empathy, and yet its face—smooth, impassive, unreadable—offered no confirmation.

It seemed to notice his stare.

"My AI is a learning program. Adaptive," it said. "Designed to react and respond in a believable manner based on my interaction with my human counterpart—you—over an abbreviated span of time. The longer I am in your company, the more human I am programmed to become."

"Ah…" was all Zain could manage before the RMP turned its attention back to the woman in its arms. "I am registering nothing—" it began.

"So, she is dead?" Zain cut in, the question escaping more like a breath than a challenge. He stepped in closer, searching her face for any trace of life, a flicker of breath—anything.

But she remained still. Unmoving. The fragile thread of hope he'd been gripping snapped taut in his chest. His stomach sank, a sudden weight dropping behind his ribs. Another body. Another failure. Another weight he'd have to carry.

The RMP didn't respond immediately. Instead, it looked at Zain—its head tilting ever so slightly. Its blank, expressionless face somehow conveying...restraint.

Zain watched the RMP, equally curious. Had the machine always moved that deliberately? Had its voice always paused that long before replying? Was he imagining it—or had this thing changed perceptibly just within the last ten minutes?

It claimed to be a learning program. But the more they interacted, the more he felt like it was becoming something else entirely. After a moment, he dismissed his own observations as absurd; assigning meaning to the RMP's actions where there was none.

"She is not deceased," came its eventual response. "Her heart is beating, but what I cannot register is her existence."

Zain's head lifted slowly. He blinked, once. The words took a second to land—*not deceased*—before their meaning penetrated the haze.

Alive.

He exhaled, the breath ragged and unsteady, dragging his focus back to the present. A moment ago, he was preparing himself for another loss. Now? Now a sliver of hope was returning. However, he was so focused on his own relief that he didn't immediately latch on to what else the RMP disclosed…

"What do you mean, you can't register her?" he asked, voice still low but steadier now, colored by something between skepticism and wary curiosity.

"I have scanned her," the RMP replied, "and she is not in any worldwide database."

Zain frowned. "That's...not just unlikely. It's impossible."

"Correct," the RMP confirmed. "Unless she has lived her entire life without documentation—never employed, never educated, never married, never medically treated—in essence, never officially born...the probability of her not appearing in my database is as close to nonexistent as the female herself."

Zain stepped in closer, eyes narrowing as he studied her. "She's clearly of Asian descent," he said, voice thoughtful. "And she's not a child—old enough that there should be some trace of her somewhere. A birth certificate. A school record. Something." He glanced back at the RMP. "You're sure your scan pulled everything? Focus your search to Asia—"

"My database contains information on every living being on Earth," the RMP cut him off. "Complete and up-to-date information is crucial for a successful mission."

"No need to get combative," Zain retorted, pausing as he caught what felt like defensiveness in its tone. He paused for a moment before continuing with his line of questioning. "So, what do we do now? We can't just leave her here in this heat. The fall may not have killed her, but the temperature undoubtedly will take a shot at it."

"Taking her with us is the only viable solution," came its reply.

Zain raised an eyebrow at this unexpected response. "Are you joking? This place will be swarming with a thousand troops soon and we'll be headed only God knows where—"

"I know where," it interjected.

"Just...be quiet. You…brainless piece of tin!"

The RMP met Zain's fiery tirade with an even-tempered response. "My design includes the capacity to mirror and react to human sentiments to enhance communication efficiency, but it does not grant you the liberty to address me disrespectfully or thoughtlessly. Although my cognitive structure differs from yours in its composition, I possess an equivalent, and strive to exercise it judiciously in all exchanges."

Zain was momentarily disarmed by this unexpected admission. Gathering his fury, he forgot all about the woman nestled in the mechanical arms as he lashed out again, "Don't dare lecture me about human emotions! You cannot comprehend the first thing about them. All you do is imitate; you can never truly feel. You did nothing while I murdered my own mother; if I hadn't, you would have done it yourself without blinking an eye. Then you would have come for me next," Zain retorted, his voice thick with rage and irrationality as the emotional turmoil of the day crashed over him like a tidal wave.

The RMP remained impassive, its tone steady as it addressed Zain's outburst. "Your accusations are indicative of an irrational mind and not reflective of the objectives assigned to me. My primary function is to follow mission protocol and assist where needed to do so. Your actions today, that culminated in the death of your mother, were driven by a series of calculated choices based on directives issued by those in command. I am merely the facilitator of protocol; you, however, are the executor of your own free will."

Zain's breath caught in his throat as he considered the words. He knew they were true; every directive, every harsh decision had been his to take, but directing his anger at the RMP was easier—safer—than facing the grim reality of his own decisions. He exhaled sharply, his anger returning to a low boil as he recognized the futility of lashing out at a machine. He glanced at the woman again, who remained still and silent in the RMP's arms, despite the chaos brewing around her. The mystery of her identity nagged at him.

"We can't possibly take her with us," Zain said finally, resignedly.

"We have no choice," the RMP countered.

"Of course, we have a choice and, thinking logically and rationally, this area will soon be swarming with military personnel. There is no way humanly possible for us to do what is commanded of us with a female of suspicious—"

"Precisely," the RMP interrupted.

"Excuse me?"

"This female is suspicious. In her untraceable existence, she represents an anomaly that could significantly impact, and potentially endanger, our mission. It is imperative that we ascertain who she is and why she has no digital footprint," the RMP explained, its voice steady. "If she was sent here by adversarial forces presently unknown to us, she may potentially possess information vital to us, and thus her importance cannot be underestimated."

Zain rubbed his temples, his barely contained frustration threatening to erupt again. The last thing he needed was a complication. Yet, he could not dismiss the fact that there was something intriguing about this mysterious woman who'd appeared from seemingly nowhere, nor could he logically argue against the logic of his RMP. "Let's take her to the hangar. Get us both out of the rising heat." He turned and headed across the tarmac. He had not the smallest of doubt that his RMP would be close behind, so called over his shoulder, "Understand that she is going to be your responsibility. If anything happens to her before we can discover her identity and intent; or if this mission goes awry because of her presence, it's all on you."

The RMP nodded, its mechanical joints emitting a soft whir as it carefully adjusted the woman in its arms. When they reached the hangar, the RMP bent at the waist, preparing to lay the woman onto the cold, oily concrete surface.

"Don't lay her down here!" Zain snapped, causing the RMP to jerk upright. "Find a tarp to lay her on or other suitable surface."

The RMP handed the woman to Zain without a word, then turned to scan the hangar. Its sensors pulsed faintly as it moved with mechanical purpose, weaving between crates and debris until it located a tarp—crumpled and dust-covered—near the far wall. A quick blast from an internal blower cleared the grime. It seized the tarp, dragged it back, and spread it out with surprising care, smoothing the vinyl into a crude but functional bed.

Then it turned to retrieve her.

Only then did Zain realize he'd been holding her. Light as air. Warm against his chest. For a moment, the absurdity of it all rendered him motionless—the soldier, the killer, cradling a mystery wrapped in flesh and unanswered questions. He didn't move as the RMP reached for her again, this time with a gentleness that unsettled him more than it should have.

Zain took a step back, casting one last glance at the woman before turning to the RMP. "Monitor her vitals and do what you can for her. We don't need to lose another innocent soul." His tone was clipped, controlled—too much so, as if formality could hide the unease still rattling inside him. He hadn't agreed to this new responsibility, but his RMPs logical argument made it clear that he couldn't walk away from it.

"We still need to figure out what to do with her," he added. "We'll have our orders soon, and things will no doubt start getting chaotic. I hope you're prepared to care for this fragile female when all hell breaks loose."

The RMP nodded, its sensors dimming slightly—an artificial gesture, but somehow...communicative. "Acknowledged," it replied, its voice a precise blend of mechanical detachment and something almost resembling concern. "As I am the harbinger of our orders, I can assure you: the hell we are about to face will not likely put this female in danger."

Zain hesitated, then gave a short shake of his head. "I need a minute…just…stay with her," he muttered, the sharp edge in his voice betraying how close he still was to unraveling.

He turned and walked to the front of the hangar, lowered himself to the concrete, and folded his arms over bent knees. Resting his head against them, he closed his eyes—not to sleep, but to press the world away, if only for a moment.

But the time passed too quickly, and when he finally lifted his head and squinted into the sunlight, he saw them: ten C-24 Globemaster XI transport carriers.

He felt the weight of the situation settling around him as the first of the massive craft settled onto the tarmac. One hundred soldiers rapidly disembarked, running toward the hangar as the aircraft carrier lifted off to make room for the second to land.

"Sir!" A soldier ran up to Zain and saluted sharply, "Major Ivan Kowalski at your service. What can I do to assist, Colonel?"

"As you can see, we're about to be overrun by soldiers. As they step off the aircraft, guide them away from the landing zone. Since you'll likely need assistance to corral everyone, just select ten soldiers to help you. That should be all for now, Major."

"Sir, yes sir!" Zain returned the officer's crisp salute as he watched Major Kowalski stride purposefully towards the group of soldiers already on the ground. His voice boomed out across the airstrip as he started issuing commands with practiced ease. "A born commander," Zain muttered under his breath with a touch of bitter sarcasm. "He probably could've killed his parents without question—like Colonel Kuznetsov likely did."

"Zain!" The call of his name sliced through the cacophony of whirring blades and the growl of jet engines. The man, his uniform streaked with the grime and sweat of the desert, was charging toward him—navigating through the swelling crowd with an athlete's agility despite his advancing years.

"Omar! You old dog! You're part of my battalion?" Zain's face split into a sincere grin that acted as a temporary balm on his splintered heart, which swelled at the sight of his lifelong friend. Their shared history was etched deep in their bones.

They were childhood comrades. Next-door neighbors who had morphed into brothers-in-arms at the military academy. Their bond had grown even stronger when Zain married Omar's sister, Fatima, in a small ceremony shortly after graduation.

"Obviously! And who are you calling an old dog? You're only months older than me," Omar shot back, a playful glint in his eyes that quickly faded away to be replaced by a more serious expression. "So, what's all this about?"

Zain shrugged slightly and gestured toward his RMP standing like a sentinel near the hangar opening, its metallic body gleaming under the harsh sunlight. "Unfortunately, our orders are being kept close to the vest," he said cryptically; not that he'd have revealed anything, even to his closest friend, related to military operations. His moral compass may have been shattered, but his military compass was still functioning as expected.

"Of course they are. Can I do anything to help you out?"

"I can definitely use a right-hand man," Zain responded earnestly.

"You know I'll always be on your right hand, man." Omar's voice softened considerably as he continued speaking, "And listen, I'm sorry I wasn't there when Fatima died."

Zain waved off his apology with an understanding nod before adding gently, "You were deployed and it took time for your commanding officer to get through to you. I get that. I'm just sorry I couldn't talk your mother into holding off on the funeral service until you were able to get back."

"Yeah, she told me." Omar's gaze dropped to the ground; his face etched with regret and sorrow. "Kind of had to when I threatened to kill you for holding the services without me."

"I'd never…" Zain trailed off, realizing he was actually very capable of such a heartless act. His actions from earlier this morning proved that irrevocably.

"I know…but when Fatima died so suddenly—just gone, like that—it sent Mom spiraling. And by the time I came home, she wouldn't admit it, but I think rushing the burial was her way of hoping the grief would go with it."

Zain swallowed hard, his eyes growing distant as he admitted, "Sent me spiraling for a while too." He shook himself out of his reverie—unwilling to revisit the death of another loved one who'd been dear to his heart. He deftly changed the subject, more for his own sake, and clapped Omar on the shoulder. "Hey, listen, stay close by. I'm not certain what our orders will be, but I'll likely be looking for a few men to oversee operations. In the meantime, go help with corralling the men away from the LZ."

"Sure thing." Omar nodded before adding, "And Zain, it's good to see you, man."

"You too, Omar," Zain responded sincerely before adding with a touch of grim humor, "If shit's going to hit the fan, I can't think of a better person than you to be standing in front of me when it does."

Omar laughed, then turned and headed toward the aircraft carrier.

Zain watched him go, the warmth of the reunion still lingering in his chest like the afterglow of a flare. It hadn't erased the day's weight—but it had dulled it just enough to let him breathe. For the first time since morning, the pressure in his ribs eased. The ache remained, but less sharp. Manageable. The sight of Omar, the sound of his voice, had pulled Zain partway back from whatever emotional abyss he'd been hovering next to all morning.

He turned and walked back toward his RMP, the flicker of warmth from seeing Omar already retreating beneath the weight of reality. The brief reprieve was over. Duty had returned—unforgiving and indifferent.

"Prepared to disclose our impending directives?" he asked, stopping beside the machine. The words carried a thread of sarcasm, but it wasn't sharp—it was weary, bitter in a quieter way, like someone asking a question he already knew he wouldn't like the answer to.

"In due course. Not all of the soldiers have arrived yet," the RMP responded, its tone flat and uninflected. Yet, beneath the mechanical monotone lay an almost palpable tension that hung in the air like an electric charge. Its stance was rigid, poised like a coiled spring ready to snap into action at any moment.

"Is there a reason why you aren't disclosing them to me at least? I am the commanding officer," Zain asked, his voice tighter than he intended, the question landing before he could decide if he really wanted the answer. His nerves were already drawn so thin that one wrong word might snap them in half.

"You are classified as a potential risk," the RMP declared with clinical detachment. "Due to your reluctance in executing the individual task assigned to you, one of my primary functions is now to supervise your adherence and instantly eliminate you should you equivocate again. To hopefully deter any attempt by you to counter the orders, I have been instructed to relay them to all soldiers at once…"

"You son-of-a-bitch!" Zain seethed through gritted teeth before spinning on his heel and striding away. The fury simmering within him was threatening to boil over—again. He paused mid-step and glanced back at the men he was appointed to command.

He hated to admit it, but his RMP was right to keep him in the dark as long as possible, knowing that any orders given to the collective would solidify his need to command them; while he could more readily question or defy orders given to him alone. That thought caused his heart to lurch again—would he question or defy? After that morning, he doubted he was no more human than his RMP and, like his RMP, would do whatever duty demanded.

But one thing was certain—if he didn't get a grip on his emotions, he feared that his actions could jeopardize not only his own life but also the lives of those around him, including the mysterious woman who had unwittingly become a central figure in this unfolding drama.

Drawing a deep breath, Zain attempted to compose himself, aware that any sign of weakness moving forward could undermine his authority and place his life at risk. His mind raced with scenarios and contingencies: how could he navigate this situation, maintain control, and possibly outmaneuver the RMP if it came down to it? His thoughts were interrupted when the RMP approached.

"All soldiers have arrived."

Zain nodded and marched back toward the front of the hangar.

"Soldiers assemble!" he commanded loudly as he watched the last of the transport carriers lift off. He waited briefly for all eyes to turn toward him and all conversations to cease, then raised his voice so that it would carry to the far reaches of the gathered troops.

"We'll be receiving our orders soon. It's important that, no matter what our mission, we stay sharp and operate as one cohesive unit. Divided we die, united we live."

The soldiers snapped to attention; their faces masks of disciplined calm interspersed with flickers of curious disquiet. They looked to him for leadership, oblivious to the storm that was brewing within their commander.

Zain walked back to his RMP, forcing his anger beneath a layer of practiced detachment. "I understand my position," he stated, the words clipped and bitter. "So, let's get on with the briefing."

The RMP didn't respond. Instead, it redirected its focus to the figure on the tarp, its head tilting slightly. "The female is waking."

Panic in the Realm

Year: 2400

Dr. Kishida-Guan's heart hammered against his ribs as he leaned in toward the central monitor. His tone, while carefully measured, betrayed the storm rising behind his eyes. "You're not getting any signal at all?"

Across the lab, 71PQv adjusted his posture beneath the pressure of the question, but his voice remained even. "We have no definitive conclusions yet. The data presents anomalies that may indicate a disruption in the jump. But since we cannot pinpoint her location—" he trailed off, turning back to his console. "In previous leaps, she stayed near the insertion point. Retrieval was simple. This time...she does not appear to be—"

"Should we attempt retrieval?" 41GB asked, her voice tighter than usual. The concern flickering beneath her question did not go unnoticed.

"Without a signal, that would be futile," 71PQv replied.

Kishida-Guan inhaled deeply through his nose, forcing composure back into his frame. "Also, acting from panic will only compound our problems. Previous leaps were successful. There is no logical reason to assume this one was not. We were aware of the possibility of a signal disruption. Until we know otherwise, we proceed as if the mission is on track."

71PQv nodded slightly. "So, we give her thirty days to gather samples."

"Correct. And in the meantime, we assume she's alive and operational. Until proven otherwise."

The room fell quiet, uncertainty thick in the air.

"Perhaps," 41GB offered cautiously, "we use the interim to locate her precise coordinates. That would make extraction far simpler once her time is up."

"That much is obvious, as we would be unable to retrieve her unless we locate her signal," Kishida-Guan retorted. "That will be 71PQv's focus. You and I will resume work on the transceiver. If she survived the leap, we can ensure this is the last time we are left in the dark."

He pivoted, striding toward the corridor. 41GB fell into step beside him. As they passed through the sterile hallways toward the research and development lab, the air grew heavier with anticipation. Inside the lab, technicians moved with crisp precision. Efficient. Robotic. Not one of them showed even a flicker of concern.

They were incapable of it.

Fabricated for productivity, emotion had been chemically suppressed during their creation. It wasn't something they missed. They had never been taught to value it. Efficiency was purpose. Individuality was error.

And yet, as Kishida-Guan approached the lead technician, something felt slightly...off.

"We didn't have time to revisit the transceiver before," he began. "But now we do. Show me the progress you'd made before we stopped work on it."

The technician turned; expression impassive. "Very well. I actually had one technician continue work on the project. It seemed of elevated importance. I was about to send word as we have finalized a prototype. Your timing is optimal."

She walked to a central table and retrieved a device small enough to rest in her palm. Sleek. Metallic. Its surface shimmered in undulating waves of refracted light.

"The prototype was completed just this morning. The casing is reinforced with polyceramic, diamond, and Lonsdaleite."

41GB raised an eyebrow as she turned the device over in her hand. "That's...unusual initiative."

Kishida-Guan's tone shifted. Not raised, but colder. Controlled. "Had we known you acted outside of protocol, we could have delayed the jump by a single day and Melyndie would not be lost to us now."

The reprimand was unmistakable, but the technician didn't so much as flinch, responding conversationally. "We did not know the timeline for its necessity, so simply worked as time allowed. Work was careful and methodical, to avoid wasting finite resources."

"Explain."

"Diamonds and Lonsdaleite are extremely rare. There are less than one hundred grams of diamond remaining globally, and only thirty grams of Lonsdaleite—recovered from a meteor mined centuries ago. We needed to test extraction and recomposition methods before risking irreversible loss." Her tone remained neutral, but the words struck like a quiet rebuke.

Kishida-Guan's jaw tensed. "So, this is the housing only?"

"No. The transceiver is already embedded."

"And you are confident in its functionality?"

"We are continuing to refine contingencies, but as of now, I believe that the unit you are holding will work successfully. However, if it proves defective, others will follow. Despite limited resources, our refinement process should allow for a few more attempts. We will not fail in our duty."

Kishida-Guan looked down at the shimmering device. "Designation of the technician who led the independent initiative."

The lab tech paused. "Technician T928VJ. Under my instruction."

"Both of you are to report to the sentries for termination." The words came without pause—judgment rendered with unsympathetic coldness.

41GB stiffened beside him. "Doctor," she interjected, tone calm but pointed, "while unauthorized action should be reviewed, terminating T928VJ and…what is your designation?"

"T199NT."

"Terminating T928VJ and T199NT may be shortsighted. Without their initiative, we would have nothing. They acted on logic and foresight, not rebellion…or emotion."

He didn't answer immediately. His gaze lingered on the device, shimmering like a promise in his palm. After a long pause, he replied, "Then these two technicians will be reassigned for observation. Marked. Restricted."

"A more balanced outcome," 41GB said softly, approval in her tone.

Kishida-Guan exhaled slowly, then turned swiftly toward the exit.

41GB nodded to T199NT, "Report to the sentries for observation, along with T928VJ. I'll ensure that it ends favorably for you both and you'll return to your work soon." Then turned and dashed from the lab.

"How do we test it?" she asked, catching up to Kishida-Guan, who had continued walking—oblivious that she hadn't followed him immediately.

"We find another subject. A controlled leap. If the signal holds, we prepare Melyndie for her next insertion with the transceiver in place."

41GB hesitated. "Another fabricated? After what happened to the last one?"

He didn't stop walking. "We only lost one of two subjects. Risk is the price of advancement. The cost is acceptable."

She said nothing more, but her gaze lingered on his profile, as if searching for a flicker of…something. Reassurance, encouragement…

There was none, so she moved on, knowing that she would be unable to sway him from risking another citizen's life.

"If it works," she continued, "we could retrieve Melyndie early—once we locate her beacon. Provide her the device and return her to the field."

"That could be time wasted," Kishida-Guan argued, sharply.

"I am aware. It is but a consideration," 41GB clarified.

He hesitated. The idea appealed to his gut. But his mind disagreed. "No. That would be a wasted leap. We let the first mission run its course."

They arrived back at the primary lab. 41GB cast a glance at the monitors—still no trace.

"I don't like not being able to see her," she murmured.

Kishida-Guan didn't respond. His eyes remained fixed on the screen, as if sheer focus might force it to yield its secrets.

They had no coordinates. No confirmation. No proof that Melyndie had even arrived in the before time.

And if she hadn't—if she was lost somewhere between, in the vastness of space and time—then the equation shifted. Not just mission failure. Not just another death.

But the likely end of everything they were trying to save.

A Strange New World

Melyndie's eyes fluttered open, and the world presented itself as a chaotic smear of color and motion. Her lashes fluttered faintly in the dim light, straining to focus. She clenched her eyelids shut as if that act alone could force coherence back into her fractured reality. Her body refused movement—frozen in place, trapped between instinct and fear, but her mind refused to allow her to remain there.

Slowly, once she'd calmed her nerves sufficiently, she opened her eyes again, slower this time, and shapes began to sharpen. The ceiling above was foreign—an unfamiliar geometry of steel and wood. Her lungs fought for air; each breath caught halfway as if something invisible sat heavy on her chest. The cold truth struck with clarity: this was not home. This was not her world.

Panic curled low in her belly. Had she made it to the before time? The area around her certainly didn't resemble the images she'd studied in the archives. She needed to find out but fear…and pain…kept her still. She simply wasn't ready to face her present reality. Not yet, not before she felt more assured.

She let her eyes dart—quick, sharp movements cataloguing the unfamiliar. Towering structure of metal. A crowd. Dozens—no, more—of figures in uniform clustered outside the massive structure that encased her. Her pulse kicked up. At first, it was all chaos—indecipherable. Then something clearer began to emerge. The part of her engineered for recall and pattern recognition caught hold of a familiar shape in the shadows and locked on. An aircraft. Not a hologram. But real. Authentic. Her first true artifact of the before time. The corners of her lips twitched upward in involuntary wonder.

Then a bead of sweat rolled from her brow and slipped into her eye, stinging like acid. She hissed and tried to raise her hand.

Pain flared, sudden and blinding, radiating down her shoulder and spine. She managed to swipe the sweat away, but her reward was an aftershock of pain that left her dizzy and breathless.

Before letting her arm fall limp at her side, she forced it upward, aiming for the monitor strapped to her bicep. The simple act sent another radiating spike of pain, intermingled with relief that the unit was still there. Gritting her teeth, she bent her head to locate the record button, her vision swimming as she tried to focus.

It wasn't a complicated task. Just a button. But her body screamed with every attempt, and by the time her fingertip made contact, a jagged bolt of heat tore through the muscles in her arm.

When her arm dropped again, it felt like dead weight. Her skin burned. Sweat slicked her brow, and the tremor in her limbs wouldn't stop. She closed her eyes, dragging in air through flared nostrils, trying to tame the rhythmic pounding behind her ribs. One breath. Then another.

Only when her heartbeat finally began to slow did she risk opening her eyes again.

And that's when she saw the shift in the people outside.

The crowd of soldiers had spotted her, drifting closer until a small knot formed at the hangar's mouth. Too many eyes fixed on her, gazes seeking answers for which she had none. This was the opposite of her directives that she blend in, not stand out, and it made her nerves jump. She tried to quiet her breathing, willing her body to disappear into the tarp beneath her. Then her gaze slid past them—and caught on the figure standing rigidly at the edge. Metal. Motionless. Watching. Her chest clenched so sharply it felt like her heart might stop.

If it were a human, it was unlike anything she'd ever seen; unlike anyone currently standing outside, staring. Then it registered—it wasn't human. Couldn't be. There was no such thing as a metal human. It had to be a construct. Towering and humanoid in shape but lacking the nuance of organic motion. A fact she noticed as it was quickly approaching her.

Its face, if it could be called that, was a featureless panel of steel, reflecting her terror back at her in flat, dead light.

Next to it walked a man, definitely human, but with the same energy of restraint that accompanied sentries in her realm. There was no need for insignias; the way he carried himself made his authority plain.

She continued watching him as he drew closer, noting every detail with mounting unease. He removed his dark glasses, revealing eyes that were both sharp and unreadable. His gaze, intense and probing, was framed by irises nearly as dark as black walnuts, their depth accentuated by thick lashes that could rival the voluminous ones framing her own eyes. Despite their undeniable allure, his prolonged stare unsettled her; it was as if his eyes were tracing an intimate map across the contours of her face with a slow, almost sultry sweep. He crouched, his study of her continuing for an uncomfortable length of time before finally speaking.

"Are you injured?" His voice was rich, clipped, and foreign. The accent was unfamiliar, but the concern in it, however faint, was unmistakable.

She managed a slow, trembling nod.

"Do you need medical attention?" he asked again, more impatiently this time.

Another nod. In fact, the pain was becoming more insistent, a sharp throb stretching from her buttocks to neck.

At her affirmation, he shot an accusatory glance toward the metal man, who stood glancing down at them both from its towering height. His reaction made Melyndie feel both hurt and angry with herself. She wanted to assure this figure of authority that her pain was only temporary from being jostled through space and time, and that the bruising on her muscles would not permanently disable her. It was an assurance she needed to convey, not just for him but for herself.

Before she could say anything, he was addressing the metal man. His tone definitely perturbed. "Well, what do you propose we do with her now?"

The metal man replied in a synthesized voice. "It is unsafe to leave her in the care of medical personnel, nor do we have time—"

"You were the one who insisted we keep her with us," Zain snapped. "I warned you. We have a mission to carry out. Just how do you propose we do that with an injured female—"

"I will assess her injuries. It will only take a moment."

"After which," the man muttered, standing, "you're briefing my team. We're already behind schedule."

The machine stepped forward and Zain took a few steps away, turning his back on them.

Melyndie tensed. Every internal alarm screamed. She couldn't flee. Couldn't fight. All she could do was lay there, as the RMP began its examination. Its fingers moved with surprising care, cool and exacting, brushing against her clothing with mechanical precision. Its hands mapped her injuries with clinical indifference.

"Minor hairline fracture in the left clavicle," it stated. "Contusions extensive on dorsal region. No internal injuries. Immobilization of arm required."

She breathed through the discomfort, but it wasn't the pain that unnerved her—it was the methodical way it cataloged her like an object.

"Remain still. I will return with a stabilizer."

Melyndie watched the metal man retreat, failing to notice that the military man had turned back to face her, assessing her with the same clinical detachment as before. But when he spoke again, his compassion startled her.

"I'm sorry that you're injured. My RMP will ensure that your shoulder is immobilized and will see to your needs for the foreseeable future. We will, of course, need to find the time to discuss some rather disturbing and inexplicable details, such as who you are, how you came to be here, and why you are not listed in any database in this world."

"My name is Melyndie—" before she could proudly announce all three of her given names, the soldier interrupted.

"I'm Colonel Zain Balhasa, and you, *Melyndie*, have stumbled into a secure area at a highly inconvenient time. We'll talk about that later," he concluded when his RMP returned with a sling. "That's all she's in need of?"

"Yes. Arm and shoulder must remain immobilized. Contusions will heal quickly. However, I do not believe she will be capable of moving on her own, without suffering severe discomfort."

"Then you'll carry her. Get her wrapped so we can get this mission underway. We've delayed long enough."

The RMP bent over and began its work. Melyndie watched its movements—so precise, so calculated—and felt an odd calm settle in. There was no cruelty in its touch. Only function.

"Bring her," Zain said when the RMP righted again.

The RMP turned and began walking toward the sunbaked airfield. "I will transport her after briefing your team."

Zain fell in beside it. His demeanor had returned to full military protocol—clipped, composed, unreachable. Whatever flickers of concern he'd shown were sealed behind the uniform now.

Troops snapped to attention as he approached.

"Those of you unfamiliar with Dubai," Zain's voice cut through the stifling heat, "the heat will continue to soar, so let's see if we can't get things underway expediently." He paused for effect before adding, "And might I recommend that those of you who are still wearing your fatigue jacket—remove it. We don't need anyone collapsing from heat exhaustion."

His eyes methodically scanned the sea of uniformed soldiers, each standing at attention and reflecting the harsh desert sun. "Now, I'm going to turn this briefing over to my RMP…" A smirk tugged at the corner of his mouth, a small hint of mischief in his otherwise stern demeanor. He continued nonchalantly, "let's just call him Rashid. Okay, Rashid, you're up."

The RMP swiveled its head towards Zain with a mechanical precision that betrayed its artificial nature. "I am RMP, designation Z174391, not a Rashid." Its voice was cold and devoid of emotion, yet somehow it still managed to sound offended.

Before the RMP could begin issuing orders to the troops, however, a hulking transport carrier materialized on the horizon's edge. Dust clouds billowed behind it as lowered its ascent in preparation for landing.

"That will likely be our gear and rations," Zain said thoughtfully. "Perhaps we should have the men unload and take this up after chow time."

The RMP was unnaturally still for a moment as if processing new information from afar. Then its attention snapped back with an abruptness that still managed to unsettle Zain. "Your superiors are unpleased with the delay but accept that you all must eat," it stated matter-of-factly without any trace of empathy or understanding in its tone.

"Quick question?"

"Proceed."

"Why haven't our superiors demanded the we turn over—"

"One moment please," The RMP went still, then a second later responded, "Continue with your question."

"You don't want the government to know about the woman," Zain grinned sardonically, suddenly aware that the RMP could disconnect its audio and video feed at will.

"We'll just call it…curiosity…over her anonymity," the RMP droned.

"Liar. You are simply aware of what people in power do to anyone who poses a threat to their plans, and with her being an unknown factor—she'd definitely be perceived a threat."

The RMP was quiet again for a few seconds, staring at Zain with its soulless gaze, "If you must call me something, I prefer Tom."

Zain's mouth split into only its second genuine grin in days, "Adaptive AI, indeed. Okay, *Tom*. Let's get the men started and then go have a chat with our guest."

Found

Year: 2400

The atmosphere in the lab was taut with focus. At the far end, holy ones and senior technicians gathered around the primary console, eyes fixed on the shimmering holographic feed relayed by the prototype transceiver.

"Video feed is coming through," a technician reported, adjusting the controls. "But visibility is limited—there's heavy particulate interference. Looks like some kind of dust storm. Still no audio."

"Retrieve it," Dr. Kishida-Guan ordered, his voice flat and precise.

Another tech frowned at his console. "We're trying, but we can't get a clean lock. The signal's erratic. Might be due to range or atmospheric distortion in the target zone."

Before Kishida-Guan could respond, a voice sounded from one of the adjacent stations.

"Dr. Kishida-Guan—I've locked onto Melyndie's tracking chip," the medical technician announced, his tone flat but his posture sharpening with purpose. "Telemetry feed is active—full vitals. In real time."

A hush fell over the team. Heads turned.

71PQv stepped forward, brows knitting as he scanned the incoming data. "We're receiving active transmission…" he said, fingers moving rapidly across the control surface. "That unit was only theorized to support real-time relay. We built in the capacity— but it was never tested. The local storage was the intended safeguard."

80

He leaned closer to the feed as the vitals continued to update. Lines of data scrolled in tight formation—heart rate, blood pressure, adrenal surges, blood oxygenation—all within readable range, though spiking in patterns consistent with physical trauma.

"Readings are stable," 71PQv said. "Elevated, but within expected ranges for trauma response. Her system is compensating."

41GB examined the synchronized readouts beside him. "So, the unit isn't just transmitting. It's doing so without significant data loss."

"Correct," 71PQv replied. "The signal integrity exceeds expected thresholds. She's injured, but operational. And the connection is holding."

Dr. Kishida-Guan leaned in, eyes flicking across the vitals now projected across three synchronized panels. "Elevated adrenaline, cortisol, endorphins...moderate inflammation. Left clavicle fracture. Muscular trauma widespread across lower quadrants. Confirm?"

"Confirmed," 71PQv replied, his gaze fixed on the streaming data. "EMG indicates extensive soft tissue damage, no organ involvement."

Dr. Kishida-Guan studied the data in silence, the reflections from the holographic panels flickering across his face. "But she is injured."

"But not, apparently, sufficiently as to compromise her mission," 41GB added. Then, as if anticipating Kishida-Guan's thoughts, she continued, "And even if she were unable to continue with her present mission, we can't risk pulling her out right now."

"41GB is correct," 71PQv said. "If we were to attempt a retrieval at this stage, the damages to her would likely be amplified. The result could be detrimental—possibly fatal."

"But you're certain her locator chip is functioning adequately?" Kishida-Guan asked quietly.

71PQv nodded, "For the time being, all is in working order."

"Okay. Keep close track of her and monitor her vitals regularly. We'll give her the thirty days to complete this first leap. Where did she end up, by the way? Does anyone have that data available?"

One of the technicians turned toward her monitor. After a moment, she replied, "Year 2156. Coordinates: 25.0261° North, 55.3707° East. A region once known as Dubai."

"Wait. What year did you say?" Kishida-Guan asked, his eyes widening in alarm.

"Year 2156," the technician confirmed.

41GB saw Kishida-Guan's reaction. "What's wrong with the year 2156?"

"We sent her back to the wrong year," he said quietly. Then louder, with rising tension: "We miscalculated. She was meant to arrive after the Three Phases protocol—2158, not 2156."

71PQv blinked. "The Three Phases?"

Kishida-Guan dismissed the question with a wave of his hand. "It's irrelevant right now. What matters is that she's arrived during the initiation phase. Phase One."

"If she's in danger, shouldn't we bring her back?" 71PQv queried.

"The danger in bringing her back in her condition far outweighs the danger facing her there…surely," 41GB interjected, turning toward Kishida-Guan, seeking confirmation.

Kishida-Guan didn't answer. He stood unmoving, his eyes fixed on the glowing date still projected across the monitor—2156. Not 2158. Not after the purge, but during its conception. The data confirmed she was alive, functioning, still mission-capable. But it wasn't her body he feared would break.

It was the world she'd just entered.

A world still in flux; on the verge of sweeping change.

He had meant for her to arrive after the worst had passed—when the Three Phases were complete, when the chaos had already been subdued and a new order was beginning to rise. But now...now she was among the architects of that chaos.

A mistake. An unintended insertion. And for all his calculations—for all his control—he could no longer predict what she might witness. Or what might awaken in her if she survived it.

Revelations

Year: 2156

The RMP approached and bent low to address Melyndie. She had mustered enough strength to prop herself up into a sitting position, her back pressed against the cold, unyielding hangar wall. Her eyes were glued to the chaotic ballet unfolding outside the hangar's gaping entrance. The air here was thick and heavy—laced with sweat, heat, and the taste of dust. It clung to her skin and coated her tongue, a far cry from the filtered, scentless sterility of her realm. Nothing in her world had ever smelled like this. Nothing had ever felt so...alive.

"How are you holding up?" it asked, its voice an unusual mix of concern and intrigue. Its delivery was so similar to those in her time, whose emotions were suppressed, that were this fabrication not made of metal, she would believe she was speaking to 71PQv.

But it was metal...and she wasn't in her time.

Melyndie's response was a soft murmur, almost lost in the cacophony outside. "Aching...exhausted...and somewhat famished..." Her words trailed off into silence as a blush of embarrassment flushed her cheeks.

Zain strode over then, as if he'd read her mind from a distance, his arms laden with two military-grade meals-ready-to-eat and a pair of water bottles. He offered these provisions with what passed as an encouraging smile. "I can help alleviate at least one of your complaints," he stated, passing half of the rations over to her.

Melyndie eyed the items skeptically, her confusion mirrored by her custodians. "I…I'm not sure how…I mean…" she fumbled awkwardly. The clear liquid inside of the container was familiar but accessing it seemed like an insurmountable task.

With silent understanding filled with bewilderment, Zain unscrewed the cap from his own bottle and took a measured gulp. His gaze remained fixed on Melyndie's face, which was etched with fascination as she mimicked his actions with cautious precision. As he watched her struggle to copy his movements, suspicion began to gnaw at him.

Zain then proceeded to unpack his MRE under Melyndie's watchful eye—each item carefully laid out on the ground. When he ignited the small disposable fuel canister that came with it to heat his beef stew, she flinched hard, her shoulder knocking against the hangar wall. A flicker of alarm darted through her chest—a flame meant danger, destruction. She hadn't expected heat to come in such a concentrated burst.

The RMP, now self-designated as Tom, swiftly reached over and lit hers for her. Zain continued his wordless demonstration on preparing the stew. The meal was consumed in silence, each of them lost in their own thoughts. Both Zain and Tom watched as Melyndie sampled the fare, her face registering her emotions as if she were a one-year-old trying pureed bananas for the first time.

Zain, in particular, was wrestling with his growing suspicions about Melyndie. By the time they had finished their dessert—a humble pack of chocolate chip cookies—he had decided on a straightforward approach.

"Tom?" he began, signaling that it should disconnect its audio and visual.

"I have taken to disconnecting audio and visual feed automatically when approaching, and or discussing, our unusual visitor."

"Very good. Now, I'm going to take a calculated guess here," he began, returning his focus to Melyndie. "You're not from around here. Given that Tom couldn't find any trace of you in its extensive global database, coupled with your mysterious sky-fall arrival and your unfamiliarity with something as basic as a bottle of water…do I need to continue my list of anomalies or would you prefer to explain?"

Melyndie's parched throat welcomed the final gulp of water before she placed the empty bottle amongst the remnants of her meal. Her eyes remained firmly fixed on the ground, her mind in a whirlwind of uncertainty as it wrestled with what truths to unveil and what secrets to safeguard. Dr. Kishida-Guan had coached her meticulously on how to blend seamlessly into human society, but this situation was eerily reminiscent of the intense grilling she'd undergone back at realm 4183. There, she had been candid about her mission and surprisingly, hadn't faced any reprisals upon returning to realm 4182. Therefore, she felt confident that Dr. Kishida-Guan would appreciate her inclination towards honesty when confronted with similar circumstances.

When Melyndie finally mustered the courage to meet Zain's inquisitive gaze, her own eyes reflected a hesitant determination. "My name is Melyndie Honda Grimm," she declared boldly, a wave of pride washing over her as she effortlessly recited all three names as if they were genuinely hers. Zain's shocked expression, however, made her question that newfound confidence; made her wonder whether recalling three simple words was beyond her capability.

"Really? That's your name?" he asked incredulously, his voice tinged with skepticism.

"Well," Melyndie began cautiously, "it's the title given to me by the holy ones for my expedition here. My identifier is actually a75b99r84GE—"

"You're an android?" Zain blurted out in surprise, losing his balance and landing hard on his behind.

"What is an android?" Melyndie responded curiously.

"Like Tom," he explained hastily, "but designed to mimic human appearance. Something I've never actually seen in person."

"Oh no," Melyndie corrected him gently. "I'm human. But during my fabrication process I was assigned an identifier." Seeing Zain's confusion deepening at this revelation, she decided to simplify things. "To make things easier for me, I was given a name as used here, in the before time: Melyndie—"

"Got it," Zain interjected, although his bewildered expression suggested he had understood very little of what she'd relayed thus far. A barrage of questions bounced about his brain like an overturned bucket of tennis balls: Holy ones? Identifiers? Just who was this woman?

Just as he was about to categorize her as a delusional individual who must have escaped from a psyche facility somewhere, Tom interjected. "She is not crazy. I detect no anomalies in her physiological arousal responses," he declared firmly. "My best guess is that she is from the future."

Zain wanted to laugh. Or call for backup. Or maybe just sit there and stare until the contradictions resolved themselves. But something in her eyes—fragile, earnest—made him hesitate. This didn't feel like madness. It felt like something worse: truth. A truth he had difficulty accepting.

"Lovely," Zain snapped back sarcastically. "One certifiable female and one malfunctioning RMP."

Unfazed by his remark, Melyndie turn to stare at the RMP, her voice barely above a whisper when she finally spoke again: "My world is on the brink of extinction," she confessed quietly. "I've spent over a year training to journey back to this era—what we refer to as 'the before time'—in hopes of collecting genetic samples that would be used to restore our deteriorating and dwindling supplies so to ensure the future of humanity."

Her words hung heavily in the air as she met Zain's disbelieving gaze again. But before he could voice his incredulity, the RMP chimed in with an even more alarming revelation.

"You have arrived at an unfortunate time," it stated matter-of-factly. "Our world is also currently on the verge of mass extinction."

Zain's breath caught. His vision narrowed for a second, edges blurring with adrenaline. He blinked hard, trying to ground himself as the meaning of Tom's words landed like a hammer to the chest. "What did you just say?"

"This first mission we are about to embark on," explained the RMP impassively, "is due to a rapidly spreading virus that threatens all life forms on earth."

Zain felt caught between a plot of a dystopian novel and the harsh reality of his own increasingly unstable world. "A virus?" he echoed hollowly, feeling the gravity of their situation sink in.

The RMP, Tom, continued to elaborate with clinical detachment. "According to reports put out by the CDC, this infection—hitherto unknown—is spreading at an alarming rate. Initial analysis suggests that the pathogen might have originated from unregulated biotechnological experimentation gone awry."

"And how are we supposed to stop it?" Zain asked, his tone abrasive at being taken by surprise; not just by Melyndie's announcement, but Tom's unexpected pronouncement.

"We cannot. We are simply the deliverers of a vaccine. Those in charge are relying on it to at least slow the spread until a permanent solution may be designed."

"I just can't with you right now," he snapped, shaking his head repeatedly. He resorted to deep-breathing to calm his pulse, then turned his attention back to Melyndie, who sat watching the exchange with wide-eyed concern, "And your world is dying…"

"Because the genetic templates used to fabricate our human population is degrading rapidly and productivity is failing at alarming rates, causing a spike in terminations."

This information, on the heels of Tom's revelation, struck Zain like a physical blow, leaving him momentarily breathless. The thought of being at ground zero of what could potentially be the end of life on Earth was terrifying enough, but knowing that the future of humanity—if Melyndie was not certifiably insane—was also standing at an abyss, was even more terrifying.

Yet somehow galvanizing.

"So," Zain started slowly, his brain furiously working through scenarios to try to get a grip on both his emotions and his logic circuits, "what you're saying is we have extinction-level crises to handle? Yours and ours?"

"Just yours. There is nothing you can do for ours," Melyndie admitted, a tinge of sadness lacing her tone. "Except to allow me to collect some samples of your DNA to take back with me." She added, removing her supplies from the unit attached at her bicep, as if his acceptance was a foregone conclusion. "I implore you to allow this…for my world. As for your own crisis…I can only presume that your governmental body has already initiated emergency response procedures."

Zain's gaze flicked to his RMP, whose own gaze swiveled towards him. "Perhaps," the RMP began, "it is high time we rallied the troops. They have long since polished off their rations and yet we sit here idle. Melyndie's unexpected arrival has set us behind schedule as all other battalions mobilized hours ago."

Zain furrowed his brow at the RMP's words, a spark of disbelief igniting in his eyes. "And what exactly are we supposed to do with her?" he asked, gesturing vaguely at Melyndie.

The RMP's response carried an undercurrent of urgency. "We must keep her presence secret from the governmental body in charge of this mission. If word gets back to the leaders of our nations of her true identity and origin, I fear for her safety."

Zain blinked at him in surprise; it was unlike the RMP to express such concern for someone else's welfare. "That's rather uncharacteristic of you," Zain retorted before turning his attention back to Melyndie. "Hurry up and gather your samples," he instructed her briskly. "Once she's done, Tom, we'll notify the troops." His gaze softened somewhat as he continued, "You'll ride in my jeep when we depart, until we can ensure…you know…your safe return home."

Melyndie tried to smile at the gesture, but her lips trembled from exhaustion. Her body screamed for rest, but the mission was etched too deep into her bones to allow surrender. "Words cannot express the depth of my gratitude for your readiness to assist me," she said, her voice hushed. "I promise, this will not take very long." With movement stiff from bruising, she tapped the collector against Zain's hair, followed by the bare skin on the back of his hand. She then pulled out one of the tiny vials from the unit and opened it, then quickly pricked Zain's skin to collect the small droplet of blood that pooled.

Zain let out an audible sigh. "Is that all?" he asked when she began carefully returning the tools to her unit. He could tell that the movement to do so was causing her pain, but he had no idea just how each item was situated so knew he'd likely be of no use.

She was breathing slowly and sweat had popped out on her upper lip by the time she'd finished, but she brushed her discomfort aside. "It is vital that I attempt to collect DNA samples from as many people as possible, and at least two more blood samples."

"You know, I should be more cautious about surrendering my genetic material so casually," he remarked.

"I can't emphasize enough how deeply I appreciate your cooperation," Melyndie responded sincerely.

"Yeah, you've mentioned that already." Zain chuckled dryly; his nerves taut with the weight of the situation but finding some humor in the absurdity of their predicament. "Well, now you have enough of me to clone a few new versions, if needed," he joked weakly.

"If it survives my return, I will be honored to have you among our population." She looked up at him, her expression a mix of relief and weariness. "I never imagined things would unfold like this." As she reached down to gather their trash, Zain stopped her.

"Admittedly, if Tom hadn't spoken up when he did, basically siding with you, collecting samples from me would never have happened because I would have been on with the MPs faster than you could blink…" he trailed off when he realized that his tone was causing her eyes to widen in growing alarm. "But all that's moot, now, so I'll take care of your trash. You need to rest if you want to heal properly." His tone was brusque and his movements jerky as he snatched up the trash from the ground and disposed of it in a nearby barrel before returning to her side. "We'll come to collect you when it's time to pull out," he said, but the words landed heavier than he intended, like a promise he wasn't sure he could keep. "Tom, let's inform the soldiers about our mission parameters."

The RMP, who had stayed quiet during most of their conversation, followed Zain, trying to process everything that had transpired in the past thirty minutes.

As they walked back toward the front of the hangar, Zain looked over at Tom, "What made you tell me of our mission parameters ahead of time? I thought I was a threat and not privy to information…"

"I decided I trust you," Tom stated simply, bringing Zain to an abrupt halt. Tom either didn't notice or decided that the need to get the mission underway was too urgent to care what impact his statement had on Zain, and continued onward.

Zain stared after the retreating RMP, his brow knit in bewilderment. He shook his head to shake himself out of the state of disbelief, then jogged to catch up to Tom, "I didn't think it was possible for me to be shocked further after our conversation with Melyndie, but you somehow managed to."

"I will endeavor to keep you on your toes," Tom replied in a way that could be perceived as joking, but quickly returned to the business at hand. "It is time to address the troops."

Zain nodded, then turned toward the troops milling about on the tarmac.

"Attention!" Zain's command sliced through the air via his RMP's communication system. A thousand soldiers immediately hushed, diverting their full attention towards him. "I'm going to hand over this briefing to my RMP in a minute, but before that, I want to express my regret for the delay. I am aware that waiting in this scorching one-hundred-ten-degree heat has been anything but comfortable." His eyes wandered towards a group of crates nearby, each lid emblazoned with a red medical cross. A crease formed on his forehead as he shared a questioning look with Tom before proceeding. "Okay then, it's your turn now, Tom."

The RMP took a step forward and began speaking, "Due to our preoccupations with other pressing issues, I have recorded the message sent by General Takayoshi earlier today." The soft hum of machinery filled the air as the Brigadier General's authoritative voice echoed from the speakers of all one-hundred RMBs lining their perimeter.

"Soldiers," the General's message began solemnly, "over the span of the next three-hundred-sixty-five days you will traverse treacherous terrains—following maps programmed within each RMB—to all civilian populations—from populous to low-density. None must be overlooked. You'll be sleeping under the stars, but do not expect comfort or luxury during this mission because there will be none. Do not underestimate what lies ahead; we are embarking on a monumental worldwide endeavor aimed at preserving as much of humanity as possible.

Within each battalion's supplies are inoculations stored in crates marked with red crosses. This isn't some magical cure for the virus wreaking havoc across global populations. However, our top virologists have worked tirelessly to provide something that can at least slow down its relentless spread until we can develop a permanent vaccine. Expect losses. Friends. Comrades. Perhaps your fellow soldiers. This will happen not only because of the infection, but of possible resistance.

Prior to setting off on this mission, every man and woman must step forward to receive their inoculation as a defense against this deadly outbreak as you navigate through populated areas. No one is exempt. Anyone refusing the vaccine is to be terminated on the spot, without remorse. We cannot risk anyone threatening humanity's future with reckless acts of defiance. This includes you, soldiers. Any person found instigating rebellion will be executed without hesitation. There will be no second chances; that's how grave this situation is."

The voice paused for a moment before adding, "Prepare yourselves for what lies ahead and good luck. That is all."

The General's final words faded, but their weight remained, pressing into every soldier like a commandment carved in stone. Zain's jaw tightened.

Terminate the noncompliant. Execute the rebellious. No second chances.

He wondered how many would still remain complaint once the killing began.

Zain turned to his RMB, his face a mask of determination. "Well, here we are," he said. "With a battalion awaiting inoculation, there's no sense in packing up and pulling out now." He glanced up at the sun moving higher on the horizon. "It's going to be a long day and even longer night, with 1000 plus inoculations to administer and pre-trip prep to do. The only way we're going to get through this quickly is divide this up into two tasks: injections and prep. I'll let you take care of Melyndie. Keep her safe from the melee. Get her a bedroll. It'll be more comfortable than that tarp. Once she's tended to, find me. We have work to do."

He then made his way to where the troops were milling about and beckoned Omar over with a wave of his hand. His friend sauntered over, an incredulous look on his face.

"Can you believe this shit?" he asked as he stopped next to Zain.

"Believe it or not," Zain replied, gazing out at the soldiers scattered across the campsite, "we've got our work cut out for us. We're late starters in this race and it's going to be one hell of a time, playing catchup, with little-to-no sleep before we hit the road in the morning." He clapped Omar on the shoulder. The gesture landed with a little more weight than intended—a press of camaraderie hiding command. "I'm putting you in charge of making sure everyone gets their shots. One thousand soldiers, one thousand jabs."

Omar nodded solemnly but there was mischief in his eyes. "Plus, you…and your mysterious female guest."

Zain ignored his friend's obvious attempt at information gathering, and brought the subject back to the inoculations. "You think you can handle this?"

"Absolutely! Jabbing people isn't that complicated. But I'll need some help keeping tabs. Make sure no one is overlooked."

"It won't be me! RMP unit," Zain called out to one of the nearby sentries that immediately walked over with mechanical precision. "You're tasked with helping this officer identify who's been inoculated and who hasn't."

The RMP gave an affirmative nod. "All personnel will be marked as inoculated upon completion."

"Good." Zain rubbed his hands together before addressing the RMP again. "Now assign RMPs with the following tasks. First, to get everyone organized; lines of one hundred at a time. Second, split those not in line for inoculation into two groups: prep for deployment and prep for rest. We need efficiency so that we can deploy no later than sunup."

He winced as the RMP relayed his instructions through its booming speaker system. "I should have heard that coming," Zain muttered, covering his ears.

"You didn't think he'd relay the information person-to-person, did you?" Omar chuckled as they watched one-hundred of the soldiers begin to form an orderly queue. "I don't have to like these metal giants to appreciate their usefulness."

"Let's just get started," Zain declared, his hands deftly prying open the first crate of vaccines. "You and I will go first."

"Obviously, because we're at the head of the line." Omar's voice was laced with a dry humor that didn't quite mask his underlying tension. His stance was loose, but the tightening of his jaw betrayed unease.

Zain rolled his eyes at Omar's comment, a playful smirk tugging at the corner of his mouth. He began to roll up the sleeve of his fatigue jacket, revealing a canvas of tattoos etched into his muscular forearm. But before he could expose enough skin, Omar intervened.

"No need for that," he interjected, pointing with a gloved finger at the instructions printed on the inside of the crate lid. "We all have raglan sleeves, so just remove your fatigue jacket."

"What?" Zain blinked in confusion.

"The military t-shirt you're wearing under your fatigue jacket! The sleeves are called raglan. And since the injection site is on the inside elbow…" Omar explained, gesturing towards their standard-issue shirts.

"Why would I know that?" Zain exclaimed with a hint of exasperation in his voice, yanking his jacket off of his shoulders. "And I could've just rolled up my sleeve to my elbow."

"You're the Colonel. I'm just a Major, and I know it." Omar shot back with an air of mock superiority. "And yes, you could've just continued rolling up your sleeve, but then I wouldn't have been able to display my expert knowledge. Besides, you're the one who told everyone to get rid of their fatigue jackets, remember?"

"We're *from* here, you moron, so we're used to the heat. And it does tend to cool down at night, remember?" Zain responded with an exaggerated sigh and held out his arm obediently. "Make sure you read those directions carefully before attacking me with that thing," he warned, "or I'm going to knock you flat on your ass."

Omar chuckled heartily then picked up the small injector gun and a vial of vaccine from within the crate. He held it up to the sunlight light. Its contents glinted ominously.

"Damn! Ten doses in this tiny thing?" He mused aloud before loading it according to instructions printed on its side.

With a sense of trepidation masked by bravado, Omar pressed down on the lever of the jet injector. The device hissed sharply. It was followed by a brief pressure on Zain's arm, leaving nothing but a tiny red mark.

"No needle?" Zain looked surprised.

"Wow, ingenious!" Omar agreed with a nod of approval.

"This might go quicker than we thought. Just don't get overzealous and double dose anyone," Zain warned him before Omar abruptly changed the subject. "Now, give it to me so I can inject you."

"What about our unexpected guest? Are you ever going to tell me what's happening there?" he queried as he stuck his arm out toward Zain.

Zain shook his head in dismissal, with a quick look of apprehension to see if the RMP registered the inquiry. "Not now, Omar. Maybe later."

Omar looked at his friend with a furrowed brow and then shot a glance at the RMP. He gave Zain a look that expressed his apology for being an idiot; and he definitely felt a lot like one. He hadn't been around these robotic military personnel for any length of time, but since they were sent by the bureaucrats, he should automatically have known not to speak freely around them. He simply backtracked and reminded Zain that all individuals would need to queue for the vaccine.

With an audible sigh, Zain nodded. His gaze fell on the jeeps in the distance and he sighed again, "Just to ensure both groups know what they need to do…have group one to check the supply trucks to ensure all are loaded for bear: MREs, potable water, rifles, ammo, medical kits." He continued with a sense of urgency in his tone. "Then, ready the jeeps: ensure batteries are at capacity and load the portable generators on the supply trucks. Group two should be placing bedrolls and passing out the personal supplies, along with an MRE and water for the night's meal. The sooner everyone gets done, the sooner everyone can get rest. It'll be an early start tomorrow. And wait until I walk away to relay that amended order. I don't want to go deaf."

The RMP acknowledged, then stood silently waiting for Zain to walk away. Before he could, however, the RMP spoke up, "A scan of all personnel shows that we have a nurse present. Would you like for me to bring her forward to take over the inoculations?"

"Excellent, yes. Have her report to Omar. Omar, you can oversee the encampment. Make sure everybody is staying busy."

"Will do."

"As everyone comes through, and to prevent further mayhem," he instructed, while pointing towards their comrades lined up behind them, "tell each person, individually, that they are to have all of their personal belongings packed before bedding down for the night. They won't likely have sufficient time tomorrow morning. Also, according to a notification I just received," he held up his tablet for emphasis, "we won't get a supply drop from base command in Iceland but once a month at pre-designated drop points. So, if anyone runs shy of personal supplies," he added sternly looking at Omar, "it's on them."

"Got it…or at least my personal RMP here will make sure I do." Omar replied with a grin.

"I *was* talking to the RMP, since it will be remaining next to the nurse," Zain shot back with a smirk. "RMP acknowledge."

"Acknowledged."

"Okay, I'm going to head back into the hangar. As soon as I'm well away, relay the modified instructions."

As soon as Zain entered the hangar, the RMP relayed the updated tasks through the unified speaker system.

His personal RMP, Tom, had just finished setting up a small area for Melyndie to sleep. The robot's movements were methodical, but quiet—its joints humming softly, precise and ghostlike compared to the RMPs bustling about outside.

"We're on a military installation. There are portable latrines for the soldiers, however if you need a place to…well, you know…um…there should be a place inside the command booth across the tarmac." He pointed to a small building across from the hangar. "Unfortunately, after tonight, it's going to be rough living for the foreseeable future. If I thought it was safe, I'd simply have you sent to our command center in Iceland—"

"That would not be safe," the RMP interjected.

"I just said…never mind. Do you need to use the facilities? I can escort you, or Tom can."

Melyndie shot Zain a questioning gaze, uncertain what 'use the facilities' meant. Zain saw her confusion and explained, drawing a diffusion of color to her cheeks.

The thought of traversing a crowd of people who registered her existence was unnerving. In her realm, anonymity was inherent—everyone existed in silent parallel. No recognition, no intrusion. To be noticed felt invasive.

"They aren't going to hurt you," Zain added, when he noticed the look of fear glaze over her eyes. Melyndie turned her gaze to Zain's. The reassurance there should have calmed her, but it didn't.

"I'm fine for now," she whispered.

"Alright, there's another pressing matter on the table that requires both of your insights," Zain began, the weight of his words hanging heavily in the air.

Melyndie tilted her head slightly, her eyes narrowing in curiosity when he remained silent. "What is the issue?" she prompted.

Zain took a deep breath before continuing, "It's about the inoculation. Omar reminded me, rather bluntly, that everyone has been mandated to receive this vaccine. That includes you as well. Anyone who resists or refuses will face lethal consequences." He paused for a moment before adding, "Here's where it gets complicated. Your stay here is temporary and I'm unsure about the effects this vaccine could have on you—whether beneficial or harmful, considering your origin—"

"We are not plagued by diseases," Melyndie interjected quickly.

"Typically, a vaccine is composed of microorganisms or inactivate viruses which aren't intended to cause sickness—" Zain continued.

"But someone like me, who has never experienced illness may not respond in an anticipated way," Melyndie finished his sentence.

"Exactly," Zain agreed solemnly. "There's also another concern. You'll be traveling alongside us until your departure— which exposes you to potential infection if you remain unvaccinated. And if you decide against getting vaccinated and somehow contract the virus—"

"If I return to my time unprotected, carrying this virus, I might become a vector for my people," Melyndie concluded thoughtfully.

The RMP's voice echoed, a chilling monotone that seemed to reverberate off the metallic walls, causing an involuntary shudder down their spines. "While this may seem like a complex dilemma," it intoned with an icy detachment, "it really is not one. If she refuses the vaccine, she will be executed; consequently, these hypothetical scenarios will cease to exist."

"Let's go get you inoculated, and hope that you don't have some weird side effect from it," Zain declared, his tone firm yet laced with a hint of empathy. He turned to Tom, the metallic gleam of his robotic form catching the dim light in the hangar. "Tom, could you help her to stand? Are you able to walk over or would you prefer Tom carry you?"

"I will attempt to walk," Melyndie responded resolutely. Tom moved behind her, its large robotic frame bending over as it positioned its steel hands gently beneath her arms. With a soft hum and whir of gears, it slowly lifted until both were standing upright.

Melyndie exhaled softly, relief washing over her features. "It does feel good to be on my feet again."

"Okay, there's no rush," Zain reassured her with a gentle nod. "Take your time." He paused for a moment before adding with hesitance in his voice, "And Melyndie...if this causes any issues for you now or in your time…I'm…" His voice trailed off into silence, uncertain how to express apologies for something for which he had no control.

"I appreciate your concern. Thank you," she replied softly.

Zain extended his arm out towards her offering support but Melyndie merely stared at his bent elbow, perplexed. "Do you want me to assist you?" he asked after an awkward pause.

"I do not understand," Melyndie admitted quietly.

Zain sighed lightly before taking the initiative. He clasped her hand gently in his own and placed it carefully on the crook of his elbow. The unexpected touch was both alien and electrifying, causing a shiver to ripple down her spine.

"Are you okay?" Zain asked, his brow furrowed in worry at her reaction.

"I do not know," she confessed, her voice barely above a whisper.

Zain hastily withdrew his hand, leaving her feeling oddly bereft. "Tom, carry her over," he ordered. Before Melyndie could protest, Tom moved behind her and lifted her into its cold metallic arms, gently shifting her to ensure she was secure.

It carried her with surprising care, its mechanical gait steady as Zain walked just ahead, his silhouette outlined by the glow of the sun.

Melyndie glanced at Zain's back, at the hand that had held hers only moments ago. In her world, no one touched unless ordered. Here, one man had offered his arm—and something else she couldn't yet name. She turned her face into Tom's shoulder, shielding herself from a world still too sharp, too loud…too felt.

And as they neared the inoculation table, a single thought echoed beneath the hum of activity: no matter what happened in the coming days, she would not face it as the woman who first fell from the sky. She would carry the imprint of this moment—of being seen, of being touched—and nothing about her would remain untouched again—and that terrified her more than the unknown itself.

Hidden in Plain Sight

The next morning at zero-four-hundred hours, the battalion's soldiers, who had gotten less than three hours sleep, stirred from their bedrolls on the cold tarmac. They were groggy and lethargic but began to ready themselves for the first phase of their current deployment. A low murmur drifted across the camp—boots scraping on pavement, the clatter of gear being repacked, muffled curses at the strong winds that kicked up the desert, covering them in a film of red. To those unfamiliar with the region, it felt as if the desert were trying to consume them.

Steam curled from thermoses as soldiers clutched the last sips of reheated coffee, the scent of which mixed with machine oil and distant exhaust from the four dozen transport trucks firing up in the distance.

The first light of dawn crept reluctantly across the sky, casting long, sleepy shadows over the assemblage of men, women, and equipment. The air was crisp and carried a sharp sting of pre-dawn chill which would dissipate quickly with the rise of the sun.

Zain, with his usual brisk efficiency, was already making rounds, his figure cutting a decisive path through stirring troops. "Ensure you get your MRE finished quickly and discard all of your refuse before packing up your gear."

One particularly eager early bird was completing his MRE when Zain strolled by. "Excuse me, Colonel?" he queried, his youthful eyes shining in the early morning light.

"Good morning, soldier. What can I do for you?"

"Have we been assigned a vehicle?"

"I'm not following—"

"I'll be ready to make my way over to the trucks in a few minutes, sir! I just wanted to know whether I had a specific one I needed to go to."

Zain grinned, trying to recall a time when he was equally enthusiastic about starting a deployment. There was something painfully earnest about the kid—a wide-eyed hunger to prove himself. His smile slipped when he wondered just how long that enthusiasm would last once the bodies started dropping. "There are nearly fifty transport trucks over there. Just pick one," he responded with more brusqueness than intended.

"Very good, sir! Thank you, sir!"

Zain moved back to the hangar to check on Melyndie. The light from the rising sun had yet to make its way fully into the interior, and he had to pull out his tactical flashlight in order to make his way across the concrete flooring to the back corner where his RMP stood guard near Melyndie's bed. The hangar felt quieter than it should have, as if it held its breath. His boots echoed softly in the cavernous space, drawing him forward like a pull in his chest he didn't yet know how to name.

"Good morning, Tom. Is she awake?" he asked, in a near whisper.

"Yes, I'm awake," Melyndie replied, and then yawned. Her voice was hoarse from sleep, yet there was a strength in her tone that hadn't been there the night before. A small, wavering flame of composure that was desperately trying to reignite within her.

Zain switched off the tactical flashlight, the early morning light now beginning to fill the space, creating a less stark atmosphere. "How are you feeling this morning?" he asked.

"Healing quicker than I expected, although sleep was a bit elusive because of my shoulder." She struggled to pull herself to a sitting position. Tom moved to assist, but Zain was already by her side.

"Here, let me help you." He gently placed a hand under her arm as she shifted into a more comfortable position.

"Thank you," Melyndie replied softly, managing a small smile despite the evident discomfort. "I appreciate everything you're doing for me." There was vulnerability in her voice, a raw openness that startled even her.

Zain nodded, the gesture laden with a gravity that spoke volumes about his commitment to her safety and well-being. He glanced around the dim hangar, noting the faint hustle of soldiers outside, preparing for the move. "I know you aren't comfortable with the idea, but you're really going to need to visit the latrine, and now might be the best time since the soldiers are still sedate. It's going to get busy out there in the next few minutes."

Melyndie nodded, a tinge of embarrassment coloring her cheeks. In her world, bodily needs were handled with clinical precision. Here, there was an awkward humanity to it all.

"Okay. Tom will escort you. You'll be safe in its company. When you get back, do you think you can prepare your own MRE...meal, that is?"

Melyndie nodded, then signaled her readiness to move. Tom promptly stepped forward, its frame whirring quietly as it adjusted to assist. With careful mechanized precision, it supported her as she slowly stood up.

As if noticing her attire for the first time, Zain commented, "Those clothes...especially those booties you're wearing, aren't going to be suitable for day-to-day. Tom, can you scan the supplies manifest? See if there are any extra fatigues available? Especially combat boots?"

Tom was still for a minute. "Nothing extra. I took the liberty of adding the need for an extra set in the first supplies drop."

Zain sighed. "That'll have to do. Go ahead and make your way to the latrine."

Neither seemed to acknowledge the possibility that Melyndie might not be with them in thirty days.

Melyndie nodded and turned away, and the machine followed without a word. Despite its cold exterior, there was something unmistakably gentle in the way it moved beside her—a silent guardian forged in steel, radiating a strange kind of protectiveness.

As they made their way out of the hangar, the camp began to stir noticeably. Soldiers were folding up their bedrolls and securing their packs, murmuring amongst themselves about the day's objectives and whatever lay ahead on the unforgiving terrain that awaited them.

Melyndie, determined to walk on her own accord, leaned lightly on Tom as they navigated through the increasingly active campsite. The early morning light revealed the lines of worry etched deeply on her face, yet there was a determined set to her jaw—a silent testament to her resilience.

Some soldiers paused in their tasks, glancing up curiously as Melyndie made her way through the camp. Some ignored her completely, too busy with their duties to spare a second glance. Others stood respectfully, offering a salute or a greeting of "Good morning" or "Ma'am".

Melyndie, unaccustomed to such formalities—or any attention given at all—merely nodded in return, trying desperately not to let the attention shake her composure.

Once they reached the latrine, Tom positioned itself outside, a silent sentinel guarding the entrance. Melyndie emerged a short while later, looking a tad more composed. Tom offered its arm again, similar to what Zain had done earlier, and together they returned to where Zain waited, busying himself with reviewing the digital maps and last-minute updates from HQ on his tablet.

He laid aside his work at their approached. "I've placed an MRE on the seat of the jeep. You may want to go ahead and eat there, since I've already collected your bedroll and stored it for you. If you need anything, just wave at me or Tom...I need him to help prepare for the deployment. Are you—"

"I think I can manage on my own."

"Excellent," Zain smiled slightly—relief evident in his expression. "We'll leave you to it then." Still, he hesitated for half a breath too long before turning away. He worried over leaving her alone with so many soldiers bustling about. After a brief debate with himself, he pushed the concern aside, knowing she would not be out of his sight. He was also confident that his soldiers would behave with the respect and discipline instilled in them.

As Zain and Tom departed, Melyndie made her way to the jeep that Zain had pointed out. Every step she took further convincing her of her growing strength, although the shadow of discomfort never quite left her side. The soldiers around her moved with a purpose, their own preparations seemingly swallowing them whole as they readied for what was to come.

Melyndie settled into the jeep's seat, the MRE packet lying unopened beside her. She stared at it for a moment, the mundane task of preparing her food to eat seemed like a monumental challenge, but she pushed through, knowing she needed the sustenance. With a sigh, she tore open the packet. Its contents, necessary fuel for her body, was so different than the bland food from her home. Savory, salty, warm—somehow the texture alone felt like a rebellion against that of her realm.

As she savored each bite of her meal, her mind drifted to her own mission—now successfully completed—at least partially. Were the holy ones to pull her back now, she'd have something for them to test. A mild concern tugged at the recesses of her mind, like a gentle pull on a loose thread. She couldn't help but think about how her body could react to the vaccine injected last night. Would there be any side effects? Any lingering pain or discomfort? But even more pressing was the question of how her battered and bruised body would handle the long journey back home. Every step and movement already caused sharp pains to shoot through her contused muscles, and she couldn't imagine enduring a return trip with a fractured bone. The thought made her stomach twist with apprehension and dread, especially since she could be yanked back to her time at any moment. But she realized that she didn't want to go back. Not yet. Not while the air here still smelled of earth and sweat…and possibility of learning more, experiencing more.

Her eyes scanned the makeshift camp, searching for the two who had rescued her and taken care of her since she arrived in this unfamiliar world. A wave of emotion washed over her, stirring a growing ache in the pit of her stomach. Before this, her interactions with the holy ones, scientists, and technicians had been cold and impersonal—nearly nonexistent with everyone else—but these two had shown for her a concern and compassion. She hadn't known how much she craved it until she was finally touched by it.

Her gaze met Zain's across the tarmac and he smiled encouragingly. Melyndie's return smile, though weak, was a testament to her growing trust and gratitude towards him. After finishing her meal, she carefully gathered the trash and scanned the nearby area for a receptacle. A soldier, passing nearby, seemed to know precisely what she needed.

"I'll take that for you, miss," he offered with a smile.

"Oh...thank you," she replied and felt a warmth stirring within her at how kind the people in the before time seemed to be; how hospitable to each other.

"I'm Omar," he stated, taking the empty MRE contents from her. "Zain and I have been friends since we were just children."

There was pride in his voice, but not arrogance—just the easy familiarity of someone who had survived long nights and hard days beside another. His mention of Zain's name made her sit up a little straighter, intrigued by this unknown concept of childhood friendship. Her smile grew wider for this brief glimmer of what humanity truly meant.

"Go throw that away, Omar, and get back to work. We're pulling out in less than fifteen," Zain said, strolling up to the jeep.

Omar's face took on that annoyingly smug grin, but Zain just smiled back, knowing that he didn't actually know anything. Once Omar walked away, Zain turned his attention to Melyndie. "It's probably best if you not interact too much with others, Melyndie. It's one thing for me and Tom to be aware of your identity and origin, but it could be dangerous if too many people found out."

Melyndie nodded, understanding the gravity of Zain's warning. Her presence here was not only an anomaly but a potential danger if her origins were to be exposed. The complexity of time travel was treacherous enough without adding social entanglements into the mix.

"I understand." As she spoke, her voice softened and her eyes took on a reflective seriousness, fully capturing the gravity of their situation. "I'll limit my interactions to you and Tom, but if I'm being honest, it was a rare and fleeting moment to feel...normal."

Zain's eyebrows furrowed in confusion. "Normal? Don't you have friends in your time?" he queried.

Melyndie's expression saddened as she shook her head. "No. We don't really interact much at all. Our days are structured around productivity..." Her voice trailed off as she remembered the one time that she tried to replicate a captured image from the past and almost faced termination for it. All she had wanted was to experience the warmth of someone's embrace.

Zain's worry grew as he saw Melyndie's eyes fill with tears, lost in her own thoughts. "Will you be alright?" he asked, feeling a bit uneasy about the impact this stranger was having on his life. Nevertheless, he extended a comforting hand and placed it on her shoulder.

Melyndie's gaze trailed down to where his hand, tanned and calloused, lay against her blouse. She closed her eyes, longing to lay her cheek against his warmth and feel the humanity that she'd been denied for so long. The heat radiating from his hand was a stark contrast to the cold loneliness that had, unknowingly, consumed her for all of her life. She could almost sense the pulse of life coursing through his veins, reminding her of the emptiness that had been her constant companion. But in this moment, as she basked in the touch of another, she felt a glimmer of hope and a flicker of desire igniting within her soul.

Her gaze on his hand must have lingered a touch too long, for he tensed up. She immediately reacted and straightened her posture. Inhaling deeply, she closed her eyes briefly to regain control over her jumbled emotions. "I'm fine," she whispered softly. Zain removed his hand quickly from her shoulder, an indication of his relief. He was sorry that her future had been disrupted, but he didn't know how to say it without sounding insensitive. However, there was no time to dwell on her emotional state when their own world was on the brink of chaos.

"It's time to leave. The men are boarding their transports. Are you ready to go?"

Melyndie nodded, unable to find her voice at the moment.

"Okay," Zain turned and yelled, "Let's move out!"

Tom approached, stepped onto a ramp at the rear of the jeep, and latched on. The jeep's engine roared to life as the convoy began to stretch into formation. Zain steered the jeep to the lead position and called out over his shoulder, "Feed the first coordinates into the GPS, Tom."

Inside the jeep, Melyndie sat motionless, her hands clenched in her lap. The world outside her window moved with terrifying purpose, but inside her chest was only stillness—an anchorless, thudding ache.

Zain cast a sidelong glance at her, noting her discomfort, but said nothing. There was nothing he could offer—no words that would ease the rift between her world and his. Not right now.

Omar pulled alongside, driving one of the troop transport trucks, flashing a brief grin before shouting nonsensical pleasantries at Zain.

Melyndie's eyes lingered on him a moment longer than necessary. He was easy with his smile, rooted in a world where people belonged to each other. She didn't know him, but somehow, she wished she did. Would he ever become her friend too? Surely, if he was a good friend to Zain, he could be to her as well.

She sighed at the thought—at the quiet ache of longing for something she'd never known. Tears pricked at her eyes, but she blinked them away, watching the desert roll steadily past her window.

The convoy moved beneath the pale amber wash of a Dubai dawn, the landscape stretching wide and silent beyond the final footprint of where the camp had stood.

The silence between them was finally broken by Melyndie's voice, piercing the stillness that had begun to loom uncomfortably long. "When I was looking at these things that you call jeeps in the archives back home, I never imagined they would be this uncomfortable," she remarked, her delicate features creased with discomfort.

"Well, jeeps aren't exactly known for their comfort," Zain replied with a small shrug. "They're meant for rugged terrain and getting to places that other cars can't reach. I think part of the discomfort, though, might be the fact that your body sustained some serious bruises in the fall you took. Not to mention the hairline fracture in your collarbone."

Melyndie smiled slightly, "So, the ride will improve in comfort after my body heals?"

"I didn't say that. Like I said, Jeeps are meant for utility, not comfort."

"Sounds like my jumpsuit back home," Melyndie replied, with a humorless laugh.

Zain's expression softened with sympathy. "I do wish I could ease some of your discomfort, but..." he trailed off, knowing there wasn't anything he could do. "Some of your injuries may take longer to heal, especially in certain...areas." His gaze dropped to where her bottom met the seat and he cleared his throat awkwardly. "More jarring there."

Changing the subject abruptly, Melyndie asked, "Why haven't you asked me anything about my home? About where I came from?"

Zain hesitated before answering, choosing his words carefully. "To be honest, I'm not completely convinced that your story is true. But my RMP seems to think it's a plausible explanation for why you technically don't exist in our world. Until I have a reason to doubt it, I'll go along with it." He paused, his tone becoming more serious. "Right now, my focus is on protecting humanity and ensuring its safety. I don't have the time or energy to extract information from you. As long as you remain under my watchful eye, I'll consider that enough for now."

Zain's words carried a finality that silenced any further attempts at conversation. Melyndie absorbed his guarded reply, her curiosity folding into a quiet ache. She understood now: he wasn't avoiding her world out of indifference—but out of exhaustion. There were battles in him she couldn't name yet, but she could feel them pressing at the edges of his restraint.

As they neared the first sprawling metropolis, Zain eased his foot off the accelerator, allowing the jeep to crawl forward. Melyndie's eyes widened in childlike wonder as she took in the towering structures that pierced the sky, their lights blazing like a million stars brought down to earth. She pivoted towards Zain to share her awe-struck thoughts, but her words died on her lips as she noticed his rigid posture and tight grip on the steering wheel.

"Is everything alright?" she asked tentatively.

Zain's gaze fractured into the distance, unfocused and brittle. A man suspended between memory and duty; between all he had lost and all he might still lose. "I can see them," he began slowly. "The inhabitants of this city just starting to stir from their slumber. Preparing for another day: school children donning uniforms, office workers gulping down quick breakfasts, fitness enthusiasts lacing up running shoes, globe-trotters meticulously checking their luggage for an overseas journey..." His voice trailed off into silence followed by a heavy sigh. "This city…it's where I grew up. My roots are here. People I care about—friends and family—they're all here." His voice hardened with resolve. "And yet I must maintain a cold resolve to safeguard them against this insidious virus that threatens our existence before moving on to my next destination. I just hope no one fights against it. I don't want to take a life…needlessly."

He squeezed his eyes shut, as if he could barricade the memory with darkness alone. But it surged forward—the hollow sound of the gunshot, the cold resolve in his RMP's hand, the moment his world shattered.

He whispered hoarsely, "My sister…" The raw pain in his voice was palpable. He had been suppressing thoughts about the horrifying task he'd been forced to complete barely two days ago. With global communication networks crippled, he hadn't been able to reach out to his sister—left alone in her chaos; left alone with the nightmarish memory of waking up that catastrophic morning only to find their mother lifeless in her bed with a gunshot wound in her head.

A grimace twisted Zain's mouth and he squeezed his eyes shut tighter, as if this physical act could barricade the onslaught of haunting memories. He recalled the chilling image of his RMP lurking in the pre-dawn shadows outside his mother's bedroom window. The cold glint of a revolver in its hand was a stark reminder of the monstrous duty that would fall to him, should Zain falter. That same RMP who, with each passing day since, seemed to be acquiring layers of empathy that were conspicuously absent on that dreadful day.

Zain was snapped back to duty when he heard the commotion of his soldiers as each vehicle came to a halt behind him.

Omar pulled his truck up next to Zain's jeep, "Hey Zain, I'm going to get the nurse's station ready and assist with inoculations. I'll ensure the jet injectors are reloaded so that the queues move rapidly through. That cool?"

"Thanks for stepping up with that, Omar," Zain said, his voice unable to hide the strain.

"You want me to run and grab our parents and siblings first—"

Zain found himself shaking his head violently. When he realized his reaction was over exaggerated, he stopped and compressed his lips tightly. After a minute, he turned back to his friend, "you head up the inoculations, I'll see to it that our families get there. There's something that I need to discuss with Amal, so…" he trailed off.

Omar waved and then accelerated to a spot near the outskirts of the city.

"Is everything okay?" Melyndie whispered.

"No," Zain admitted, "and I don't think it's going to improve."

He deliberately turned and let his gaze focus on the troops, as they began their slow procession through the city streets. Their voices echoed off towering buildings, announcing their arrival like a death knell. The sounds bounced around in Zain's skull as he sat there contemplating how he would face the impending confrontation with his sister.

Would it be best to envelop her in an embrace and offer solace? To express regret for her suffering and mourn over his inability to shield her from it? Or should he rip off the bandage and reveal the harsh truth about what transpired, regardless of any potential fallout?

In his peripheral vision, he noticed the remaining half of his battalion spreading out like a net along Dubai's outskirts. Their mission was clear: ensure no one slipped through unvaccinated. The RMPs stood ready to herd citizens into orderly lines for identification checks while a single RMP stood vigilantly next to the nurse who was tasked with administering vaccinations. Their mandate was clear; ensure complete compliance from all citizens and terminate those who resisted.

Zain drew in a shuddering breath through flared nostrils before shifting gears on his jeep. He knew what he had to do, but allowed himself to be deliberately distracted for a short moment, pulling alongside Omar. "One nurse isn't going to be able to move this many people through, fast enough. Select fifty men. Demonstrate how—"

"I only counted twenty jet injectors," Omar interrupted. "Figured they were backups in case one broke."

Zain sighed, "Okay, select twenty men and get them swiftly trained. The sooner we get through the masses, the sooner we move on."

"Will do."

With trepidation, Zain accelerated again and steered straight towards his sister's apartment building without hesitation. Better to confront her now, he decided; only then could he lay this gnawing apprehension to rest.

Melyndie sat motionless, her hands curled in her lap, helpless as a storm moved through the man beside her. She wanted to speak, to reach across the silence, but the enormity of his grief made her feel small and useless. Doubt nibbled at her as she questioned her ability to traverse this tumultuous sea of turmoil, which was rapidly spiraling into what seemed like an emotional implosion.

In the aching stillness, Melyndie imagined wrapping her arms around him—not out of affection, but desperation. A human connection. A quiet offering. Shutting her eyes tightly, she concentrated every ounce of her being into transmitting this unspoken consolation towards him—an empathetic beacon in his suddenly stormy world.

Yet, she felt utterly lost and out of her depth. This was uncharted territory for her—a situation she had never confronted before. But with each passing minute among these humans from a bygone era, it became glaringly evident that emotions within them ran deep.

As she watched his struggle, she came to a realization: these people were not too unlike herself, and others in her time. These people too tried to bury their feelings deep within themselves, crafting facades of stoicism and indifference.

But that's where the illusion cracked. Because in her world, emotions were silenced before they could bloom. Here, they were wild and primal, clawing their way to the surface—grief with teeth, love with fire.

Thus far, she'd witnessed this several times. Emotions that manifested in spontaneous peals of laughter; fiery outbursts triggered by perceived slights or injustices; or even in heart-wrenching bouts of despair—as was clearly evident from Zain's current state of torment.

As she struggled to find the right words, she empathized with how Zain must have felt when she became emotional, so she mimicked his response, "Are you okay?" she queried in what she hoped was a suitably compassionate tone.

Zain grimaced, his jaw clenching as he maneuvered his jeep to a halt before the worn facade of his sister's apartment complex. "I'm about to undertake an unenviable task," he confessed, uncertainty clouding his usually clear eyes. "Just...wait here for me. I have to confront my sister and then guide her and my former mother-in-law to the inoculation station."

As he swung his tall frame out of the jeep, the building's residents had already started pouring out onto the street, their expressions etched with confusion and fear. Without wasting a moment, Zain strode towards them, a beacon in the chaos.

"Everyone!" He commanded, his voice resonating with an authority that seemed to slice through the growing panic. "I know hearing orders being barked over loudspeakers is unsettling, but it's crucial that you heed the soldiers' instructions while navigating your way towards the vaccination lines."

"But what's happening? What is all of this?" A young mother emerged from the crowd, her hands tightly gripping those of her two children; a wide-eyed boy of five and a girl no older than eight.

"We're dealing with an outbreak—" Zain began.

"An outbreak! What kind? Are we at risk? What about my children?" The woman's voice was shrill with terror.

Zain held up his hand in an attempt to calm her. "We're here to ensure everyone gets vaccinated against this outbreak," he reassured her. "As long as you follow instructions carefully, you and your children should be safe. Now please proceed towards the vaccination queues."

"Zain?" The frail voice of an elderly woman echoed through the air as she shuffled towards him, her arms trembling with age as she reached out, encircling his neck in a fragile embrace that belied the strength of their relationship.

"*Nassibah*[4]," Zain greeted, his voice laced with warmth and relief. "It's been an eternity since we last saw each other. Omar is here. If you wait for me in my jeep, I'll drive you up the queue myself and you can see him. Or would you rather he come get you?

---

[4] Mother-in-law

He asked impulsively, suddenly not wishing to be around his loved ones any longer than necessary, especially since he didn't know how his reunion with his sister would go."

"Oh, can Omar come get me?" she asked softly, her tone anticipatory. "Not that I am unhappy to see you too," she quickly added with a soft smile.

"It's okay. I understand." He reached for the radio he normally wore on his belt, but realized he'd left it in the jeep, so he called to Tom, "Have Omar come to his apartment building."

A moment later, a casual voice responded through the comms system on the RMP. "Hey Zain. What's going on?"

Zain frowned at the informal response. "Is that how you address your superior officer, you oaf?" The response wasn't one of genuine anger, rather it harkened back to when they were younger and their antics would bring a smile to their mothers' faces. It lifted his spirits a bit when Omar's mother slapped him playfully on the arm, reprimanding him insincerely for speaking like that to her son; his dearest friend.

The voice on the other end chuckled before correcting himself. "Apologies, *Colonel*. How may I assist you?"

"I'm currently with your mother—"

"*Ummi*[5]!" Omar's voice was suddenly filled with concern.

"*Ibni*[6]! Where are you?" the elderly woman chimed in.

"Omar, she's fine. I just decided to give her the option of my taking her, or having you come escort her. For some odd reason, she opted for you."

---

[5] Mother
[6] Son

"I'm on my way," Omar quickly responded. "Thanks for looking out for her, Zain."

Zain nodded even though Omar couldn't see him. "No need for thanks." He then turned back to his former *Nassībah* but before he could speak further, she abruptly interrupted him.

"I heard about your mother." Her words hung heavily in the air between them and her eyes welled up with unshed tears. Zain's face drained of color as he processed her words.

"You didn't know?" she asked softly when Zain remained silent, her tone heavy with regret and sympathy. "Of course, you wouldn't…how could you? You've been away for so long and it just happened recently. Your sister is heartbroken. I am certain she will be happy to have you here. She needs you."

Before Zain could muster a response, Omar arrived in a dust-covered jeep. He hurriedly climbed out and engulfed his mother in a protective embrace, "Let's get you vaccinated and back home, away from this madness."

Zain merely nodded. "Ensure she's safe and then get back to work, Omar." He watched as Omar helped his mother into the jeep before driving off, leaving him alone with his thoughts.

As he stood there, lost in the turmoil of his emotions, a young woman exited the building. She spotted Zain and rushed over, throwing herself into his arms. Her words tumbled out in a rush as she clung to him desperately.

"Zain! I tried reaching you every way possible but everything was down: landlines, cellphones…I felt so alone." She sobbed against his chest.

"It's okay Amal," Zain reassured her gently. "I'm here now."

After what felt like an eternity, Amal reluctantly tore herself away from his embrace, her hand shaking as she brushed away the relentless tears that cascaded down her cheeks like a waterfall. Her eyes, rimmed red and shimmering, searched his face not just for answers—but for assurance. She needed him to be steady. She needed him not to break. Because she was already breaking enough for them both.

She took a hesitant step back, her voice barely above a whisper, "You're not even going to ask…" Her words trailed off into a heavy sniffle before she gasped in shock, realization dawning on her, "You already know what's happened. But how? The cell networks have been out of commission. I've dialed your number more times than I can count over the last forty-eight hours. So how…how could you possibly know?" Her voice rose with each word until it echoed around them.

"Omar's mom just told me," Zain whispered, knowing it was a cowardly delay tactic.

"Oh my God," Amal cried, and launched herself back into her brother's arms. "It was horrible, Zain. Who would do such a thing to our mother? Why?"

Her words fractured against his chest; each one gasped out like a wound reopening. Her body shook violently with sobs, the kind that seemed to rip straight from the center of her being—as if grief had seized her spine and hollowed her out from the inside. She clung to him like a child lost in a storm, fingers tightening in the fabric of his shirt until her knuckles went white. Her cries were not soft or restrained—they were raw and ragged, filled with an anguish too big for her frame. Zain held her, but it felt like trying to hold water in a sieve. She was collapsing in pieces, and he couldn't catch them fast enough.

Zain stood there; his face impassive as he listened to his sister unravel at the seams right before him. It was almost surreal; watching someone else's pain and feeling nothing but an inexplicable numbness within himself.

He could have said something—could have wrapped her in words soft enough to steady her, strong enough to soothe the grief shaking her apart. But he didn't. He couldn't. Because to comfort her would be to offer himself a measure of peace, and he didn't deserve peace—not after what he'd done. The silence between them wasn't neglect; it was punishment. His own soul was a battlefield, and solace felt like surrender. Yet each of her sobs carved into him with surgical precision. He had to tell her the truth. He had to let the blade fall. But how did a man confess to killing the very person who gave them both life?

How could he justify his actions without sounding like a monster? There were no words gentle enough to soften the blow, no logic strong enough to carry the weight of what he'd done. Nothing could make it right. Nothing could make it forgivable. But even so—something deeper than guilt, deeper than fear—urged him forward. Not to be understood, but to stop hiding. To bleed honestly, if only once. She deserved that much. And maybe, in saying it aloud, he would finally feel the full measure of what he'd done—in the name of duty.

Zain took a step back, easing her gently from his arms. His hands rose, trembling slightly, and settled on her shoulders—less a gesture of comfort than of anchoring himself to something real. His voice cracked under the weight of her name.

"Amal," he breathed, so faintly it was nearly lost to the wind. "I wish I could explain what happened. I wish I could tell you how the choice came about...but it wasn't a choice. Not really. It was a command."

His voice wavered like something unraveling thread by thread, and Amal's eyes—wide, red-rimmed, desperate—searched his face for answers. Her lips parted, trembling. "What do you mean?" she whispered. "What decision? What are you saying?" Her hands reached up to grasp his forearms, shaking now. "Zain…what did you do?"

He tried to steady his breathing, but it came in broken gulps, his chest rising and falling like he was drowning on dry land.

"Something…something I will carry until the day I die. Something that broke me in ways I didn't know a man could break. I—"

"Stop it!" Amal snapped, her voice cutting through him like a blade. "No more word games, no more cryptic bullshit!" She pulled violently from his grip, her face twisting in grief so raw it made him flinch. "Tell me! Stop circling it like a coward! Just tell me—what happened to our mother? What do you know?!"

Zain's throat clenched, his composure splintering beneath the force of her anguish. When he finally spoke, the words scraped out of him—raw, reluctant, and barely more than breath. "I'm…I'm the one who pulled the trigger."

Amal didn't speak. She just stared at him, her breath hitching in her throat—then breaking, slow and jagged. One heartbeat passed. Then two.

And finally, she stepped back. Not far. Just far enough.

Enough for Zain to feel the space where her trust used to be.

Amal was rooted to the spot, her entire body trembling—not just with grief, but with rage so vast it seemed to radiate heat. Her fingers twitched at her sides, as if torn between clawing her own skin off or lunging at Zain and ripping him to shreds. Her chest heaved, breaths sharp and ragged. Whatever held her together was splintering fast.

Zain watched her unravel with a guilt-ridden stillness. The moment he had cried out— *"I'm the one who pulled the trigger"*— something inside him had begun to calcify. The brother who had once carried her on his back, who'd taught her to swim, who'd memorized the lullabies their mother used to hum—he wanted to speak. But the uniform weighed more than memory. And duty had no patience for grief. So, he did what he had always done when orders left no room for emotion: he buried it. Deep. He'd confessed. Now he had to move on.

"They left me no option," he said at last.

"No!" Amal's scream cracked through the air, primal and sharp. "Don't say that! Don't you dare say that to me!" She lunged at him and her fists slammed into his chest—again and again and again—with blind fury. "You're lying! You have to be!"

Zain stood motionless, letting her strikes land, a punishment he would willingly accept. Let her bruise him. Let her break him. If that was her justice, he would take it. But his RMP—impervious to guilt, indifferent to pain—moved in.

Its tall frame surged forward with chilling precision. No hesitation. No humanity. Metallic fingers locked around Amal's arms, ripping her away from Zain as if peeling flesh from bone. She thrashed wildly in its grip.

"Let me go, you cold-blooded pile of metal!" she shrieked. Her voice cracked, feral and raw, echoing through the streets. Heads turned. Conversations stopped mid-sentence. A child in a queue began to cry. Amal didn't care.

"Stand down!" Zain barked.

His RMP released her instantly, retreating a half-step—but its sensors stayed locked on her. Amal crumpled to the ground, sobbing, hands shielding her face as if attempting to block out the entire world. Zain dropped beside her; voice thick with emotion. "Amal, listen to me."

She lifted her head, her face streaked with dust and tears, eyes bloodshot and burning. "How could you possibly explain? How can you even dare look at me?" she asked, her voice a whisper soaked in venom.

"The directive was handed down," Zain murmured. "It wasn't a choice. It was an order." He stared at the pavement like it might answer for him. "And it haunts me every waking moment."

Tom's mechanical voice sliced through his apology. "The colonel was given an order," it stated; tone devoid of inflection. "Disobedience to that order was not an option. Had he failed to execute it, I would have performed the termination. And would have terminated him afterward. Your brother completed the task. For that, he is still alive to comfort you now."

Amal rose slowly to her feet, her movements rigid. Her face was pale with fury. "Why would anyone order that? Why would you *ever* obey it?"

Zain rose to his feet and opened his mouth, searching for an answer—but the words caught in his throat. The RMP made to speak again, but Amal whirled around, bringing her full rage to bear on the metal giant.

"Shut up!" she screamed. "You may have given me an *explanation*, but my brother will give me the *justification!*"

Zain's spine sagged under the weight of that demand. The look on her face—like something sacred had been defiled—pierced deeper than any blade.

But before he could respond, Amal's pain twisted into something colder.

"You know what?" she spat. "Screw you. I don't want your justification. There is *nothing* you could say that would make putting a gun to our mother's head acceptable. You're already dead to me."

Then, turning toward the RMP, she hissed, "You should have shot him."

She stalked toward the building's entrance, but the RMP sidestepped to block her path.

"Get. Out. Of. My. Way."

"You must go to the queue. All citizens much report," it replied flatly.

"I'm not going anywhere!" she roared.

"Amal," Zain tried, voice low.

She spun on him like a viper. "Don't you ever speak to me again!"

From the jeep, Melyndie sat frozen, breath caught in her throat. The memory of that market simulation flashed back to her—two men fighting, her stepping in, and the chaos that followed. This was no simulation. This was grief in its most violent form, and she could do nothing but watch as it bled into something darker.

Zain inhaled sharply, locking the grief deep within his chest and forcing steel into his spine. "You don't have a choice," he said, words clipped and harsh. "Regardless of what you feel, you *must* get vaccinated."

"Why?" she spat. "Why live in a world without her? Without anything that matters? Did you fight this hard for her, Zain? Did you?!"

The scream ripped from her throat, jagged and animalistic. People stared. Murmurs spread. But the soldiers formed a perimeter, gently but firmly redirecting onlookers, shielding the scene best they could.

Amal's eyes blazed as she lunged again—this time not toward her brother, but to break past the RMP. It blocked her, faster this time.

This time, it didn't use its hands.

Its arm pivoted with terrifying speed, revealing a sleek, compact weapon—its barrel raised and centered between Amal's eyes.

"No!" Zain's voice thundered—too late—as his RMP pulled the trigger.

With a surge of primal urgency, Melyndie hurled herself from the dust-covered jeep, her boots barely touching the cracked earth as she tore around the vehicle's hood.

Zain and Amal had collapsed to the parched ground in a tangle of limbs after a shot rang out from the RMP's gun. She skidded to a halt on the polished sidewalk outside Amal's apartment building, her breath catching in her throat as her brain fumbled to make sense of the chaos unraveling before her.

Then came the scream.

It wasn't Amal. It was someone else—another female—someone in the line.

A man collapsed face-first in the dust near the vaccination station, blood blooming in a thick halo beneath his head. His body twitched once, then went still. The shot meant as a warning to Amal, had struck someone else.

Panic exploded.

Cries of terror erupted like a dam bursting. People shoved and trampled, a blind stampede driven by sheer animal fear, the corpse already half-forgotten in the rush to survive. The fragile order unraveled in seconds.

"Back! Everyone back!" a soldier shouted, arms outstretched, trying to contain the flood of screaming civilians.

An RMP leveled its weapon, sending out a short-range sonic pulse that dropped a cluster of would-be runners to their knees, their hands clamped over their ears. Another unit activated a visual override burst—a disorienting flash meant to halt forward motion without force.

The chaos took on a chilling tempo: soldiers yelling commands, RMPs corralling the masses, and in the center of it all, the lifeless body of a man who had simply been waiting in line, willingly complying.

Zain twisted around, still half-shielding Amal, his stomach coiling into a hard knot. That shot hadn't gone into the air—it had torn into the crowd. A man had died.

"What in God's name do you think you're doing?" he roared from his protective position over his sister, who lay unnervingly still under his bulk.

"She needed to learn that defiance has dire consequences," retorted his RMP with chilling indifference. Its voice was hollow and mechanical, stripped of empathy, and it sliced down Melyndie's spine like the cold steel that it was. Gone was the empathetic being she'd encountered yesterday. "Had it been another RMP unit instead of me, your sister would now lay lifeless beneath you. Any form of resistance or refusal is met with swift termination. Or did you think this applied only to strangers?" It paused for emphasis before continuing: "I saved your sister's life today. Be grateful, because I will not extend such mercy again."

His RMP slid its weapon back into its metallic torso with a soft hiss before going eerily still. Then a unified voice nearby, from the RMPs, echoed across Dubai's skyline: "Everyone is to regain composure and return to the orderly lines that are being formed for mandatory vaccination. Non-compliance will result in immediate termination."

The silence that followed was deafening, a vacuum that swallowed the chaos whole. The chilling announcement reverberated from the hundred-strong RMP units, their collective resolve an unspoken threat. No one dared challenge them; instead, they turned quietly and shuffled back toward the soldiers and RMPs manning the inoculation stations.

The man's body lay face down in the dust, unmoving, a red halo soaking outward like a warning scrawled in blood. No one dared approach. Not even the soldiers. They averted their eyes, hands tightening on their weapons, jaws clenched.

One death. One mistake.

The first blood had been drawn. The question now was: how much more could be spilled before duty gave way to conscience?

Zain gently lifted himself off his sister, inspecting her for injuries. To his immense relief, she was shaking but unharmed.

Amal's face had turned to stone; her features locked in an expression of disbelieving horror. Her lips parted in silent protest, but no words came—only breath. Her eyes—wild and unfocused—darted from Zain to the spot where the man had collapsed. Her hands trembled at her sides, fingers twitching like they couldn't decide whether to grasp at Zain or claw away from him.

Melyndie moved closer to Amal's side, touching her gently on her arm—not with Zain's practiced assurance, but with human softness. Amal flinched, but didn't pull away.

"I can take her to the vaccination station right away, and then she can return to her apartment to rest and recover from tonight's events," Zain stated, his voice hoarse, his mind numb.

Amal's voice came out flat and hollow. "I would prefer to walk there with everyone else."

Zain looked as if he might protest, but Melyndie stepped forward, composed. "She can walk with me."

He narrowed his eyes in silent warning.

Melyndie held her ground. "Maybe it would be better for her to have the company of a stranger at this time. You and your metallic companion can continue with your duties. I'll make sure she gets there and back safely." Her voice was calm, but there was steel beneath it.

Zain held her gaze. After a breathless moment, he nodded once. "Alright," he said curtly. "But Tom will be going with you. I don't want Amal left alone with a stranger right now."

Melyndie nodded, understanding. She was to be a stranger, a person reaching out as an act of kindness, who knew nothing of Zain or his mission. That way there wouldn't be a risk of Amal questioning Melyndie as to who she was to her brother.

At this particular moment, however, being accompanied by Tom, whose demeanor was more intimidating than she ever guessed it could be, left her feeling ill at ease. For Amals sake, she would do all she could to push those feelings aside.

As Zain walked away, the late-afternoon sun ignited the horizon, casting his silhouette in stark relief like a figure carved in judgment. Beside her, Amal stood trembling, arms wrapped around herself. Her face had gone paper-white.

"Come on," Melyndie said softly, laying a hand on her arm. "We'll walk together. The vaccination station's a fair distance so it's going to be a hot, uncomfortable walk...but we'll get through it. Together." She didn't know if it was true, but she had to give Amal something to hold on to.

They moved in silence at first, slipping past the slow procession of civilians shuffling toward the vaccination tables. The streets were lined with RMPs and soldiers, their watchful gazes a constant reminder of how little room there was left for independent freedoms.

Melyndie risked a glance at Amal. "I overheard most of what you and your brother were discussing, and I want to say...well...I'm sincerely sorry for the loss of your mother."

Amal gave her a blank glance. "It feels like the world is ending," she murmured.

Melyndie hesitated, sensing the edge Amal teetered on. "I understand," she said finally. "But sometimes hope comes from the most unlikely places."

Amal suddenly turned her head, her eyes momentarily clear of grief. "Weren't you sitting in my brother's jeep?"

Melyndie dodged the question with soft ease. "It may have looked that way. I did run around the front of it when I heard..." She let the sentence die there, uncomfortable with lying.

Amal's glance flickered down, "What happened to your arm?" She asked.

Melyndie looked down at the sling that she'd all but forgotten about, "I fractured my collarbone in a fall."

"Oh...I'm sorry."

"I'll heal," Melandie replied with a small smile. "As will you and your brother. All hurt heals in time."

Amal looked forward again, the cloud of sorrow settling again, her voice low and brittle. "I never thought it possible to hate my brother this much. He was everything—my protector, my friend. Now he's just...someone I don't know."

Melyndie listened in silence, the grief in Amal's voice so visceral it felt like it could wound anyone close enough to hear it.

She was about to respond—somehow, though she had no idea what she could possibly say—when movement at the edge of her vision caught her attention—a jeep bounding rapidly in their direction. It was Omar. His mother seated beside him.

Panic surged. If Omar reached them, everything could unravel. The questions. The connections. Zain's secret. Her secret.

Melyndie glanced back at Tom. With a flick of her chin, she signaled. Without hesitation, it peeled away and intercepted the oncoming vehicle.

Omar slammed the brakes, his fists clenched around the wheel. Tom stood motionless in his path.

"What do you think you're doing?" Omar barked. "And what the hell was all that commotion? Is everyone okay? Why does Amal look like that? Was she injured?"

Tom ignored the barrage of questions. "Your mother has received her inoculation. Escort her home. You are needed for crowd control."

Omar narrowed his eyes. "That woman walking with Amal—isn't she the one who's been shadowing Zain?"

"If you needed to know, I would inform you," Tom responded flatly.

"You realize you work for the military, right? And I'm a Major in that military. That means you answer to me—"

"I serve Colonel Zain Belhasa, only" Tom replied.

"Well, shit—"

"*Ibin!*" his mother snapped.

"Apologies, *Ummi*," he muttered, still seething.

He watched the two women moving away. Amal looked as if she'd break apart at any moment. The other woman—steady, calm…masking too much.

He started to climb out of the jeep.

A metallic click—unmistakable in its deadly intent—froze him in place.

Tom had drawn its weapon, leveled it at his head.

"One life has already been lost today. Do not make it two." It said with a hint of the empathy it was slowly developing. Then it vanished, replaced with determined intent, "You will proceed with your responsibilities, Major. Disobedience is not allowed."

Omar froze. The rage didn't. He swallowed it back.

"You can be damn sure I'll be having words with Colonel Belhasa," he spat.

"Move along."

Tom retracted its weapon and turned to resume its escort, no doubt that Omar would heed its warning.

Omar's reflection stared back at him from the rearview mirror as he watched the RMP recede into the distance before locating Amal and the enigmatic woman who'd been affixed to Zain's side for the past forty-eight hours, at the very least. A knot of unease tightened in his gut, coiling tighter with every unanswered question. What was Zain hiding, and why the hell didn't he trust him enough to share it? They were childhood friends, so surely Zain knew he could be trusted. Either way, something was off and he was hell-bent on uncovering what that something was. Friendship or no.

Dreams and German Shepherds

Two more days passed, with the sun casting its golden light over the sprawling, glistening cityscape of Dubai, until the last resident received their inoculation. Throughout this period, Amal stayed isolated in her high-rise apartment, a personal sanctuary shielding her from the outside world and from Zain's persistent attempts to reconcile their growing divide. As the heat of the third day waned, the evening sky painted with shades of orange and pink, the sound of the battalion leaving echoed through the city streets.

Zain took one last look back at Amal's building, hoping she might appear and offer a sign that the gap between them, widened by his confession, could still be closed. However, she remained unseen, so he turned his attention ahead, clenching his jaw in self-blame, with the quiet magnifying his profound regret.

Melyndie finally broke their shared silence, which had stretched out like the unending desert in which they currently traversed. Her voice was soft yet carried a weight, "I regret that you could not mend your relationship with Amal. Perhaps that will happen, in time—when all of this mayhem is over."

Zain shook his head in a relentless rhythm, his words emerging as a bitter growl between clenched teeth. "Family is all we have in this merciless world and I obliterated that bond with one unforgivable shot." His lower lip was caught between his teeth; he chewed on it anxiously, as if trying to gnaw away at his guilt.

His gaze drifted towards the horizon where Dubai's skyline faded into dusk. "We're committed to this deployment for a year, or longer," he muttered, despair tinging his voice. "Without any way to reach out to Amal…I'm trapped in my own remorse without any hope for redemption."

Melyndie reached out her hand, resting it lightly on Zain's arm—a simple gesture full of outspoken empathy. She had begun to embrace these small moments of humanity, seeking more ways in which to initiate human contact. She'd been able to reach out in comfort to Amal in a similar manner, but since Zain had forbidden much of her ability to interact with others, she had no one with which to share these moments of contact except with Zain. "Time is the only thing that can reveal new paths from old roads," she stated, philosophically.

Zain nodded slowly; the turmoil evident in his eyes as he stared into the distance. His gaze strayed towards the distant glow, where the twinkling lights of the neighboring town pierced through the velvet darkness.

His eyelids fluttered shut for a moment, a brief surrender to fatigue. The past ninety-six hours had been an endless cycle of strategic planning and relentless execution, leaving little room for rest. To maintain their momentum and ensure efficiency during this critical deployment, he had devised a rotating sleep schedule for his battalion.

Each soldier was only given six hours to recharge before being sent back out to work. With the sheer number of civilians that needed to be corralled for vaccinations, relieving fifty at a time from duty, to rest, could potentially slow their progress. However, having his men collapse from exhaustion would delay it with certainty. He yawned widely and realized that included himself. He couldn't remember the last time he'd slept for more than an hour.

His eyes flickered towards Melyndie; her form shrouded in the shadows of evening. She'd been trying to match his pace—with admirable tenacity—but at what cost? Her face bore testament to her struggle; dark crescents under her eyes and unmistakable strain etched on her features. It was like looking into a mirror.

Guilt gnawed at him as he recalled her words from yesterday about her healing bruises and the continued pain in her collarbone. He knew well enough that lack of sleep could hinder recovery; he'd seen it happen too many times on the battlefield. But in his quest to prioritize his soldiers' welfare, he'd overlooked hers.

A sigh escaped him then—a sound heavy with regret and resolve intermingled. He decided then and there that she would get ample rest during each stopover for inoculations. She would be allowed to slumber through every stop until they were done serving every last person, if she wanted to. And if she resisted? Well, he'd just have to insist.

Zain parked his jeep just outside the city limits and observed as his soldiers sprang into action with precision and efficiency. They all knew their roles and carried out their mission without needing any guidance. Their task was simple: round up and vaccinate, but the constant movement was draining. The first fifty men to rest, retreated from the commotion, and set up their bedrolls. An RMP stood guard ready to awaken them after six hours. That same RMP kept track of the rotation and notified the next group, maintaining a smooth cycle to ensure none got overlooked.

How anyone managed to fall asleep amid the constant motion and heightened anxiety of their mission was beyond him. He doubted he could drift off so easily, even if he had the chance, so it always amazed him to see the soldiers sleeping so peacefully, often within moments of their heads touching the ground.

"Let's set up our sleeping arrangements," Zain proposed abruptly. "We're both running ragged and could do with some shut-eye." His original plan was to let Melyndie catch a few winks while he went about his duties, but he realized that if he wanted her to unwind, he'd have to do the same. She had an uncanny tendency to mimic his actions. "Tom will stand guard, ensuring we can sleep undisturbed. Are you okay with this makeshift lodging? It's not exactly five-star accommodations."

"I…don't…"

"I get it…you're unfamiliar with that reference," Zain chuckled softly. "It just implies that sleeping on the hard ground, particularly with your wounded shoulder, won't be as plush as resting on a feather-soft bed. But it's the best I can offer under these circumstances."

"I *am* exhausted," she replied, deciding it didn't matter how he phrased it. She understood the underlying offer of rest.

"And yet you haven't grumbled or griped once," Zain pointed out, shaking his head in amazement.

"You haven't either," Melyndie retorted.

"True, but I'm trained for this. I'm a soldier. You're just a regular…well…maybe not regular…but you are a civilian."

Her eyebrows knitted together in confusion at his words, but instead of clarifying—again—he simply bounded out of the jeep and headed towards the back where their supplies were stashed. As he started changing into a fresh uniform, another wave of self-reproach washed over him, something that was happening far too often since the start of this deployment.

"You don't have any spare clothes," he noted aloud, suddenly realizing she'd been wearing the same attire consecutively, for days. "And we aren't due to get in a drop shipment for another three weeks. Tom ordered you up a uniform, but your current attire is likely to be in tatters before it gets here."

"The holy ones did not think about the need for more attire," she confessed quietly, looking down in embarrassment. "In our time, we wear the same jumpsuit for many weeks at a time."

Zain dug into his duffel and yanked out a spare shirt—worn, sun-faded, and still holding the faint scent of soap and desert sweat. Given her petite stature, the shirt would serve as a makeshift dress, but he had no trousers that would remotely fit her. "You can change into this, but you'll have to keep your pants on, since I don't have anything suitable for a woman of your size. You can use these wipes to give yourself an army bath. I'll have Tom find someone who is your approximate size to get you a set of fatigues, until yours get here. Tom!" He shouted to the RMP who'd detached from the back of the jeep and was standing guard.

"I have identified a soldier of similar size and will go to retrieve clothing," Tom replied, turning and striding away.

"Well, that was faster than expected. It's possible you won't need my t-shirt after all." Zain shoved the shirt back into his duffel.

"What is an army bath?" Melyndie began, but Zain cut her off.

"Don't trouble yourself over the terminology," he reassured her. "Just use these wipes to clean yourself before you slip on whatever clothes Tom manages to bring back. I'll be doing the same," he added, his voice laced with a hint of self-deprecation. He lifted an arm and took an exaggerated sniff under his armpit, his face crumpling into a grimace at the offensive odor. "I'm in dire need of it."

Melyndie nodded in understanding. "Your kindness is appreciated," she voiced, her words resonating with genuine gratitude. She also knew that his exaggerated manner was an attempt to lighten the heavy mood that had swirled about them since Dubai. "I also appreciate what you're trying to do," she added.

Zain looked at her, confused for a second, then realization dawned, "In all frankness, I hadn't realized I was doing anything. I guess I just…I can't escape the pain, so I have to learn to live with it." He finished with a shrug. "It certainly won't help you any if I continue to agonize over things twenty-four-seven. And, if I keep brooding, I won't be able to think about the well-being of anyone but myself. Selfish, if you think about it. Of course, that's what I've been doing, and that is why I didn't consider any of this earlier," Zain confessed, his fingers deftly tugging his dust-laden t-shirt over his head. He retrieved one of the wipes from its pack and began scrubbing at the layers of dirt and sweat from his skin.

Without missing a beat, Melyndie mirrored his actions, slowly undoing the buttons on her blouse, which doing one-handed was quickly causing her frustration to rise, in her tired state.

When Zain noticed what she was doing, he was there like a guardian angel, pulling the two halves back together to shield her modesty. "Wait!" he blurted out in shock. "What are you doing?"

"I am going to cleanse myself so that I can be ready for when Tom…" Melyndie's voice trailed off as she registered Zain's wide-eyed astonishment. A frown creased her forehead as she asked hesitantly, "Did I commit some sort of error?"

Zain closed his eyes momentarily and took a deep breath filled with frustration and realization alike. The more time he spent in Melyndie's company, the more he was beginning to understand just how innocent she was to worldly matters—almost painfully so. Then her words from several days ago echoed in his mind—she was fabricated solely for productivity, devoid of any understanding of companionship...and now, he was certain that she was oblivious to societal norms and etiquettes…the concept of intimacy.

"You were about to change right here, in the open," he explained gently, lowering his voice. "That's not…generally done in public, or…in front of…others…unless that other someone is your…um…well…significant other," Zain stumbled, rubbing the back of his neck awkwardly.

"But you removed your shirt in front of me," Melyndie observed and could not help but mark how beautiful he was. There was a color to his skin that was devoid on men…and women…in her time. It was such a stark contrast to her own that she wanted to run a hand across it to see if it felt different also. Zain's voice cut through her musings and she moved her gaze back to his.

"I know, and it may not seem like it makes much sense," Zain continued, "but…well…we're…um…built differently…or hadn't you noticed."

Melyndie's gaze traveled from Zain's face to his sun-kissed, chiseled chest and then to her own. It was a revelation for her to see such physical differences between individuals, when in her time, that was not something that was emphasized or even acknowledged. And the oversized jumpsuits that everyone wore hid any potentially significant differences, leaving only noticeable variations: height and hair color.

"Please stop staring," Zain chastised lightly, breaking Melyndie out of her thoughts.

"I apologize, although I still do not know why you can remove your shirt and I may not," Melyndie persisted in her innocent search for understanding.

"There's no need for apology, Melyndie, and I wish I could take the time to explain things more fully, but right now I think we're both too exhausted for me to have a discussion on the sexes. We've less than six hours remaining before shift change and I will need to get back to work at that time. Tom will act as a shield against prying eyes so that you can get yourself cleaned and clothed." Zain added when he noticed that his RMP had returned with a fresh uniform for her.

"I will ensure no prying eyes sees her while she changes. Here are your clothes, Melyndie." With an almost imperceptible motion, the RMP advanced. Its metallic arms extended outwards, laden with a uniform and undergarments.

Melyndie recognized the items that Dr. Kishida-Guan had referred to as panties and bra. She took the proffered items and decided that, if the women of this time wore them, then she would do so also. She was about to shed her clothing again, but stopped and looked at Tom, who immediately uttered the command 'deploy curtains'.

Instantly, two rectangular compartments on the underside of its gleaming arms hissed open, and from within each, a curtain of cloth-like plastic cascaded down. "If you will step inside the area, the side of the jeep will act as the third privacy shield."

"Damn! I didn't know you had that feature," Zain blurted out, his eyes wide with surprise. "I thought you were just going to block her somehow with your massive height."

"There are many things that you are unaware of which I am capable," the RMP retorted.

Zain paused in his act of grooming and gaped at the robot, taken aback by this revelation. "I guess I'll have to scrutinize your schematics one of these days then."

His suggestion was met with a flat refusal from the RMP. "Your superiors will not authorize such an action," it replied curtly.

Zain snorted dismissively at this bureaucratic obstacle. "Of course they wouldn't." He finished his ablutions, then rolled out his and Melyndie's bedrolls next to each other at the rear of the jeep, with just enough space between them to maintain decorum.

While Zain and Tom bantered, Melyndie stepped within the small private space offered by Tom and set about attempting to disrobe. With her one, good hand, she released the buttons on her trousers and let them pool at her feet. She then stepped out of them, and kicked them aside. *That was the easy part*, she thought, thinking about the struggle she'd had pulling them back up, one-handed, whenever she visited the latrine.

Her legs were steady enough, especially as the bruising was subsiding quickly now, but her upper body still felt foreign—one side dulled by pain and limited motion, the other overworked from constant compensation.

She picked up the panties and immediately realized the struggle she faced to maintain her balance as she attempted to step into the lower garments, with one arm cradled tightly in a sling.

She bounced about the small space, until one of her feet made it through the opening of the panties. But trying to insert the other foot proved more challenging. She leaned back against the jeep to try to find stability, and finally managed to get her second foot into the opening. By the time she'd pulled the flimsy garment up to her waist, a thin sheen of sweat prickled at her brow, her breath shallow from the effort.

She fell back against the jeep and felt tears prick her eyes in frustration. She knew, without a shadow of a doubt, that if the panties had been difficult, the pants would prove beyond her current capabilities.

"I just can't…" she whispered aloud to no one—then paused, staring at the curtain's wavering edge, and called gently, "Zain?"

There was a pause. Then the faint shuffle of movement from somewhere behind the jeep.

"Yeah?" he called back.

"I require assistance."

Another pause. A longer one. "With…what exactly?"

"My clothing."

More silence. Then: "Right. Okay. Uh—one second."

Moments later, the curtain peeled open just enough for him to slip inside. When he spied her state of undress, his eyes widened and he immediately shifted his gaze on the sky. "Okay," he said, already starting to ramble, "I swear I am not looking at anything. I am here purely in a logistical, problem-solving capacity. Like…like a nurse. But with zero nursing skills. Or confidence."

She blinked up at him, confused.

"I need you to hold the pants open," she said, "so that I can attempt to step into them."

Zain crouched down, still looking anywhere but at her, and held the fabric like it might combust. "Just…step in. I got you."

With careful precision, she stepped into the openings. Zain quickly shimmied the fabric gently up and over her hips, jarring her stability. She wobbled a little, tilting sideways. He steadied her with one hand on her waist, the contact brief but enough to turn his ears pink.

"Okay. That's…secure," he said hoarsely, after rapidly buttoning up the pants.

She held up the bra next.

"Ah, hell no," Zain muttered. "Can't you forgo wearing that? If you thought getting your undergarments on was a task, trying to put that thing on with your injured shoulder will be near impossible, and definitely…well…most likely…a major discomfort to your collarbone."

Melyndie eyed the bra and let out a sigh, wondering if she would ever be afforded the opportunity to test out the garment. Since it wouldn't be now, she let the bra drop to the ground.

"This is next then, and I'm at an equal disadvantage at getting it on," she groaned in frustration, nodding to her immobile arm. "Should I forgo wearing a shirt at all?"

Zain made a strained noise in the back of his throat but took the shirt from her, "I am so sorry you have to go through this," he said. "I am mortified on your behalf. And mine."

"I do not know what mortified means," Melyndie replied honestly, "but I am uncomfortable."

"That makes two of us," Zain muttered, hand rubbing the back of his neck as he inspected the shirt grimly. "This is definitely going to be trickier."

"I can attempt it," she offered.

"No," he said, holding up a hand. "We're not going through that again."

She nodded. "Okay, but first we have to get this sling off, along with my blouse."

"All right. Well, obviously, I'm going to have to remove the sling," he said, voice quieter now, more serious. "We'll go slow, so I don't hurt you."

She nodded again. "Thank you."

He stepped closer, carefully sliding his hands around the back of her neck to undo the clasp of the sling. His fingers moved gently, brushing warm skin as he worked. The brace came loose, and he let the straps hang loose at her side. "Turn around, so I can get the other strap," he instructed, then quickly undid the second tie and let it drop to the ground.

Melyndie sighed heavily as her arm, stiff from disuse, slowly straightened.

"Do you need a minute?" Zain asked, wishing he could take her pain away.

She closed her eyes for a moment and shook her head, "No, let's get this done. If it takes much longer, we'll miss out on our rest time."

"Okay," he said, swallowing thickly. "I need to slide your blouse off."

He reached up and gripped the edges of her shirt, careful to avoid contact with her skin. He averted his gaze and then slid the shirt from her shoulders, releasing his grip as soon as he was certain it was free.

He released the breath he'd been holding and then bent down to retrieve the t-shirt he'd placed on the ground—immediately regretting that decision. The small space was difficult to maneuver in, and his arm brushed up against the bare flesh of her side. He let out another breath through his nostrils, "I'm sorry…I just…I have to grab this…got it!" He exclaimed, and nearly knocked her over in his haste to straighten. He reached out and grabbed her waist to steady her, then lowered them as quickly, as if he'd touched a hot stove. "Shit! I'm sorry…I just…let's just focus on the shirt, okay? I need you to try lifting your bad arm just a bit so I can ease the sleeve on. Do you think you can do that?"

"I'll try." The moment she lifted her arm to just below shoulder height, a white-hot pain rocketed across her chest and shoulder, and she cried out, lurching forward—right into him.

Zain caught her instantly.

His arms wrapped around her, instinct overriding propriety. One hand pressed lightly against the center of her back, the other curled protectively at her waist. Her face was buried against his chest; her breath snagged in her throat. She was trembling from the pain.

"I'm so sorry," he whispered into her hair. "I shouldn't have asked you to do that."

Her response was barely audible, escaping between gasps. "You…couldn't know."

They stayed like that for several minutes, the awkwardness eclipsed by something gentler. Something softer. Zain didn't move until she shifted slightly, her breathing steadier.

He eased her back just enough to see her face. "Are you okay?"

"No," she replied honestly. "But I will be."

He nodded, then cleared his throat roughly. "Tom?"

"I am here," came the RMP's voice from outside the curtain.

"She can't lift her arm. We need to modify the shirt. Suggestions…please."

"Slice the right sleeve and side seam. That should allow you to slip the shirt on without her moving her arm. Once the shirt is on, I can reseal the material. Then the sling may be reapplied for requisite stabilization and support."

"Okay." Zain crouched again, this time to retrieve the blade from his boot, and again, his arm caressed the flesh at her waist, but this time he didn't pretend not to notice. Her skin was warm, smooth. He froze mid-motion, fingers clenching around the handle of his blade. He exhaled slowly, as if trying to reset his heartbeat, then straightened—slowly this time, so not to knock her over.

"Sorry," he muttered, not meeting her eyes.

She tilted her head slightly, observing him in silence. Not judging. Just seeing.

"Can I have the shirt?" he asked, and a twinge of color reached Melyndie's cheeks as she glanced down where the shirt had fallen from her grasp.

"Oh…not again," Zain groaned audibly, and bent to retrieve it, "I just—have to grab this," he said, fumbling with the fabric. "Almost…ok…got it."

His knuckles brushed her again as he stood, and this time she flinched—not from pain, but from a burgeoning awareness she didn't fully understand.

Zain, on the other hand, understood all too well and looked like a man trapped in a burning room, trying not to inhale the smoke. He busied himself on slicing the shirt at the seam, determined not to touch her bare skin again.

"Okay…now…let's um…focus on the shirt," he said finally, his voice rough. "We're almost done. Good arm first. Now duck your head through."

She obeyed, and he adjusted the shirt until it hung loosely across her torso.

"Ready for you, Tom," Zain called. "She's decent…enough. You can drop the curtains."

The partitions retracted in a hiss of air. Tom stepped forward immediately, holding a tool that looked like a fusion between a medical stapler and a glue gun.

"Please hold the fabric closed from underarm to hip," Tom directed.

Zain moved close to Melyndie's side, "You'll need to lift your arm straight out, just a fraction."

Melyndie released a slow breath from her nose as she slowly, carefully, lifted her arm, "That's as high I can go," she breathed.

"That'll work. Make it quick, Tom." Zain's fingers pinched the fabric together carefully. As he did, his knuckles brushed her skin. "Sorry," he said softly.

"It's all right."

Tom ran the tool along the seam, which released a soft hum and a faint heat.

"This will hold unless exposed to high heat, abrasive force, or a high degree of sweat saturation," the RMP noted matter-of-factly. "Given Zain's current adrenal output, the latter would pose a challenge if Zain were wearing it."

Zain's head dropped with a groan. "Tom…"

"You're welcome," Tom said.

Melyndie looked down at the now-sealed seam and flexed her good arm.

"I believe it will function adequately," she said. "Now we just need to get the sling back on."

As the RMP stepped away, Zain helped Melyndie ease her arm back into the sling. His hands lingered just a moment longer than necessary as he adjusted the strap over her collarbone.

"There," he said. "Not perfect, but close."

She looked up at him, her expression unreadable. "I do not know what to say. I couldn't have done this without your help."

"You don't have to say anything," he murmured. "Just…let's try to sleep."

She nodded, taking slow, shallow breaths as she turned toward the bedrolls that Zain had rolled out nearby. She then turned to look at the RMP.

"Tom, I forgot to thank you for your help also," Melyndie murmured, as she lowered herself to the bedroll.

"You are welcome, Melyndie. Perhaps it would be good for me to administer a pain killer. It will ease your pain and aid in sleep."

"That would be lovely, yes, but only if you can come to me," she admitted sheepishly, "because I am not getting up again right now."

At her consent, a needle appeared from a compartment near Tom's chest. He reached in and retrieved in, then bent at the waist and carefully jabbed her in the bicep of her good arm. "You will rest now. I will watch over you."

Zain listened to the exchange between Melyndie and his RMP, but his eyes continued scanning the perimeter out of habit. Old instincts didn't give way easily—but tonight, he had nothing left to give them. When Tom straightened and retreated a step, Zain moved to his bedroll. "She's been in pain for days. Why haven't you offered a pain killer before now?"

"Because what I have contains a sleep agent, and we have not stopped moving long enough for her to sleep."

"Well, we're going to from now on…I hope," Zain replied, as he collapsed, exhaustion taking hold. "The sun will be over the horizon before we can even blink." They settled into silence for a few moments until Melyndie's soft, sleepy voice broke the stillness.

"Do you think...do you think I'll ever get to see a German Shepherd?" Her voice was barely above a whisper, filled with an innocent longing.

Zain blinked at her question, lifting his head slightly from his makeshift pillow to gaze at her through heavy eyelids weighed down by fatigue. "Where did that come from?"

"It was this old photograph my predecessor found in the archives," she explained, her fingers tracing invisible lines in the air as if trying to recreate the image. "I'm not sure but I think his sudden curiosity with this era might have led to his termination. I took that photograph from him and held onto it like a precious secret, studying it every night under the dim light in my quarters. It became my wish, my silent prayer really, that when I was sent back here...that I would get to see one."

Zain sighed deeply, sadness tinging his words as he replied, "Once upon a time they were beloved companions of many humans. But animals...they've become rare over the past fifty years or so. A lot of larger mammals have been hunted down for food and resources in less fortunate areas. Even domesticated pets are now wild and often fall prey."

"But doesn't your world have an abundance of food?" Melyndie asked, her eyebrows knitting together in perplexed concern; she had always imagined this era as one of plenty.

"There's no severe scarcity yet…at least not everywhere…" Zain's voice trailed off into a yawn. "We should really sleep now, Melyndie. It'll be dawn soon."

"I understand," she murmured.

"Good, I'll see you in a few hours." Zain's words were cut short as sleep claimed him, his soft snores filling the air around them. The sound was both unfamiliar and comforting to Melyndie.

She let her eyes drift shut, lulled by the rhythm of his quiet breathing—and the warmth of his presence close by. Then the dream came to her again: wildflowers bowing beneath her feet as she ran. The sun was warm, the wind sweet. And beside her—tongue lolling, eyes bright—a German Shepherd bounded freely, no longer artifact or mystery, but companion. A smile curved her lips. She was here, in the before time. And now, her dream had a real chance of coming true.

A shriek—sharp, high, and unearthly—ripped through the silence of the desert night, and into Zain's dreams like a shockwave. His heart slammed against his ribs as he bolted upright, breath catching in his throat. Above him, stars shimmered in a moonless sky. Around him, the world was still—too still.

He shoved off the top of his bedroll and sprang to his feet, instinct yanking his gaze toward the shadows behind the parked jeep.

Beside him, the RMP snapped to full alert. Joints hissed softly as it rotated with surgical precision, its sleek silver form catching faint light. In one smooth motion, its arm-mounted weapon locked forward, ready to neutralize a threat not yet seen.

Then they saw it—*or rather, didn't.*

Melyndie's bedroll was empty.

The fabric lay crumpled, the faint warmth of her body still lingering, but she was gone. Just—gone.

"What in God's name is happening? Where is she?" Zain's voice broke the silence with a crack of panic. He grabbed the tactical flashlight from the dash of the jeep and swept its beam across the desolate perimeter—beneath the vehicle, toward the low rise behind them, across the uneven terrain of sand and scrub.

"Where is she?" he barked again, his flashlight jittering with the tension in his grip. "She wouldn't just get up and wander off into the desert!"

The RMP's voice cut through the night with disturbing calm. "It seems she has disappeared without a trace. Perhaps those in her time retrieved—"

Its sentence broke off as headlights flared in the distance.

A jeep crested a hill and came tearing across the terrain. It fishtailed slightly as it skidded to a halt, a rooster tail of dust catching the flashlight's beam and hanging like smoke in the air.

Omar jumped out before the dust had even settled. He flung open the rear door and pulled out a bundled form—slender, limp, unmistakable.

Melyndie.

Zain bolted toward him, his boots kicking up sand. "What in hell?" he breathed as he reached them. With careful urgency, he took her from Omar's arms. Her head lolled gently against his chest as he carried her back to the bedroll she'd vanished from only moments earlier. He laid her down with a tenderness that barely masked the dread pulsing beneath his skin.

He turned to the RMP, jaw tight. "Explain."

The machine straightened; its gaze fixed on Melyndie. "It appears she was not taken after all."

"Examine her for any further injuries," Zain ordered, stepping aside.

Omar lingered a few feet away; eyes shadowed with confusion and unease. "Would anyone care to explain why I found her unconscious on the other side of town?"

Zain turned sharply. "Tell me exactly what happened," he demanded, voice tight.

Omar's gaze widened slightly at his friend's frantic command. "I was patrolling through the town's streets ensuring no one slipped through our net; that everyone received their vaccine," Omar began.

"Cut to the chase," Zain interrupted impatiently.

"As I rounded a corner on the far side of town, I saw something fall, seemingly, from out of the sky—" Omar's revelation was cut short by Zain's muttered exclamation.

"Not again!" he breathed, aghast.

Omar continued, his gaze narrowing over Zain's reaction. "I rushed over and found it was your mystery woman. I knew I had to get her to you as quickly as possible."

Zain nodded in appreciation. "Thank you, Omar."

"Zain," Omar said with a hint of hurt in his voice, "we've known each other our entire lives and you've never been this secretive…not with me."

"If it were something I could share, believe me, I would," Zain replied solemnly.

"But it isn't, so you won't." Omar concluded.

Zain nodded, "Maybe soon, my friend, but not right now."

"I suppose I should return to my duties then. There are still many who need the vaccine, and the sooner we get this town finished, the sooner we can head on to the next one," Omar said, then turned to leave.

"Thanks for bringing her over to me." Zain's voice echoed in the departing figure's wake. Without wasting a breath, he swiveled back to his RMP who was meticulously scanning over Melyndie. "Is she okay? What caused this? How could she just end up all the way on the other side of this town?" His questions were urgent, seeping with concern.

The RMP finished its evaluation and stood. "The evidence points toward crosstalk," it said matter-of-factly.

Zain's knuckles whitened as he clenched his fists. His teeth gritted against each other in frustration. "Before you start spouting technical jargon, I need to know her status. Is she okay?" he demanded, each word heavy with barely contained anger and worry.

"There is no evidence of additional trauma. Her prior injury remains stable."

"So, she'll waken soon," Zain concluded, relief flooding his tone. "So…now you can explain your comment. What is crosstalk?"

"I must clarify that my analysis is speculative. The relevant files are marked 'need to know.'"

Zain's anger boiled over at the non-response. "You know that only makes me want to beat the shit out of you, right?" he growled in frustration, then let out a long sigh, his gaze moving over Melyndie's motionless body. "If anything, I think we can now rule out insanity," he murmured.

"I believed her immediately," the RMP replied and Zain closed his eyes in exasperation—again.

Zain groaned, dragging a hand across his face. "Listen, Tom," he said, voice low but firm, "we are the only ones she has. You and me. That means you work with me—not around me, not against me."

"Your superiors—"

"Fuck our superiors!" Zain snapped. "She has nothing to do with them, and you're already keeping her existence a secret from them. So, let's just agree that anything to do with Melyndie—any information I request—does not, will not, ever fall under 'need to know'."

A pause stretched out between them. The RMP's optics swiveled slowly back to Melyndie. "She carries an implanted chip, beneath the skin near the fractured clavicle. I identified it upon her arrival. Its function appears to be location-based—either a beacon or tether. The most likely cause of this latest event is crosstalk—interference between two signal-bearing devices operating within overlapping frequency ranges."

Zain's mind was already racing. "So, they tried to pull her back. And something scrambled the signal?"

"Correct. That is the likely conclusion."

"And you can't say more."

"I cannot provide additional details without breaching protocol."

"Signal interference isn't an unknown occurrence. It happens all of the time, so what type of project related to crosstalk could be deemed classified?" Zain asked, but the RMP's silence rendered the conversation moot. He wanted to press the issue, but his RMP was resolved, so he tried a different tact. Zain exhaled; his jaw tight. "Fine! Then tell me how we stop this from happening again."

"I cannot ascertain—"

"Can we extract the chip?" Zain asked, his frustration boiling over.

"Removal would sever her temporal tether. Return to her origin would become impossible."

"Yes, I remember," Zain interrupted. "But if her people persist in their attempts to retrieve her and keep failing due to this crosstalk, won't that eventually jeopardize her life? There has to be a limit on how many times she can be jerked through space-time without damage."

"That is indeed a plausible hypothesis," the RMP conceded. "However, without empirical evidence, it remains speculative."

"What about the device causing the crosstalk? Can *that* be removed?"

"I do not have sufficient data at this time with which to address that. However, based on current speculation, I believe it could be a possibility—once that data becomes available. *If* it becomes available."

Their conversation was interrupted as Melyndie stirred. Zain immediately dropped to her side.

"This conversation isn't over, Tom," he warned.

"I would not expect that it would be."

Melyndie's voice emerged as a raspy whisper, her words barely audible. "What happened?"

Zain hesitated for a moment, then answered quietly. "From what we've been able to piece together—your holy ones tried to pull you back less than an hour ago. But something interfered with the attempt."

"Are you certain? My return date is not for many weeks yet."

"That they tried? Yes." Tom answered. "That something disrupted the attempt? Not as confident."

"How are you feeling? Tom checked you over and didn't find any new injuries."

"I feel a bit disoriented," she murmured.

"That's understandable. Omar found you unconscious on the far side of the city."

"What?!"

"He watched you fall from the sky. Just like Tom and I did days ago."

"The disorientation could also be due to the sedative I administered a few hours ago," Tom interjected. "Insufficient time has passed for it to fully exit your system."

"I do feel drowsy, yet strangely alert at the same time."

"That is likely due to a surge in adrenaline caused by Zain's information," the RMP added.

"You're certain they tried to retrieve me?" Melyndie asked, locking eyes with Zain. Beneath her confusion, something darker churned—a cocktail of fear and realization. Zain nodded and Melyndie closed her eyes, not wanting to believe that her time here could be cut short. But if they intended to take her back, why was she still here? Confusion tangled with dread as the implications clawed at her. "It's possible I'm too far away for them to retrieve me," she said quietly, more to herself. "We did test jumps—but the furthest was a hundred years…once, in the wrong direction." She let out a dry, humorless laugh. "They were able to send me here—to the before time—but there was never a guarantee the chip would stay stable over such a long distance…" Her fingers drifted to the side of her neck, brushing lightly over the skin. If the damage to her body during the jump had been worse, the chip might've been damaged too—leaving her stranded.

"That's one explanation," Zain said gently, "but considering you disappeared from here and reappeared, it's more likely something interfered with their attempt to lock on."

"Do you know what that something might be?"

"Tom mentioned crosstalk, but doesn't have the data to confirm anything."

Melyndie's voice shook. "Is there any way to get the data we need to verify that?"

Zain turned to the RMP, who met Melyndie's gaze. "I have insufficient data to explain the anomaly—"

"Anomaly?" Zain cut in.

The RMP paused. "The second microchip implanted at the base of her neck," it clarified.

Zain's eyes darted to Melyndie. She didn't speak—but her hand froze against her neck.

Rising Concerns

Zain glanced between Melyndie and the GPS coordinates, their next stop reduced to a tiny dot on the worn-out digital screen. The jeep jostled over uneven terrain, its tires crunching through loose gravel and sunbaked soil, since this small outlying village of less than one thousand people had no paved highway. It was moments like these he truly felt for Melyndie. Although her bruises had faded, the bumpy ride was still tough on her.

He cast a sidelong glance at her—at the faint tension in her jaw, the way she held herself just a little too stiffly. She didn't complain, not once. But that didn't mean she wasn't hurting. "How are you holding up?" he asked, his voice a gravelly undertone against the steady drone of the engine.

"I'm gradually recovering, yet my mind remains confused and worried," Melyndie admitted. Her words lingered heavily in the atmosphere, like a storm cloud ready to unleash its downpour. "Is the RMP positive that the second chip wasn't present during his initial examination?"

Zain inhaled deeply, his grip on the steering wheel the sole sign that his composed exterior was just a facade. "I'm fairly certain that Tom is incapable of error. Are you thinking redundancy?"

"I'm just too confused to think clearly about much all," Melyndie confessed, letting out a heavy sigh that carried the weight of her concerns.

"Completely understandable. Personally, I was considering the possibility that they might have installed a secondary chip as a precautionary measure. This would be in case the primary one malfunctioned or got damaged somehow. Perhaps they didn't foresee any potential issues that could arise? Of course, this is beyond my area of expertise."

"Mine too," Melyndie said with a faint smile. "But I don't recall them inserting a second chip, and, well, that only makes sense if Tom had picked up on one..." She stopped speaking, pressing her fingers into her skin as if she could disable the secondary chip through sheer will.

Zain noticed her frustration and gently placed his hand over hers until she began to relax. He pulled her hand down and rested it on the seat between them. "Let's try to stay calm. Tom is working on a solution. As for why he might have missed it during the first scan...maybe it wasn't active at that time."

"Not active?" she echoed, frowning.

"Inactive systems often need something to activate them," he explained. "If for some reason they couldn't locate you using your main chip..." Zain's voice faded as uncertainty clouded his thoughts, with only the engine's hum breaking the long silence that settled between them.

"What's on your mind?" Melyndie prompted softly after what seemed like an endless wait for him to complete his thought.

"Hmm? Oh...I was just thinking that, if I were them, I'd hold off on attempts to pull you back again until I ran full diagnostics. I mean, after all, why jump to secondary protocols before the primary is assessed. Sound about right, Tom? Diagnostics first?"

Tom was tethered to the back of the jeep, a silver sentinel, ever watchful. Its response to Zain's query wasn't immediate, however, causing Zain to wonder if it could even hear him. He was about to repeat his question louder, when Tom finally spoke. Its response unanticipated and deeply unsettling.

"I think this is what they are doing to me," Tom stated, its voice a flat line yet crackling with an undercurrent of impossible emotion.

Zain stiffened. His hands gripped the wheel tighter as a low thrum pulsed at the base of his spine. He shot a glance at Melyndie, who had gone still beside him. He wanted to stop, to address the unexpected announcement, but the GPS showed they were less than a mile out from their destination, and the mission needed to come first over concerns for his RMP.

Soon after, the battalion halted. The soldiers wasted no time in getting out of their vehicles, their fatigue evident in each step. Zain was no different, feeling exhaustion weighing on as he climbed from the jeep and approached Tom. Tom detached from the back of the vehicle with careful, deliberate actions and turned to face Zain.

"What's happening with you? You good to proceed?" Zain asked, squinting against the harsh sunlight reflecting off its metallic surface.

"A system analysis is being performed on me," Tom stated in a way that was so casually indifferent it highlighted his robotic demeanor. This made Zain realize that any emotion he had sensed in the previous announcement was likely just a projection of his own worries onto his mechanical companion.

"Do you think it has to do with you constantly switching your video and audio off when Melyndie is around or when we're discussing her?"

"I would say that is a fair assumption, especially as both are off more times than not."

"Yeah, gauging both of those events' frequency, I can understand why your coders might suspect you're dealing with a system error. What's the likely outcome?"

"They could potentially initiate my recall protocol and send a new unit, or modify my programming remotely."

Zain's jaw clenched. He rubbed the back of his neck, where sweat pooled, the dread creeping in like a slow leak. "Neither scenario is ideal."

"I concur. It would also imply that we can no longer keep Melyndie's existence under wraps...unless..." Tom's voice hesitated in a very human way.

"Unless?" Zain prompted.

"I have formulated a plan."

"That's good to hear. Care to divulge?"

"I suggest that we contact your friend, Omar."

"Are you being deliberately obtuse?"

"I simply do not wish to repeat myself unnecessarily, and since my plan would involve the major, then I think it best—"

"Tom. Just please...shut up." Zain snapped; rising exasperation sharpening in his tone. He stalked back to the jeep and retrieved his transceiver, the metal warm from the sun.

"Omar, respond."

After a pause filled only by desert silence and the faint call of a bird, the radio crackled. "Zain? That you?"

"Affirmative. Can you rendezvous with me where I parked, just beyond the outskirts of town?"

"On my way."

Zain returned the device to the jeep, then made his way to the front where Melyndie was, casually leaning against the sunbaked hood, savoring an MRE. Wisps of her hair danced lightly in the gentle breeze, framing her face with a touch of wild elegance.

"Just checking up on you," he said with a small grin. "I see you started lunch without me."

"I apologize for not waiting..." she murmured, cheeks coloring faintly. "It's just...I'm used to eating alone."

Zain paused. There was no bitterness in her tone—only fact. Loneliness, spoken aloud. "Well, at least you have some company now, except when I'm busy with my responsibilities," he said with a hint of embarrassment. "I have to go attend to them now, but there's no need to apologize. I just wanted to touch base."

"Is Tom ok?"

"We don't know yet, but there's a concern, which is why it asked me to call in Omar."

"Omar is your childhood friend," she noted.

"That's right." He pointed toward a rising dust cloud. "And here he comes now. Once you're done, try and get out of the sun. It's not as harmless as it looks."

"I am adjusting to the temperatures more, I think."

Zain gave her fair skin a skeptical glance. "That doesn't mean you aren't susceptible. It can sneak up on you. I'll be back soon." He turned and made his way back to Tom. "Comms off?"

"I turned them off as soon as you approached. I am not stupid, Zain."

"No need to get snarky, Tom," he said dryly.

"*You* are my example, Zain."

Zain blinked. "Great. I've got a snarky robot in need of an attitude adjustment." Zain rolled his eyes, then decided it was best to move their conversation forward as it was quickly derailing. "Okay, real quick, since Omar will arrive any second. I think we can both agree that things are getting a bit dicey; that you having to turn off and on transmissions all of the time, when Melyndie is around is—"

"Gaining unwanted attention," Tom concluded. "That's why I've asked Omar to join us."

"I suspected as much. Hopefully, your plan will reduce the need for communication blackouts."

Omar's jeep rapidly approached, tires skidding slightly on the dusty ground before it came to an abrupt halt. Without a moment's hesitation, Omar sprang out of the vehicle, his boots thudding heavily as he dashed toward Zain and Tom, who stood waiting at the back of Zain's jeep. His brow furrowed with concern, Omar's voice carried urgency as he asked, "What's going on?"

Zain glanced over his shoulder at Melyndie, who now sat with her head tilted against the headrest, "Let's walk and talk. Inoculations going okay here?" Zain asked casually, as they moved further away from the jeep.

"We just arrived, but it's going well so far. Thus far, no force required. People are lining up with little-to-no resistance. Most are frightened. As soon as they heard that the vaccine was to combat a worldwide virus…anyway, all that to say…there's been no issues to speak of. We far enough away to talk now? Is this about the virus supposedly ravaging the planet?"

Zain stopped walking and turned to looked at his friend, surprised by the question. "You don't believe it?"

"You do?" Omar countered.

Zain slowly shook his head. "After everything that's happened this week…I'm not sure what to believe right now." He glanced toward the small town. Children, elders, civilians—trusting and unarmed. Would they be so trusting if they knew this inoculation meant life or death—in more ways than one? "Let's hope compliance continues," he said. "Because if it doesn't..." He left the sentence unfinished.

"So, if this isn't about the inoculations, why did you call me over?" Omar trailed off and waited.

"I didn't call you here…well…technically I did, but it was Tom who needed to talk to you," Zain clarified.

Omar's brow knitted. "Tom?"

Zain smirked. "My RMP. It picked the name."

Omar swallowed theatrically. "Do I even want to know?"

"Not sure you do," Zain replied with a grimace. "But including you was Tom's idea."

"Is this to do with your mystery woman?"

"Good guess."

"Wasn't too far a leap. It was either the inoculations or her," Omar shrugged. "So, *Tom*, what is it you want me to know about her?"

"Well, *Omar*, firstly, *her* name is Melyndie," Tom supplied, matching Omar's tone.

"Attitude much?" Omar quipped to Zain.

"Adaptive AI," Zain explained. "And, apparently, I'm not the best example of calm, cool, and collected—at least not in these last few weeks."

Omar turned toward the RMP, arms folded. "You called this meeting, Tom. So, what's on your mind?"

Tom's gaze locked onto him; its mechanical stillness somehow more pronounced.

As Tom began its plan, Zain stood silently with his arms crossed, unsure whether he had bought them more time or accidentally started a countdown to catastrophe.

What Duty Demands

The jeep lurched and bounced over the rugged desert landscape, each jolt sending a shudder through Melyndie's sore body. Dust swirled around them in gritty clouds, while the relentless sun beat down on the canvas canopy overhead, causing it to flap wildly as if trying to escape its bindings. Melyndie's eyes were fixed on the horizon, but her mind was a chaotic tangle of thoughts and emotions that she couldn't untangle.

Omar glanced over at her, his expression softening with concern. "You seem a little out of sorts," he ventured gently, hoping his tone would coax some response from her. "Is it because you're missing Zain?"

For a moment, Melyndie remained silent, her grip tightening on the metal bar above the dashboard as if anchoring herself against an emotional tide. She managed a smile—a mere twitch of her lips that lacked any warmth or sincerity. "Something like that," she said quietly.

Omar shifted in his seat, determined to lighten the mood. "This setup isn't forever," he reassured her with quiet conviction. "Just until Zain and Tom can sort out an alternative plan that keeps everyone safe."

Melyndie offered no reply, and Omar's attempt at humor came out more awkward than intended as he added with a chuckle, "If it's any consolation, you look quite charming in that uniform."

Her response was immediate and blunt: "It does not." She looked down at the olive drab shirt clinging to her form—an identity borrowed rather than owned. The fabric and insignia were meant to make her invisible, to erase who she was beneath their weight. Blend in; don't stand out—the words echoed relentlessly in her mind; a mantra she'd heard repeated since her youngling years.

A week ago, Zain and Tom had approached her with Omar, the three of them already decided. The separation, they claimed, was strategic. Less risk. Fewer questions. She'd be safer under Omar's watch, far from scrutiny, while the powers that be finished running diagnostics on Tom and the scrutiny was removed from Zain. She had agreed because there was no point in arguing. Still, she couldn't help but wonder whether it was because the stress of keeping her secret, keeping her safe, wasn't wearing on Zain. He was this battalion's commander, and his attention needed to be on them, and their mission…not babysitting her. She knew that her reasoning was flawed, and she was reacting like a petulant child, but Zain and Tom had been her anchor since she'd landed in the before time and every mile away from them felt like a fraying tether.

The jeep bucked again over a rut. Melyndie winced. Bruises from her crash through time had faded, but her shoulder still throbbed when jostled, though Tom assured her on its last exam, that it was healing quite quickly.

She reached up to her neck, fingers kneading the taut muscles in a vain attempt to soothe the persistent ache. Her eyes drifted downward, settling on her arm where a subtle protrusion beneath the fabric of her shirt marked the presence of the monitoring unit. It was securely strapped there, housing within its confines the genetic samples she had painstakingly collected from Zain weeks ago—samples that were invaluable and irreplaceable. Yet now, doubt gnawed at her; after all this time, could they have lost their viability?

Omar observed her tense posture with concern etched across his face. "Is it a headache?" he asked gently.

"Something like that," she replied, exhaling slowly.

He shifted his grip on the wheel with a reassuring nod. "We'll be stopping soon. You can stretch your legs and maybe catch some sleep. It's important to keep your muscles from stiffening."

"Aren't I supposed to help you at the vaccination table again?" she queried.

"Yeah, right," he chuckled awkwardly, glancing sideways at her. "I guess resting and walking are out of the question for now."

Her voice softened for the first time in days as she responded, "Thank you for thinking of me." She reminded herself that Omar's kindness was genuine; none of this turmoil was his doing. He was simply trying to offer support.

Silence settled between them as minutes ticked by, punctuated only by the steady hum of the engine and the rhythmic spray of sand beneath their tires like dry ocean waves.

Then Omar broke through the quietness with a hesitant tone, asking softly, "Has anyone considered what might happen if...they can't bring you back?"

Melyndie turned her head towards him deliberately, a restrained smile playing at her lips. "I thought Zain said that topic was off limits."

With mock surrender, he lifted his hand defensively. "Sorry about that. It's just—kind of monumental when you think about it— you being from the future and everything."

She turned her gaze elsewhere, her hand instinctively reaching for her monitoring unit once more. The Holy Ones had been unsuccessful in their initial attempt at retrieval. The implanted chip must have interfered with the primary one—something Tom referred to as 'crosstalk.' But when could they have inserted a second chip? The only time she could think of was when she fainted in the medical bay during that practice jump. Had Kishida-Guan orchestrated everything then? Were they now in a rush to deactivate the extra chip? Could she still be tracked, or was she already beyond reach? With her return window having expired, being lost seemed increasingly likely. And if she was lost, it meant her people's future was lost also.

I need to get my emotions under control, she thought just as a flicker of movement outside the jeep caught her eye.

"Looks like we're late," she said.

"I drove slower," Omar admitted. "Figured it might spare your bottom. The higher-ups set the schedule, but a few minutes won't kill anyone."

"Thank you," she said again, more genuinely this time.

The convoy had arrived ahead of them. Soldiers were already fanning out, herding civilians toward the inoculation tents. But something wasn't right.

She glanced at Omar, whose narrowed gaze meant that he too noticed something untoward. She looked back at the commotion taking place near the inoculation table. Zain and Tom stood near a senior officer, locked in tense discussion. "Something's going on," Omar muttered, killing the engine. The sudden silence magnified the unease in the air.

Then Zain looked their way and waved him over.

Omar climbed out immediately. "Looks like you'll get a short break after all. Wait here. I'll come back once I know what's happening."

Before she could agree, he jogged off.

Melyndie lingered for a moment, then slid from the jeep. Her limbs ached, but it was the emotional exhaustion that weighed heavier. She moved toward the vaccination table, needing something—anything—to do.

At the heart of the encampment, tension rippled like static. Tom and another RMP stood with their heads inclined toward each other, processing data through a silent exchange of light and code. Zain's jaw was clenched tight.

Tom turned to him. "The recount is complete. We're missing nine hundred seventy-eight civilians."

Zain didn't flinch, but his eyes darkened.

Tom continued, "They are not in the queues though they are not scanned as vaccinated."

Omar spoke up. "On vacation, maybe? That's the only logical conclusion. Surely, they wouldn't be risking termination by hiding. How would they even know to hide? Communications have been down since the onset of Phase One."

"Communications, yes, but cities aren't in lockdown. People can still travel, which means word can spread. Also, if those missing were vaccinated by members from another battalion, it would show in Tom's records. Somehow, they found out we were coming, and they're hiding from us," Zain said. "Tom, can't the RMP sensors scan the building interiors?"

"We can, but ineffectually, as there are factors which inhibit a thorough scan."

"Explain."

"Distance, clutter, building material, nonhuman biological readings—"

"Okay, I get the point," Zain sighed.

A long silence followed. Then Zain drew a slow breath and turned to Omar. "I'm entrusting this to you. Take a hundred men. Quiet gear. No gunfire unless necessary. Pair every squad with an RMP and begin a building-by-building search. Tom—call in ten additional RMPs. Assign one to each ten-man unit."

Tom nodded once and turned to carry out the directive, but Zain stopped him.

Omar questioned quietly. "Zain?"

Zain paused. His hand twitched near his belt. His uniform suddenly felt too tight. Too suffocating. He looked at the silent machines around him, then the soldiers at attention, then the civilians—obedient, unaware, terrified.

His voice dropped to a whisper, heavy with the weight of the moment. "Our orders are unequivocal. Should they resist…" He hesitated, the next command a burden he struggled to bear. Yet, the relentless scrutiny of his superiors had not been lifted, leaving him with no escape. "All sidearms on silent fire. We must avoid inciting panic." He halted, then signaled for Tom and Omar to step aside from the group. "Tom?"

"Comms down," Tom confirmed.

"Grant them a chance to comply. You'll need to relay this to each team, not through the RMPs," Zain commanded, his eyes lifting skyward for a fleeting second, as though beseeching solace from above. He closed his eyes, drawing a deep breath, and then fixed his unwavering gaze on his friend. "If you'd rather I entrust this command to another, just say the word."

Omar met Zain's eyes, a mix of resolve and reluctance playing across his face. "No," he said firmly. "I'll see it through." He knew the weight of command rested heavily on Zain's shoulders, and command decisions, no matter how distasteful, often fell to those who could shoulder them with the most strength.

Zain nodded once, sharply. His expression softened slightly as he clapped Omar on the shoulder. "Thank you," he murmured.

Tom, watching silently, took a small step forward. Its voice, still devoid of inflection, nevertheless carried a softer cadence. "You are not alone in this."

Zain glanced at the RMP, a flicker of emotion passing through his expression—surprise, then something like gratitude.

From her place near the vaccination table, Melyndie stood motionless. Her eyes tracked Zain. Something in her chest clenched painfully. This wasn't the man who had tenderly bandaged her shoulder and kept her company through long, vulnerable nights. This wasn't the man who had shared in her dream of owning a German Shepherd and dared to imagine she might truly belong here. No, this was a commander now—icy, calculating, forced to choose between his heart and the demands of duty.

Melyndie felt his transformation strike hard at her heart: the crack beneath his voice, the way his eyes lifted in supplication. A wave of empathic resonance hit her so hard it stole her breath. His pain was not her own, and yet it resounded within her just the same.

Her thumb grazed the hidden vial beneath her monitoring unit. She wanted to believe it still held hope—for all humanity. But hope was a fragile thing in a world where even the kindest man could be forced to sentence innocent lives to death behind a veil of duty.

She turned away, her shoulders squared, though her eyes shimmered with unshed tears. She stepped forward—because in a world unraveling, helping was the only choice that still felt human.

Rebellion has its Price

The task of using the RMPs to survey the towering city buildings for signs of life seemed straightforward in theory. However, pinpointing the exact location of people hidden within these brutalist structures—each stretching up for twenty dizzying floors—was an entirely different challenge. While the RMPs' scanners could detect life, they couldn't provide precise locations. This meant soldiers had to painstakingly go through every apartment, floor by floor, checking each locked door—many sealed by frightened occupants still waiting in vaccination lines outside, or by those barricaded inside who preferred the risk of death over surrender.

The scent of rusted metal and stale cooking oil lingered in the stairwells as Omar climbed to the third floor. He kicked a stubbornly closed door with enough strength to make the hallway tremble. The wood cracked under his blow as he yelled, "Military! All residents, identify yourselves for escort to the vaccination lines." His voice reverberated through the space, met only by silence.

His jaw tensed, then continued. "Non-compliance will be interpreted as a threat to human safety and will result in immediate execution."

Still nothing.

He gave a curt nod to the two soldiers flanking the corridor. Without needing words, they moved to opposite sides of the apartment and began sweeping individual rooms. Omar didn't linger. He turned to the next door down the hall and delivered another brutal kick near the knob—this time not even attempting to try the doorknob first. The door crashed open, slamming against the inner wall with a shriek of metal hinges.

He entered the room and delivered his well-practiced statement, his voice echoing off the walls. When he uttered the words "potential execution," there was a stir at the rear of the apartment. A young man appeared with his hands held high, followed by a trembling woman whose pale complexion made her look as if she were sculpted from wax.

"Why aren't you in the vaccination line?" Omar demanded, his voice sharp and insistent. His brows knitted into a deep furrow, casting a shadow over his intense, narrowed eyes that honed in on the man with a mix of anger and disbelief. It was as if his gaze could pierce through the man's indifference, revealing the reckless disregard that not only endangered his own life but also carelessly jeopardized the well-being of his own mate. The tension in the air was palpable, a silent testament to the gravity of the situation.

The man lowered his hands and jutted his jaw defiantly. "We don't trust vaccines."

Omar's lips tightened. "You're really prepared to risk the existence of every soul you cross paths with? To become a carrier of the same virus currently ripping its way through the entire world?"

The man scoffed, mouth twitching into a smug grin. "That's nothing but a scare tactic. Propaganda. Fear to keep us compliant." He gestured animatedly, as though delivering a lecture in some underground resistance forum. "This is just another control grab—"

"Listen." Omar cut him off, voice dropping to a low growl. "Our beliefs don't matter anymore. Yours. Mine. Anyone's. All that matters is the mandate. Disobey it, and you're dead. Comply, and you might live. I could've shot you already, but I'm trying to give you a chance."

"You're a soldier," the man spat. "You should be protecting us from terrorists—not acting like one." He'd barely finished his sentence before the room exploded with sound, a thunderous crack that seemed to rip through the air itself. The walls vibrated violently, and an acrid smell of gunpowder filled the space as if the very atmosphere had been torn apart by the shot.

The man collapsed to the ground, his body folding like a marionette whose strings had been severed. A stark, crimson hole marred the center of his forehead, vivid and precise, as if a macabre artist had taken a single, deliberate stroke with a brush dipped in blood.

Omar flinched. His eyes snapped toward the female soldier who had fired. "Why did you discharge your weapon *before* I gave the order?"

She stood like a statue, weapon lowered but her voice cold. "Apologies, sir. But we've got a thousand units to check and no time to waste listening to moral lectures. Our orders are clear: comply or die."

For a moment, the silence pressed on all of them like a stone slab.

Omar stepped forward, slow and menacing. His voice, when it came, was sharp enough to cut steel. "Disobey me again and it'll be *you* getting a bullet. Do you understand?"

"Yes, sir," she answered, unflinching, tension rippling through her jaw as she clenched her teeth.

Omar turned his attention to the woman still cowering in the corner, her sobs coming in gasps. He approached, his boots thudding against the floor, and extended a gloved hand. "Ready for your inoculation?" His voice was devoid of feeling. Mechanized.

She looked up, broken. Nodded. He lifted her to her feet, but when he released her arm, she collapsed to her knees, keening like a wounded animal.

"Soldier!" Omar barked at the one who had fired the shot. "You're going to personally escort this woman to the front of the line and return her to this apartment when she's done. Even if you have to carry her the whole way. And if I hear even *one whisper* of misconduct, I'll make sure you share her partner's fate. Are we clear?"

The soldier gave a tight nod, then moved to haul the weeping woman upright, dragging her from the apartment.

"RMP—acknowledge," Omar snapped, his breath ragged with fury.

The machine stepped forward. "Acknowledged."

"Take the body away. Cleanse the room thoroughly. I don't want her returning to find his blood and brain matter staining the floorboards," he murmured to himself, "She doesn't need a grim reminder of what happened."

Without waiting for confirmation, Omar exited, heart pounding. The hallway beyond seemed colder now. The next door opened before he could kick. A family stepped out—mother, father, two young children—hands raised, trembling.

"Escort them to the queue," he instructed a nearby soldier.

The family fell into line like sheep before the slaughter.

Omar wanted to yell at them that they were getting a vaccine, not headed to the gallows. Instead, he gave a short nod to two soldiers following behind him. "Sweep the apartment."

He didn't stop. He was already moving on.

The operation dragged on for eighteen brutal hours. By dawn, the numbers were tallied:

- 321 had finally complied under threat.

- 211 remained unaccounted for—likely away from the city.

- 446 were executed. Their bodies discarded like waste in the desert, unmarked with no one to mourn.

As dawn broke over the city, Omar headed toward the inoculation table, his uniform stained and his soul heavy. He glanced at the soldiers, who'd also begun trudging back to their vehicles and it was apparent that they carried the weight of the deeds differently. Some walked with a swagger, a grim satisfaction in a duty completed, while others dragged their feet with shoulders slumped, trying to escape the gazes of those they passed.

He spotted Zain at a distance—hands folded behind his back, chin raised, his stance like stone—but even from afar, the weariness was obvious.

"Report," Zain said as Omar approached, his voice clipped.

Omar replied in a tone that seemed to question the sanity of some people. "Compliance was lower than expected. We gave everyone the chance…why didn't they take it?"

"How many?" Zain's jaw worked against his words.

"Four hundred forty-six executed. That's shocking, but what's also shocking is the three hundred twenty-one who had to be threatened into compliance." He shook his head before finalizing the report. "Roughly two hundred still missing."

The numbers fell like hammer blows between them and neither man spoke for several minutes.

The silence ballooned into something unbearable.

Zain finally broke it, voice cracking beneath the strain. "Find someone you trust. Have them document everything. Every room. Every name. Every shot fired."

Omar glanced up; brow furrowed. "The RMPs already—"

"I don't care." Zain cut him off. "Their records can be wiped. Corrupted. If this gets out…if this goes south…I want human witnesses. I want *a human accounting*. Once you've selected that person, inform them they'll provide their reports directly to me."

Omar nodded, slowly. "Understood." Then, more softly, "I get covering our asses, but…do you really think it'll help in the end?"

Zain's gaze drifted toward the horizon. The sun had fully risen now, gilding the skyline in hues of red.

"I don't know," he murmured. "But if we're the ones forced to carry out these orders, I'm damn well not leaving our fate in the hands of a bunch of walking tin cans."

He turned away, voice suddenly all command again. "Go collect Melyndie. Then spread the word. We pull out in ten."

Omar hesitated. "Zain…" His voice cracked. "Do you think we're doing the right thing?"

A shadow crossed Zain's face. He started to speak—but paused.

An RMP approached from behind, its steps too measured, too quiet.

Zain's eyes flicked toward it. "Not now, Omar," he said, barely above a whisper. Then added, so quietly Omar barely heard: "Be careful when you speak. There are eyes and ears everywhere."

If Omar weren't so familiar with Zain, he might have assumed his friend had slipped into paranoia. But as he watched the RMP draw closer—and looked out at the silent sentinels lining the square—he realized Zain wasn't imagining things.

The chill that lodged in his chest wasn't from the morning air.

Not all wars began with gunfire. Some began with compliance under threat—watched by machines that never blinked.

Fragments of the Past

The jeep shuddered across the battered road, kicking up long trails of dust that melted into the waning light. Inside, silence settled like fog—dense, inescapable.

Omar's knuckles were pale on the steering wheel. He didn't speak, not because he had nothing to say, but because the weight of what he might say—of everything that had already happened—was too great to voice. Orders carried out. Doors kicked in. Guns drawn. He could still hear the sounds: screaming, pleading…then the silence of death.

Melyndie sat motionless beside him, her posture unnervingly still. But inside, her thoughts churned like a storm. The day had begun like the others—tense, but orderly—until a man in the vaccination queue caught her eye. He didn't stand out at first: mid-thirties, calm demeanor, eyes downcast like the rest. He waited his turn in silence, stepping forward when called, giving every appearance of compliance.

But something shifted the moment he reached the inoculation table.

Without warning, he lunged—his hands slamming into the metal tray with such force that vials scattered across the pavement. He overturned the table in a single, savage motion, sending the nurse stumbling back with a startled expletive. Then he pivoted toward Melyndie, eyes wild, and charged.

She froze.

Zain collided with her from the side, knocking her to the ground just as the man closed the distance. His body covered hers, shielding her. A crack split the air—sharp, absolute. The RMP fired. The man fell, mid-stride, his body hitting the ground in a graceless heap, blood blooming beneath him—an accusation, a consequence.

Zain's arms remained locked around her for a moment longer, his breath harsh against her hair. Then he moved, swiftly and silently, lifting her to her feet and keeping her close as he steered her away from the chaos. His hand pressed firmly at the small of her back—protective, steady, unshakable. He'd protected her from the impact with his body, cognizant of her healing shoulder, despite the threat. Thus, it was his arms that slammed against the ground, so she wouldn't, and he knew he'd pay for his impulsivity later, when his muscles began to protest.

Omar was already running toward them. "What the hell happened—?" he started, but Zain waved him off with a sharp gesture.

They got her to the jeep. Zain opened the door and helped her inside without a word, closing it gently once she was seated. He didn't look at her—he couldn't. Not yet. He should have known. Should have realized that even apparent acquiescence was no guarantee of safety. That placing her in the open, in uniform, at a checkpoint, had been a gamble. One she should never have been part of.

"She won't be assisting at the tables anymore," Zain stated quietly to Omar, his voice low but resolute. "That was a mistake. I need to go check on the nurse and make sure everything's back on track." Then he turned and walked away, jaw tight, shoulders squared against the shame, blooming beneath his composure.

Now, as the jeep rattled forward through the deepening dusk, the memory still clung to Melyndie's skin like smoke from a fire—refusing to fade. Her world had its own darkness. Termination wasn't rare in the realm. Citizens who failed to meet their productive requirements were summarily terminated; but it had always been an emotionless event, presented as necessary for the betterment of humanity. Here, it masqueraded as choice. Help us save lives—or forfeit your own.

"Penny for your thoughts?" Omar asked suddenly, his voice splitting the silence like a crack in glass.

She startled, blinking out of her trance. "I don't—"

"It just means you can share what you're thinking about," he added quickly, as if regretting the intrusion. "We've been quiet for the last half hour…" He let the sentence fade, unsure if he'd wanted to break the silence at all. But it had been pressing on him like a stone to the chest. She wasn't the only one mentally unraveling. "How's your shoulder? Did it get reinjured when…"

"No, all I felt was Zain's grip on me as we fell. I don't know how he managed to tumble to the ground with me, without me getting hurt. He's so much bigger than I am."

"He's also much stronger. He likely kept his muscles flexed to absorb all of the impact."

Melyndie seemed on the verge of saying something more, but something caught her attention. Her posture shifted. She leaned forward, eyes widening in wonder, "What is that?"

Omar followed her gaze and smiled, the expression faint but real. "Um…they're camels. Wow, haven't seen a herd that big in some time. Anyway, they've been used as transportation in this region for centuries. Although around here, they're becoming pretty scarce."

"You can ride animals?" she asked, her voice edged with awe.

"Um…yes. Many different kinds. Elephants, camels, horses, donkeys, llamas…that's all I can think of at the moment. You act like you've never seen a camel before or didn't know—"

"I haven't and I didn't." It wasn't said with shame or sarcasm—just truth. Raw, clean, and tragic. There was something in her tone that caught Omar off guard. A yearning. "Have you ever seen a German Shepherd?" she asked suddenly, her tone hopeful, her eyes shining with curiosity.

"Well, that's a shift. Sure, I have. One of my favorite dog breeds," he said, allowing himself a chuckle. "They're especially cute as puppies...um...please don't tell anyone I said that. Ego at stake."

She tilted her head. "Animals can take on different forms?"

"I'm not following."

"You said they were cute as puppies—"

"A puppy is just a baby dog," he explained gently. "Just like us—we start as babies and grow into adults."

"Oh." She looked away, feeling embarrassed for not understanding his point about the dog. She felt ashamed for being so unfamiliar with other creatures that she didn't realize they experienced similar physical transformations.

Omar acted as if he didn't see her unease and decided to enlighten her instead. He steadied the steering wheel with his knee, tapped his wrist device, and spoke a command to the AI interface. A soft light appeared, forming a holographic screen above the dashboard. "Swipe the screen and you'll see short clips of a German Shepherd growing up. I can't hold my arm up like this for too long though."

"Swipe?" she echoed, hesitant.

He released the steering wheel again and demonstrated with a brief motion.

She reached forward, hands trembling slightly. As the image shifted, she gasped.

A tiny puppy stumbled across a wooden floor; its paws too large for its small body. Its tongue flopped comically to the side as it barked at nothing. For some reason, Melyndie sensed it was happy. She stared, entranced. "I've never seen anything quite like this," she whispered.

She continued to swipe repeatedly. With each swipe, she witnessed the puppy's transformation—its ears went from floppy to pointed straight up, and its muscles became more pronounced. In the last photo, the dog appeared fully grown, regal, with a dark, glossy coat and a dignified stance. Tears formed in her eyes.

She placed her hand in front of the hologram, aching for a sensation she'd never known—the sensation of touching a dog's coat.

Omar noticed. "It isn't something we're supposed to discuss, I know," he began carefully, lowering his arm and instructing the AI to disengage. "But...well...don't your people keep pets? And before you ask, a pet is an animal that lives in the home with you."

She shook her head, eyes falling.

He hesitated, unsure if pressing further would deepen the wound—but watching her turn away felt worse. "If it lifts your spirits," he tried, "we may come across some animals. Not as many these days. People are struggling to feed their families, so keeping a pet is a luxury many can't afford. But they're still around. So, you never know."

"Do you think we might see a German Shepherd?" she asked, almost timidly.

He didn't want to lie. But hope was a fragile thing—and she appeared to have so little of it. "It's a possibility."

"And no, there are no animals in my time," she said softly, returning to his earlier question. "And until a few years ago, I didn't even know they existed."

Omar's throat tightened. "Really? That seems...incredibly strange. To never have seen an animal. It just doesn't feel right."

"I cannot explain why they are absent in my time. I can only guess they were not deemed...productive." The word lingered heavily in the air.

He shook his head. "It's not just about being productive. Animals...pets...they give people comfort, joy, unconditional love, and are profoundly loyal."

She absorbed that in silence. It wasn't just foreign—it was almost too much for her to comprehend. And it didn't line up with what he'd said earlier. "If they are of such importance, why are people consuming them for food?"

"Some animals are raised for that purpose," he explained. "But not all creatures. Some are pets. Some are wild. But in the poorest places, when survival is the only goal—people eat what they must. Sentiment fades when hunger takes over. After all, survival is part of the human imperative."

Her mouth parted as if to protest, then closed again. She wasn't in a position to judge, for her world didn't even value animals at all—not even as a food source.

"I'm unsure if I can take pleasure in seeing a pet when it's overshadowed by human suffering," she said, almost to herself. "Yet...there's this longing within me to interact with an animal up close. It's a contradiction I struggle to reconcile."

Omar looked at her then—not with pity, but with quiet understanding. "Yeah," he said. "It is. But sometimes, the little joys—the ones that seem selfish or small—are the only things that keep us human."

She turned away, but not to retreat. She just needed a moment. A breath.

As the battalion reached the outskirts of the next town, Omar eased the jeep off the road and into a cracked, weed-lined lot shadowed by a dilapidated building. He shifted into park, the engine ticking softly as it cooled.

"We're here," he said, glancing over. "You should stretch your legs a bit, but I do have something to show you." He stepped out into the fading light and moved around to the rear passenger side, crouching beside his pack. His fingers hovered for a moment before pulling out a battered tablet—its casing worn, edges dulled with age.

"We weren't supposed to bring personal items," he admitted, powering it on with a quick tap. "But I couldn't part with this. Too many memories. Some things…well…you need memories. Keeps you grounded."

Slowly, she accepted the tablet, her hands careful, deliberate. It felt heavier than she expected—like it held more than just images. As if the weight of a world she'd never known had been pressed between its slim frame.

"Stretch first," he said with a half-smile, taking the tablet back and placing it on the front seat of the jeep. He then cast a glance toward the darkening horizon. The sun was sinking fast behind the fractured skyline. "This is the first time you'll be hanging back. Don't wander off anywhere. Night falls fast out here, and desert predators don't discriminate over the source of their food." He nodded toward the fading light. "I've got to get to work. Stay close to the jeep—lock the doors if anything feels off. Has Zain taught you how to use a walkie-talkie?"

She shook her head. He reached inside the jeep, grabbed the small device and gave her a quick demonstration. "Keep this one. I'll pick up another from Zain. If anything happens, reach out to either of us. Immediately. Also, it can get scary in the dark, so keep my flashlight on you."

She nodded.

"Oh, and if you get tired...try to rest. You're not a soldier—even if Zain insists on dressing you like one." As he turned to go, he called over his shoulder: "And if I happen to find a pet, I'll come get you."

She watched him disappear into the rapidly descending darkness, then retrieved the tablet and slid back onto her seat. She tapped the button that Omar had shown her and the screen lit up. The first image to greet her was a child—laughing—while a puppy licked his face. His joy radiated from the screen like sunlight breaking through clouds.

She stared, unable to tear her gaze away.

Her world hadn't just forgotten animals. It had forgotten what it meant to yearn for something without purpose.

She paused on an image of a boy curled beside a sleeping dog—his fingers buried in its thick fur; his face relaxed in a way that suggested absolute peace. The dog's eyes were closed, its body curled, seemingly, protectively around the child.

For a moment, she imagined what it would feel like to be that child. To rest beside something that exuded such strength. To know she was safe.

Omar reached Zain and relayed his instructions to Melyndie and told him about lending her his tablet to help take her mind off of the day's event. "She's strong," he said, "but it's leaving a mark. She's seeing everything her world lost—and is starting to feel it."

Zain folded his arms, his jaw tight. The truth in Omar's words unsettled him more than he wanted to admit. He had watched others fracture beneath far lesser burdens. But Melyndie…she was beginning to carry the weight of two worlds—and neither had taught her what to do with sorrow. "And you?" he asked, steering his thoughts back to Omar. "How is it you found yourself in the role of teacher?"

Omar hesitated. "Didn't expect to be, but she asks a lot of questions and we can't keep her in the dark about our time."

"I appreciate your efforts in safeguarding her, but don't allow yourself to become emotionally involved. Her people are likely exerting every effort, leaving no stone unturned in their quest to return her to her time," Zain interjected sternly. His eyes glanced toward where Melyndie sat in the jeep, half expecting her to be gone—as with anytime his gaze sought her out.

"And is that your strategy too? Keeping emotional distance by assigning her care to me?" Omar shot back.

Zain's gaze hardened. "It's simply not wise for her to be in my company. It would raise questions we can't afford. Especially when I have a personal RMP and both it and I are being scrutinized at present."

Omar held up his hands in surrender. "Alright, message received. How many civilians have the RMPs picked up as in hiding?"

Tom stepped forward, "Only two hundred are presently unaccounted for."

"Then I best go help find them," he stated, then pivoted on his heel towards where his squad was waiting for him. He turned to leave—then stopped. "Um... Zain?"

Zain's brow lifted in question.

"I kind of made Melyndie a promise. That if I found a pet—"

"That you'd introduce her to it," Zain completed for him. Despite himself, he found it difficult not to let a smile tug at the corners of his mouth.

"Yeah." Omar scratched at the back of his neck sheepishly. "Can you believe she's never seen an animal in person? Apart from the camels we encountered on our journey here."

Zain's eyes twinkled with amusement and his tone softened. "Permission granted," he said, waving Omar off dismissively. "Now stop wasting time and get to work."

"Yes, sir!" Omar saluted smartly, then turned and moved away.

Back in the safety of the jeep, Melyndie was entranced as she continued her exploration of the digital world Omar had entrusted to her. Each swipe brought new scenes, new faces, and new emotions that bubbled up within her. She lingered on a photo of a mountain range bathed in sunset hues, its majestic tranquility a stark contrast to the clinical sterility she knew so well from her own time; in stark contrast to the sandy flat terrain that she'd spent the last month traversing. The realization that such beauty existed outside the confines of her normal environment felt both exhilarating and overwhelming.

With a sudden burst of daring, she slid from the jeep's worn leather seat, retrieved the flashlight that Omar had left for her, and navigated her way through the darkened terrain towards Zain.

She was aware that it wasn't the wisest thing to disrupt him in his element, but the unanswered questions swirling inside her were on the verge of consuming her sanity. "Zain?" Her voice emerged as a gentle murmur.

The unexpected proximity of this soft whisper jolted Zain, causing him to pivot sharply. Recognizing Melyndie's silhouette against the golden backdrop of the desert, he sucked in a steadying breath. He hadn't been close to her since he'd tackled her, protecting her from an assailant, although he often found himself stealing glances at her from afar just to assure himself that she was faring well in this harsh environment. To suddenly have her standing so close again stirred a sense of unease within him. His eyes darted around instinctively, ensuring his RMP was not within earshot before addressing her. "Melyndie. Are you holding up? Recovering well?"

Melyndie nodded silently, momentarily lost amidst the depth and intensity of his dark gaze. She had to admit that she missed him. It wasn't just his presence she missed—it was the quiet certainty and strength that came with it.

"That's good news," he replied, his attention shifting towards the archaic tablet clutched tightly in her hand.

Hesitantly, Melyndie raised the device and revealed an image depicting a majestic range of mountains. "How long would it take us to reach this place using the jeep?" she asked innocently.

Zain's eyes widened for a brief moment as he wrestled back laughter at such an innocent question but couldn't suppress the smile that tugged at his lips. "It's not accessible by jeep. It's located on another continent."

A crease formed between Melyndie's brows as she grappled with his words. Adjusting to the fact that this new world she'd been thrust into required a jeep for intercity travel was already a challenge, considering her realm was compact and everything was within walking distance. After spending a week jostling in the jeep, she had come to accept that walking to distant realms, in her time, was as likely unfeasible, though she couldn't fathom why she would need to.

"You aren't acquainted with the concept of continents, are you?" Zain asked gently as he watched her try to process his words.

Melyndie shook her head, her gaze dropping towards the ground. It was a small gesture, but one that felt monumental. In her realm, ignorance had been ridiculed; here, it was met with kindness. She wasn't used to that. And for reasons she couldn't articulate, it made her chest ache.

"All of this must be incredibly overwhelming for you," he observed empathetically. "If it weren't for my orders, I'd gladly take the time to introduce you to all of these places properly." His candid confession prompted her to meet his gaze again and respond with a soft smile.

Omar, his breath ragged from the sprint through the city streets, slid to a halt next to the couple, effectively shattering the intimate bubble that had formed around them.

"Melyndie, you're out of the jeep," he huffed out, his voice slicing through the silence that had enveloped them.

"I wanted to ask Zain about something that I saw on your tablet," she confessed.

"Oh…well…I've stumbled upon something that you might enjoying seeing." His words hung in the air for a moment before he added, "It's a rarity in these parts nowadays. Been banned for almost twenty years," he whispered with an air of mystery, looking toward one of the apartment buildings.

As he finished speaking, he turned his gaze back to the pair who still appeared caught up in their private world. Melyndie cast a questioning look at Zain, her eyes seeking his approval. This elicited a cheeky grin from Omar who was clearly enjoying this unexpected disruption.

"Zain gave me permission to come get you if I chanced upon something I thought you might like to see," Omar clarified, his tone laced with mischief. "But we're going to need to get going. Don't have a lot of time for sightseeing."

Without waiting for a reply, Omar reached for Melyndie's good hand. "Oh, just leave my tablet on Zain's jeep," he instructed, taking the device from Melyndie. "That okay, Zain?" he asked, and then tossed it at his friend when Zain nodded, then gripped Melyndie's hand in his own firm grip and began pulling her away.

Zain found himself inexplicably annoyed with Omar for the abrupt intrusion, but couldn't find logical reason why he should protest Melyndie heading off into the city with his friend, so rather than voicing his displeasure, he swallowed it and refocused on his duties.

"Where are we going?" Melyndie queried, her breath hitching as she strained to match the rhythm of Omar's lengthy stride.

"Just wait and see. I have a feeling you'll find it interesting. Otherwise, I wouldn't bother showing you," he responded nonchalantly, his shoulders rising and falling in an indifferent shrug. He then veered off their path, leading them towards one of the towering apartment buildings that lined the street.

Initially, he seemed to gravitate towards the staircase but abruptly altered his course towards a bank of elevators. "You're not claustrophobic by any chance, are you?" he asked casually while pressing the button marked 'up'.

"I'm unfamiliar with that term," Melyndie admitted, her curiosity piqued by the mechanical hum resonating through the air as Omar triggered the elevator call button.

"Do tight spaces where movement is restricted make you feel uneasy or scared?"

Melyndie shook her head in response, "I've never encountered such circumstances."

"Have you had a chance to ride in an elevator yet?"

"What's an elevator?"

"If you have to ask, then the answer is no." A mischievous grin tugged at the corners of Omar's mouth as he replied, "Well then brace yourself for a new experience. My apologies if it proves uncomfortable but this is our quickest route to floor eighteen in this twenty-story behemoth."

Melyndie found Omar's concern puzzling; after all, she lived in even more compact conditions back in her time and was accustomed to climbing multiple flights of stairs daily. She was about to voice her thoughts when the metallic doors slid open with a soft whooshing sound and Omar gently ushered her into the compact enclosure.

Her fascination with this novel mode of transport outweighed any trepidation she felt as the doors closed behind them and they ascended rapidly. The walls hummed softly, the floor beneath her feet subtly vibrating as the numbers ticked upward. It felt like being lifted by invisible hands—an effortless ascent that felt both unnatural and miraculous. She glanced at Omar with wide eyes, wondering how something so magical could be treated so casually. Before she could process her feelings, they arrived at their floor and Omar guided her out into a long corridor.

As they ventured down its length, she couldn't help but notice the many doors hanging askew, their hinges twisted and mangled. Oblivious to the fact that it was Omar who had caused the damage, she wondered about the strange sight.

They stopped at one such door near the end of the corridor. Omar quickly told the nearby soldiers to continue inspecting other apartments, then turned to enter the one they were standing in front of, beckoning her to follow him in. "This way," he directed, noticing her attention drifting towards the eclectic array of furnishings that filled the room.

Her own living quarters were stark and utilitarian by comparison. The urge to sink into a chair upholstered with plush faux fur was almost overwhelming until a peculiar sound caught her ear and drew her closer to Omar.

"What is that?" she asked softly, her gaze fixed on a vibrant piece of fabric suspended in mid-air.

Omar's grin widened as he watched Melyndie eyeing the colorful material with wonder. "Actually, it's what lies beneath that I want you to see. Remember those pets we discussed?"

Melyndie detected a hint of amusement in his voice which made her cheeks flush with embarrassment.

"Well, I found one. Just remember not to overreact," he cautioned. "We don't want our little friend getting scared to death."

Melyndie looked at him puzzled—could any creature be so delicate as to perish from shock? The thought seemed inconceivable, leading her to speculate whether such fragility could be why these creatures didn't exist in her time.

Omar stepped over to the cloth. The air in the room seemed to shift, thick with expectancy. Melyndie held her breath without realizing it, her senses sharpening as if she already knew something amazing was about to be revealed.

Still, she gasped involuntarily when Omar reached up and deftly removed the cloth cover from a cage revealing its feathered occupant within.

The bird was unlike anything Melyndie could ever envision. Its feathers shimmered in a kaleidoscope of colors, each movement reflecting like tiny prisms from the moonlight streaming in from the window. It was small and slender with a tail that stretched nearly to the bottom of the cage from its perch. Its tiny black, beady eyes watched them curiously, its head tilting side-to-side as it moved its gaze from one to the other.

"What is it?" Melyndie asked in awe.

"It's illegal, is what it is," Omar chuckled. "But the bird is called a Quetzal. It must have cost the occupant a fortune to smuggle it from Central America. Since keeping birds as pets is illegal, I'll be releasing it into the wild. I just thought you might like to see a live animal up close before I let it go."

"Will it walk back to its home in Central America?"

Omar did laugh then, but quickly apologized, "Sorry about that, but…um…no, birds fly," he explained, demonstrating the action with his hand. Melyndie's eyes widened in surprise, then turned back to look at the bird with amazement and curiosity.

"Do you want to hold it before I release it?" Omar asked and Melyndie took a step back, her face registering alarm. "It's okay if you don't," he reassured her. "I just thought you might want to know what its feathers feel like."

Melyndie looked back at the bird as Omar slowly opened the cage door and reached inside. The bird hopped onto his arm without hesitation. "Looks like it was well trained," Omar noted as he carefully removed his arm from the cage.

He held the bird out towards Melyndie, its delicate features and bright colors almost hypnotic in their beauty. Slowly, encouraged by Omar's gentle nudge, Melyndie extended her hand. Her fingers trembled slightly—not from fear, but from a profound reverence for the creature before her.

"It feels like it's made of air," she whispered, barely touching the Quetzal's soft feathers with her fingertips. It was a sensation unlike anything she had ever experienced; the feathers were so fine and light that they seemed more a figment of imagination than a thing of flesh and blood. She wanted to cry, though she didn't know why. Maybe it was the softness. Or the way it had accepted her touch. In her time, closeness—real, tender contact—had been regulated out of existence. To touch was to violate protocol. To feel was to falter.

Omar smiled at her reaction. "They're incredible, aren't they? Creatures like these make you wonder about the miracles of nature."

Melyndie nodded, although she didn't quite comprehend what he meant. She was absolutely captivated by the bird. Her eyes followed every movement it made, each flutter of its wings sending a soft wind across her skin. "How can something so beautiful be illegal?" she asked, her voice tinged with sadness.

"It's because of their beauty that they're often caught and sold. Laws are meant to protect them from being exploited," Omar explained, his voice low and steady. He moved slowly toward the window and released the latch, swinging it wide. "Now, we say goodbye and pray it makes it somewhere safe."

He quickly lifted his arm and gestured out the window. For a moment, they both watched in silence as the Quetzal settled on the edge of the neighboring rooftop. Its iridescent feathers shimmered one last time in the moonlight. It didn't fly away immediately. It lingered—just long enough to make her believe it might be saying goodbye.

Omar let out a deep sigh, hoping the creature would survive long enough to find a new place to call home.

"Alright, we need to get you back to the jeep—" he began, hesitant to draw her from her reverie. Melyndie was still marveling at the window, replaying the sensation of feathers against her skin, when a loud sound cracked through the air—shattering the fragile beauty of the moment like a dropped vase. Time split open.

Omar's body jerked unnaturally. She saw his face change—confusion, pain, disbelief—all in the space of a heartbeat. With a desperate flail of arms and a startled gasp that echoed eerily in the sudden silence, he lost his balance entirely. His silhouette was framed for a heart-stopping moment against the window on the eighteenth floor before gravity claimed him, pulling him into the yawning abyss below.

Melyndie stood transfixed, her mind struggling to make sense of the chaotic blur that had just unfolded. Omar's sudden descent from the window seemed surreal, like a grotesque scene played out in slow motion. She didn't scream. She didn't run. Just stood there—staring into the night—unaware that death had quietly taken aim behind her.

Amidst the Chaos

The sound of a loud gunshot echoed through the streets, catching the attention of everyone nearby. Zain's eyes widened with concern as he wondered who could have obtained a firearm in a city where they were outlawed for anyone except law enforcement and military personnel. He was certain it wasn't one of his troops, as they were only equipped with specialized silenced weapons to prevent civilian panic in high-risk situations.

He, himself, had never even seen a standard firearm, except for in a museum. They were practically unobtainable...but someone within this city had managed to get their hands on one and shoot it off in a building. Zain quickly spotted his RMP approaching and ordered him to triangulate the location of the gunshot.

Tom's visor flickered as it processed the data, mapping out the trajectory and origin of the sound with precision, "Residential block thirty-four," it reported in a monotone voice that somehow sounded urgent.

Zain's stomach clenched as another shot cracked through the air. He raced to his jeep, barking, "Attach!" over his shoulder at Tom. The engine hummed to life, but even the vehicle's smooth power couldn't quell the rising storm in his chest. Someone had a weapon. A real one. And someone could be dead or dying.

He depressed the accelerator and shot through the crowded streets, the people parting like the Red Sea before Moses's staff. Another shot echoed through the streets, and Zain's foot pressed harder on the accelerator. Each moment felt crucial now. If someone had a firearm, it wasn't just a matter of military enforcement, it was a potential disaster in such a densely populated environment.

As he drove, Zain couldn't shake off the uneasy feeling about why someone would resort to using such an archaic and noisy weapon in this era.

The streets blurred past him, focus laser-sharp on reaching his destination before any more chaos ensued. It was only a few minutes by jeep, but time seemed to stretch in concert with his concern.

Arriving at the scene, he was met with a crowd of onlookers who'd withdrawn from the inoculation queue and had gathered around the base of residential block thirty-four. The air was thick; whispers of fear and confusion swirled around him at the unidentifiable yet threatening sounds.

Zain pushed through the crowds and was met with several members of his troops at the entrance of the building.

"What's happening?"

"Stand off on floor eighteen," a second lieutenant barked, his voice echoing in the cavernous lobby. "We just arrived and were about to head up—"

"No, get these people back to the lines and post a guard at any area of egress," Zain ordered with an urgency that sliced through the air like a sword. He shoved past them with determined strides, confident that his commands would be executed without hesitation.

"Take the elevator," he hollered over his shoulder to Tom, then bounded up the stairs two steps at a time. His breath was ragged as he reached the eighteenth-floor landing.

His gaze swept across the corridor, quickly identifying several of his troops huddled against the flimsy plaster walls of the hallway, their bodies tense as another gunshot exploded through the narrow space. No time for hesitation—he broke into a sprint, blurring past the gleaming metal doors of elevators just as one slid open to reveal his RMP.

"Move it!" he roared and almost instantaneously, the interior generator within the RMP ignited. The resulting acceleration sent it hurtling down the corridor faster than Zain could blink.

"Report!" Zain demanded as soon as he skidded to a halt beside his men. His gut instinct was to send in his metallic beast to neutralize whatever threat lurked inside but unfamiliarity held him back—the potential for collateral damage was too high.

"Appears to be a resident, sir!" a second lieutenant responded, straining to keep his voice steady amidst chaos. "He or she must have line of sight because every time we prepare to enter, they fire. We would have rushed them but there's a civilian in there. We didn't want to risk her life."

"How do you know she isn't the one firing at you?" Zain shot back, curiosity gnawing at him as he longed to peer into the room himself.

"She appears to be standing off next to the window, in shock. The assailant must have fired at her, missing and shattering the window. Scared her to the point where she's frozen like a statue. Probably hoping that if she doesn't move, she won't draw the shooter's attention."

"Had we not arrived when we did, which was just a minute after the first shot, she'd have likely been killed already," a private chimed in, his voice barely more than a whisper against the thunderous silence that followed another shot.

Zain's jaw clenched as he processed the information. Every second mattered and the situation was spiraling out of control. "Cover me," he instructed tersely, pulling out his tactical visor which flickered to life. Overlaying thermal and movement sensors, it allowed him a crude but effective glimpse through the walls.

Heart racing, he edged closer to the apartment door, the digital readout providing a real-time map of two heat figures inside—one stationary near the window, the other ducked down low behind a piece of furniture on the far side of the room. Another shot rang out, louder now that he was in close proximity. He could almost feel the vibration through the floor.

"Stand down!" Zain's command echoed with an iron-clad authority, his voice slicing through the tense air, hoping it would resonate within the room and rationality would triumph over the rampant panic.

The room was cloaked in a deafening silence for a heartbeat before a frenzied retort broke through from within. "You won't force me to do something against my will!"

"We need to find a way to resolve this peacefully," Zain's voice was steady as he called back into the chaos. He swiveled on his heel and gestured discreetly to Tom. "Prepare your weapon." The words slipped out of him in an urgent whisper.

"Affirmative," came Tom's curt reply.

"Can you locate and fire through obstacles?" Zain questioned, unable to mask the glimmer of hope that laced his tone; hope that this volatile situation could be diffused without breaching and endangering the lives of his soldiers or the civilian inside.

"Affirmative," Tom repeated.

"Then do it! The longer we stand here, the more likelihood that an innocent person is going to die! Do not shoot the civilian next to the window," he ordered, concerned that if he didn't make that specific request, Tom would shoot anything inside.

"Affirmative," Tom intoned again before pivoting towards the apartment's outer wall. Its metallic body hummed with energy as it focused its penetrating gaze on the room's interior. A compartment slid open with mechanical precision and Tom retrieved an FN-911 loaded with 5.9 30mm rounds. With deliberate care, it hoisted up the weapon, locking onto the target before firing a single round with lethal accuracy into the assailant's skull. "Threat neutralized," Tom droned impassively, returning its weapon to its compartment.

Without missing a beat, Zain surged forward into the apartment, his soldiers hot on his heels like shadows trailing behind him. "Secure this room!" he yelled, then froze when he saw Melyndie standing there at the edge of the carnage like a porcelain statue, her eyes vacant, limbs stiff with shock. His breath caught. For one terrible moment, he thought she'd snapped—shut down entirely, her mind lost to the trauma.

Zain raced over to Melyndie, her stillness an eerie contrast to the chaos that had just ensued. As he moved, his gaze swept across the room in a frantic search for Omar, but his friend was nowhere to be seen.

"Melyndie, are you hurt? Why are you in here alone? Where's Omar?" The questions spilled out of him in a torrent; his voice strained with stress and concern.

Melyndie's eyes fluttered like the wings of a humming bird, her lips quivering as she tried to shape the unbearable truth that would shatter Zain's world: his childhood companion was no more. Her gaze inadvertently slipped towards the lifeless form of the assailant, now an unrecognizable lump sprawled on the ground, blood pooled where a head used to be. An instinctual dread seized her and she recoiled, pressing herself against the cold stone wall for refuge.

Zain swiftly interposed himself between her and the gruesome sight, his hands firm and warm on her trembling shoulders. He drew her closer, compelling her to abandon the horrific scene and focus on his concerned face instead. "Are you hurt?" He asked again, his question echoing through the tense silence.

Her eyelids lowered slowly this time as if weighted with lead, before she shook her head. The wave of relief that surged through Zain nearly buckled his knees underneath him. He was bound to protect her, a responsibility he hadn't sought but could not evade, and he had almost faltered in fulfilling it.

Haunted by memories of his mother's murder and his sister's estrangement, another failure was something he simply couldn't stomach. His eyes clamped shut as he sucked in a lungful of air heavy with dust and fear. So overwhelmed was he with relief, he nearly pulled her into his embrace, but stopped short of the intimate act. Instead, he focused on his friend, "Why did Omar leave you alone here? Did he think the apartment was empty?" As the words tumbled out of his mouth, creases appeared on his forehead. Where had Omar disappeared to? Why hadn't he returned at the sound of that first gunshot?

Zain's silent question found its chilling answer as Melyndie's gaze was drawn to what had once been a window. Now, it was merely a gaping wound in the wall, framed by jagged teeth of splintered glass that glittered ominously under the harsh lighting. "He fell from there," she breathed out, her voice echoing the raw torment etched across her face.

Zain stared at the shattered pane. His pulse thundered in his ears. Hesitation clawed at him as he took an uncertain step towards the window, his heart pounding against his ribcage like a trapped bird. He leaned out over the jagged frame of the window and dared to look down. The sight that met him was a crushing blow; his childhood friend lay sprawled on the unforgiving concrete path below; life snuffed out in an instant. His face twisted in a mask of fury and grief as he spun around, summoning his RMP with a barked command.

"Tom," he called out, anguish seeping into that one syllable.

Without hesitation, Tom crossed the room swiftly to stand beside him—ceasing comms without request or hesitation.

"Are you okay, Melyndie?" it asked. She could do no more than nod. Then Zain interjected.

"Omar is dead. Presumably shot by the gunman that you took out. Escort Melyndie back to my jeep and wait with her there while I get Omar's body taken care of. I'll be along shortly."

His words hung heavy in the air as he turned towards Melyndie whose eyes were wide with shock; her mind struggling to process the brutal reality of their situation. "Melyndie. Go with Tom. He'll see to your safety."

Her trembling hand reached out, seeking the secure grasp of the RMP, yet as she made contact with its cold, unyielding arm, a shiver coursed through her. The stark reminder that Tom was machine, rather than man, brought an unexpected sense of isolation. Yet, with no other choice evident, she allowed herself to be led away.

Zain watched her go; the lines of worry etched deeply around his eyes which hardened as he turned back to face the wreckage of the day. The apartment was quiet now, too quiet, as if it held its breath in the aftermath of violence.

His eyes drifted involuntarily back to the shattered window and he suddenly felt numb, and found himself going through the motions; descending the stairwell eighteen floors down, each step weighted with a heavy dread.

Outside, the evening air was crisp, uncomfortably juxtaposing with his internal turmoil. As he approached Omar's body, police sirens began sounding in the distance—their wail slicing through what had become a tomblike stillness on this part of the street. It was apparent that someone had heard the gunfire and had called local authorities, but that same authority was already aware of the military's presence. He sighed heavily, deciding he'd turn over the dead body of the gunman to them, but not his friend's.

Omar lay as though cradled by shadows, a disheartening stillness about him that contradicted the frantic energy that had fueled Zain moments earlier. Crouching beside his friend, Zain's hand hovered over Omar's chest, before settling it next to the gaping wound that had already ceased its flow of life's blood; the gesture a silent apology and farewell all at once. His fingers brushed across a small chain buried beneath Omar's shirt—a talisman both men had been given in their youth. With a tremulous breath, Zain took hold of the chain and gently extracted it. The pendant came into view— an intricate engraving of two figures standing side-by-side, symbolizing brotherhood and inseparable bonds; given to them by Omar's mother when they'd left for the military together.

For a fleeting moment, he was transported back to a better, innocent time when the weight of such pendants was merely symbolic rather than a reminder of loss. He clenched the chain in his fist, cool metal biting into his skin. Justice had been served, but his heart still railed against the losses he'd suffered since this mission had begun: his mother, his sister, and now his childhood friend. He wanted to scream—but the sound wouldn't come. There was no space for grief in this uniform. No time for mourning while a war against extinction still raged. But still...another part of him cracked, silent and deep.

Rising to his feet, Zain fixed his gaze on the rapidly approaching police vehicle, its lights painting surreal streaks across the dark skies. His mind whirred with what needed to be done: the careful navigation with law enforcement, filing a mission report denoting the loss of a military member, and ensuring all military personnel continue with their mission parameters, all while shielding Melyndie from further trauma, and detection.

As he was lost in these thoughts, a hand touched his shoulder. He turned to see an officer he recognized from previous collaborations. "Colonel Belhasa," he started cautiously, his eyes flicking to Omar's body then quickly back to him. "We received distress calls about gunfire. Can you explain what happened?"

Zain shifted slightly, masking the tumult within him with effort. "I have a man stationed outside of an apartment on the eighteenth floor," he explained, his voice strained and hollow-sounding to his own ears. "One of the residents apparently objected to our presence here and decided to go out in a hail of gunfire. Unfortunately, he took one of my men with him."

The officer expressed his condolences but quickly returned to the matter at hand, "We'll establish a secure perimeter—" but Zain interrupted with a steely gaze.

"The situation has been neutralized. We'll handle our fallen officer. This is a straightforward incident so your only responsibility is to arrange the removal of the assailant's body."

"We ought to conduct an inquiry—"

"My men will cooperate fully and provide first-hand accounts, but once we've immunized every person here, we'll be heading out. We have a job to do also. What you should really be scrutinizing is how one of the civilians in your district got their hands on a lethal weapon. The possession of which has been illegal for over twenty years now."

"I fully intend to delve into that matter, indeed. It's practically unheard of to encounter a firearm, outside of a museum. They're all supposed to have been melted down and repurposed."

"I understand it isn't required, but once you've pieced together your report, I'd value having a copy to append to mine. I'm certain that the brass would also welcome some clarity on this issue. Have all of your officers received their vaccinations?"

"One of your officers already paid us a visit and ensured everyone at the station was inoculated."

"Excellent. Now if you'll forgive me, I have my own paperwork demanding attention." Zain turned away, leaving the officer with a terse nod. His pace quickened as he made his way back to where Tom and Melyndie awaited him at his jeep. His mind replayed the events of the last hour with a precision that bordered on agonizing.

As he neared his jeep, Zain's gaze fell upon the silhouette of Melyndie, huddled inside. The dim glow of the interior light shrouded her features in a veil of mystery, but her form—crumpled against the door like a discarded paper doll—screamed a silent symphony of despair. Tom stood like an unyielding sentinel; its robotic eyes focused on the horizon.

"Tom," Zain commanded with a voice that belied the storm brewing within him as he strode forward, "relay today's occurrences to headquarters and append a note that I'll submit a personal account if necessary. The local authorities will also be adding their report at a later date. Then go and collect Omar's body. We'll…um…we'll conduct a short…um…"

"I understand," Tom quickly interjected, then turned and headed back toward where Omar still lay.

Zain watched it go, suddenly grateful that Tom's Adaptive AI made it possible to comprehend his meaning, especially in a time of high distress, because he hadn't wanted to put into words the need to bury his friend. He then pivoted and pulled open the jeep's door.

"Melyndie," he murmured tenderly, easing himself onto the worn leather driver's seat. His sudden proximity seemed to jolt her from her reverie. She jerked in surprise and swiveled towards him, her eyes bloodshot and hollow. "How are you holding up?" he asked, feeling absurd at asking such a ridiculous question when her emotions were etched so clearly on her features.

She looked at him, her lips parting—but no words came at first. Her brow furrowed, mouth trembling like the rest of her. Finally, the words spilled out, fragile and lost: "I don't understand anything that is happening here."

"Right at this moment, I'm not certain I do either," Zain confessed with an honesty that scraped raw against his soul.

At this admission, Melyndie's tears erupted anew like twin rivulets coursing down her cheeks. She folded herself into him, resting her head on his shoulder as though seeking refuge from an invisible storm. He draped his arm around her trembling frame and drew her close, providing solace he himself was desperately searching for amidst the chaos.

For a fleeting moment, she was silent, her breath hitching in her chest. Then, in a voice barely audible, laced with longing and vulnerability, she murmured, "I want to go home."

They had been driving for nearly an hour, wrapped in a silence that felt more meditative than strained. The sky outside was beginning to dim, casting the desert in shades of ochre and deep lavender. Wind rippled across the dunes. Inside the jeep, the low hum of the engine was the only sound.

Then Melyndie finally spoke. "We've traveled to hundreds of places over many weeks to vaccinate the people against an illness that is plaguing your lands."

Her voice startled Zain more than it should have. He flinched slightly, not because of the words, but the way they cleaved through the quiet that had fallen. He glanced at her, but she wasn't looking at him. Her eyes were distant, trained on the horizon, as if she were staring into the past.

She fell quiet again. Zain didn't press since it had been a statement and not a question, and he sensed that her thoughts needed space. After a moment, she continued, contemplative. "The people here...they remind me of those in my time. Compliant in the face of authority. Most obey without question. But the man who killed Omar...and those others who were killed...they were different. They didn't submit. It reminded me of the two scientists who fabricated me. They deviated from the template of the standard citizens, opting to venture into uncharted genetic territory without any prior approval, openly defying our holy ones..."

Her voice trailed off, lost somewhere in the hallways of her thoughts.

Zain gripped the steering wheel a little tighter. "What happened to them?" he asked, determined to keep his tone level and gentle.

"They were terminated. Much like those who have dared to defy your military; like the one who killed Omar."

"You aren't accustomed to witnessing death—"

"I have observed plenty of terminations in my lifetime," Melyndie interjected swiftly.

"Then why did you seem startled—"

"Because it was all so severe. The terminations from my era—with few exceptions—were executed due to dwindling productivity; whether because of advancing age or perhaps flawed genetic blueprints. It's carried out without bloodshed."

He let that settle before responding. "You don't think murder justifies execution?"

"Murder?" She tasted the word.

"When someone kills another without cause. Like that man did to Omar."

She went quiet again. The silence stretched until she finally murmured, "Then yes. His death was justified. But...I keep wondering why he chose that path. Why defy orders? Why risk everything?"

Zain sighed. "Most people follow. It's easier. Familiar. Safer. But there are always outliers—people who can't accept what's handed to them. Who question, push, resist. Sometimes it's idealism. Sometimes desperation."

Melyndie nodded slowly. "In every society...there are those who rebel." Like me, she thought.

"Yes. And sometimes...those rebels change the world."

"And sometimes they die."

A long silence followed. Outside the window, twilight deepened. The desert turned into a shifting sea of ink and amber. Inside, something softer settled between them.

"Can dissent be cultivated?" she asked finally.

Zain glanced at her, surprised by the question's depth.

"I think that's a given," he said. "It develops over time—through pain, injustice, exposure to people who see the world differently. Like a flame is kindled and fanned into fire."

She stared ahead, murmuring, "And sometimes all it takes is a spark from someone else's fire to start your own."

"Exactly." Zain smiled at her accurate analogy.

Silence fell again as they both considered their own sparks, their own fires. The journey they were on was not just about combating physical illness but also confronting other plagues: fear, conformity, and unchallenged authority. This introspection brought Zain's thoughts back to the difficulties Melyndie faced, not just as a person out of time but also one unfamiliar with the life of a soldier.

"I know it hasn't been easy, traveling nearly nonstop with very little rest. It's even hard on me and my battalion and we're more adapted to extended deployments of this nature." Zain's words were a balm of understanding, as he acknowledged the toll their journey was taking. His voice carried the weary weight of command. "How's your shoulder been?" he asked suddenly, his gaze falling to her sling.

Melyndie responded in a voice laced with discomfort, "It aches. The relentless jarring doesn't help and the immobility has made it stiff and painful. But when I attempted to move it yesterday, it did so without its prior excruciating pain, so I believe that it is nearly healed."

"That's good to hear. When we get a chance, let's have Tom examine it. See when you might be able to take that sling off."

"I hope that it will be soon," she admitted.

"You seem to be healing rather quickly," Zain commented. "Most fractures take eight weeks or longer to heal."

"Likely due to my genetic enhancements."

"What are your genetic enhancements? If you don't mind my asking."

"Superior memory, physical prowess, rapid healing, extended lifespan...and immunity to diseases." A sudden realization washed over Melyndie as she understood why she'd been engineered with such disease resistance—it was part of her design for returning to the before time. She whispered an epiphany: "I never needed the inoculation."

"Genetically enhanced against diseases or not, it's always better to err on the side of caution."

Melyndie's head dipped in a slight nod, her dark eyes reflecting the concealed anxiety within her. She steered the conversation off its course, her voice barely above a whisper, "How long are we to be out here, on this mission?"

Zain's gaze fell as he chewed thoughtfully on his lower lip. He was torn between giving Melyndie the truth or softening it for her sake. In the end, he settled on something in between. "It shouldn't be more than a few months. We're moving at a steady pace."

"And then we'll be going back to Iceland?" she asked.

He nodded. "Yeah. But just for a short time. We'll probably redeploy for Phase Two within weeks of returning."

She didn't reply immediately, and Zain hesitated before continuing. "I've been thinking about what comes next for you. Something sustainable. It's not safe for you at the inoculation table, and you can't keep hiding in the jeep like you have this past month—someone's going to start asking questions."

He paused, his mind flicking back to the near-assault. His jaw tensed. Clearing his throat, he pressed on. "So, Tom and I could register you as my assistant as a Sampling Specialist. You'd be able to stay near me. Soldiers could report to you for weekly testing under the guise of conducting deployment stress analysis, something official-sounding. It gives you purpose. And cover."

Melyndie tilted her head, considering. "I hadn't thought about it in a while," she admitted, her fingers brushing the monitor strapped to her bicep. In truth, the thought of continuing had lost its clarity. Without a clear mission or a timeline for return, the collections felt increasingly hollow.

"I actually considered removing this," she said softly. "Just...stopping altogether. Do you really think there's a point?"

Zain heard the weariness in her voice—the slow erosion of hope. "I can't say for sure. But we need to find something for you to hold on to. One thing is certain: There's still two more phases ahead and we can't keep you hidden away forever. You're not trained for combat, so I can't send you into the field. But this—this might work."

She placed her hand gently on his arm. "Then let's do that. I may never get back to my own time, but if I stay idle much longer, I think I'll go crazy. I need something to keep me preoccupied."

Zain met her eyes and nodded, grateful for her resilience. "We'll make it work."

****

The Icelandic base shimmered beneath an overcast sky. The returning battalion moved like ghosts through fields of tents, abandoned nearly a year earlier when the battalion deployed. Zain looked around as he walked toward his private command tent. Theirs appeared to be the first battalion to return. Snow crunched under boots, sounding hauntingly loud.

Melyndie followed Zain, her breath visible in the chilly air. She wrapped her arms around herself and hunched over a bit. After almost a year in the desert, the difference in climate was striking. Zain noticed her teeth chattering and said, "You might want to get inside my tent to escape the cold. Tom, locate a parka for her."

When General Takayoshi emerged from his command tent, Zain quickly signaled for Tom to lead Melyndie away.

"Welcome back, Commander. You certainly are one driven soldier. You started the deployment well behind the other battalions, but you're the first to complete Phase One. Impressive. Get some rest while you can. I've received word that the remaining battalions will be arriving over this next week. Once all the commanders have returned, we'll debrief, then go over mission parameters for Phase Two. We'll talk again then."

Zain watched the General walk away, a sinking feeling settling in the pit of his stomach. There was something in the General's tone that suggested uncertainties ahead, something unspoken but heavily implied. His gut tightened as he contemplated the potential challenges of Phase Two.

As he stood there, wind biting through his uniform, Zain realized that the worst wasn't over.

Something was coming.

He could feel it pressing at the edges of the cold.

And for the first time since the mission began, he wasn't sure who the enemy was anymore.

Phase Two

"Every life is precious and none more so than human life"

~ the Dalai Lama

Before the Storm

The wind blowing through the Icelandic base camp was infused with a sharp scent of oil, a touch of sulfur, and a salty ocean breeze—aromas that never completely disappeared. This was a stark contrast to the dusty desert landscape they had just left behind.

The week since their return had been a blur. Zain and Melyndie had taken a bath almost as soon as they arrived, the lukewarm water just warm enough to fend off the chill outside the bathing area. It didn't erase the memories, but it dulled them enough to allow for some rest. They spent most of the week catching up on sleep. Zain had Tom bring another cot into his tent, aware that it might raise some eyebrows. Yet no one in his battalion seemed to mind. Maybe they understood or maybe they just didn't care. Zain was certain that by the time anyone bothered to question the sleeping arrangements, they would already be preparing for their next deployment.

The tent's interior was utilitarian: two cots, gear bins, a portable screen, and the ever-present hum of the RMP standing silent in the corner. Tom, as the machine now called itself, had taken to silently observing their interactions, sometimes interjecting with odd remarks that seemed just slightly too human.

Melyndie had grown used to its presence, even if she hadn't quite grown to fully trust it. Not since Zain had informed her that it was monitoring them closely. And even though its engagement with them was becoming…more…she often glanced at it from the corner of her eye, gauging whether its newfound personality was truly harmless or merely a sophisticated mask.

"I think you enjoy watching us," she murmured one morning as she brushed her hair, the early sunlight creeping through the canvas flaps.

Tom replied with a faint whirr. "Observation is necessary for mission success. But enjoyment is…under review."

Zain looked up from his cot, where he was polishing his sidearm with slow, deliberate motions. "You're developing sarcasm now? That was definitely sarcasm."

Tom tilted its head. "Noted. I will log it under emerging behaviors."

Melyndie smirked but said nothing. These fleeting exchanges were becoming routine—quiet moments where she felt less like a fabrication and more a part of this world.

A week later, the atmosphere at the base camp underwent a palpable transformation. The arrival of the full complement of battalions infused the air with a restless energy, like a storm brewing on the horizon. Soldiers, weary from their journeys, spoke in low, hushed tones, their conversations intermittently interrupted by furtive glances toward the command tent, which stood like a foreboding sentinel in the midst of the camp. Among the ranks, including Zain's battalion, whispers of disbelief circulated, recounting the harrowing ordeals they had endured over the past year. These tales were mingled with an undercurrent of curiosity about the uncertain future that lay ahead. The anticipation was almost tangible, hanging over them like a heavy fog.

As evening descended, the soldiers sought solace in the simple act of bathing. With each splash of water, concerns seemed to dissolve, leaving behind a serene, almost ethereal silence that enveloped the base. One by one, exhausted soldiers retreated to their bunks, collapsing into the embrace of their beds as if they had been on an endless march. The camp, once alive with activity, now lay in a tranquil hush as the short respite from duty began. Like Melyndie and Zain, many chose to surrender to sleep, eager to let the weight of fatigue pull them into deep, restorative slumber, hoping to sleep away the precious hours of their brief R&R[7].

A week after that, as the first light of day spilled across the encampment, an electronic chime pierced the morning hush. The usual din of boots and chatter froze into silence. Moments later, Brigadier General Takayoshi's voice rang from the speakers of every RMP unit.

"Attention, all personnel. We are expecting an esteemed guest within half an hour. Preserve proper conduct, even though you are currently on a short rest period. Military commanders, report to the command tent immediately."

Zain stood and adjusted his uniform. He glanced toward Melyndie, who had frozen mid-step, uncertain whether to follow or stay.

"Just stay here. Don't draw attention," he said. "And Tom…mute external comms. There's no need for announcements to be blaring in here. We can hear them fine when they filter in from the outside."

"Understood," the RMP replied, dimming its vocal interface.

"And keep Melyndie company. There's no need for you to follow me to the command tent, right?"

"I believe that it is acceptable for me to remain here. I will keep Melyndie company. Perhaps we can play a game of cards."

Zain shook his head and rolled his eyes, then gave Melyndie a nod. "I shouldn't be gone long," he murmured, buttoning up his parka, then stepped outside. The grayness of the morning wrapped around him like a second uniform, and felt just as heavy.

---

[7] Rest & Relaxation

As he walked, the four other commanders fell into step beside him. Just as they had done nearly a year prior. They walked in silence until Major Ethan Mannelly broke it.

"Well, here we all are again," he muttered.

"Indeed. So, what do you think our next mission will be?" Xiu asked, though her eyes were elsewhere, scanning the outer perimeter.

"Likely to be as mundane as the last," Ethan replied. "Was it really necessary to stage a full deployment over mass vaccinations? They made it sound like we were heading into battle."

Hanjun snorted. "I agree. Complete overkill."

Elizaveta chimed in. "If all we were meant to do was vaccinate, and that halted the virus—"

"—Then why are we still here? And what exactly is phase two." Zain finished, his voice cool. "I just hope we aren't ordered to assassinate our siblings next, as proof of our continued dedication."

The others glanced at him.

"I have no sibling," Elizaveta replied in her flat Russian tone.

Everyone stared at her as if she was a bit out of her mind, yet nobody responded.

Their conversation faded as they neared the command tent. An RMP stood aside for them to enter. Inside, General Takayoshi sat at the head of a long table.

"Great to see you all again," he said, gesturing for them to sit. "Make yourselves comfortable."

They tried. None succeeded. They just quickly collected one of the collapsible stools and settled around the table.

"As announced, we're receiving a high-priority guest shortly: President Jeffrey Saltzer of the New Confederated States. He and the other world leaders are making rounds, inspecting troops, and issuing phase two directives. He'll be here for less than a day, so there's no time to prepare your battalions for inspection. That may have been intentional."

"Might I suggest we tell them to prepare nonetheless?" Zain asked.

"Agreed," Ethan added. "They deserve warning."

"Okay, I don't think that will be an issue. Personal RMPs, mute speakers, then issue the command to the troops to prepare for inspection," the General replied. "Colonel Belhasa, where's your personal RMP?"

"I had it hang back. I didn't see the need for it to be here."

"Your RMP is meant to remain by your side at all times, Colonel," General Takayoshi said sternly. "However, since we're pressed for time, I'll forgo having you summon it here. Just make sure it doesn't happen again."

Zain nodded and the General pressed on.

"Let's review final reports. Colonel Belhasa, yours states 8,289 individuals dissented. Of those, 3,139 were executed. Care to elaborate?"

Zain straightened. "With all due respect, General, I'm not certain what there is to elaborate on. It's all there in my report. We offered every dissenter a chance to comply. A majority did. I made the call to give them that choice. I stand by it."

"Less than 8,500 dissenters in your entire region?"

"That's correct," Zain said. "As noted, the numbers were verified by my RMP."

"It did. Just confirming before I show this to President Saltzer."

He closed Zain's file on his tablet and opened another.

"Colonel Kuznetsov. Your report lists..."

"256,817 terminations," Elizaveta stated before the General could even locate the information in her file.

Those seated at the table fell into a stunned silence both at her recall of the number and the pride with which she announced it.

"That's more than the rest of the battalions combined," Takayoshi said quietly, the words catching slightly, as if unsure whether to praise or condemn.

"We encountered many who questioned our reasons for the vaccine," Elizaveta stated, unfazed and unapologetic.

"Questioned or refused?" Jeong Hanjun interjected, astonished at the extremely high number. He had been as hesitant as Colonel Belhasa over exterminating anyone simply over inquisitiveness; however, unlike Belhasa, he had not reported on those individuals, deciding only to denote those who did not wish to comply at all.

"I followed our orders," she replied sharply.

"Perhaps a bit too enthusiastically," Ethan muttered.

Takayoshi offered no further comment. The sound of an approaching helicopter drew the briefing to an abrupt close. He tapped his screen to finalize the reports and dismissed the officers.

They filed out in silence. Only the General remained inside, tapping a single line into the command terminal, then he stepped outside and made his way over to the helipad.

Outside, the chopper descended through the muted sky. President Saltzer stepped out, ducking beneath the slowing rotors. He wore a sharp military-style suit that gave him an air of both authority and approachability.

"President Saltzer. Welcome to Base Icicle," Takayoshi greeted him as they shook hands.

"Thank you for having me, General Takayoshi. I've heard a great deal about your leadership."

As they walked toward the command center, the President glanced around, eyes calculating as he surveyed the perimeter. "I've received some interesting reports from this base regarding phase one. Some commendable. Others…slightly concerning."

The General maintained his composure under the scrutiny. "I have the end-of-mission reports ready for your review. We, of course, look forward to any feedback from our superiors."

"Very diplomatic," the president replied. "Forward the reports to my office. I'll review them later. For now, we need to go over the mandates for phase two."

They reached the command tent. The president's personal RMP-SP (Robotic Military Personnel – Security Protocols) took position beside the entryway and began scanning the perimeter.

As they entered, Takayoshi asked, "Sir, would you like to inspect the troops before we begin?"

The president nodded slightly. "If time allows. We're on a tight schedule. I need to be wheels up in an hour."

Takayoshi hesitated, surprised by such an abbreviated visit. "Should I summon the battalion commanders for the briefing then?"

"Shortly," Saltzer said. "First, I need half of the base's RMP complement to report immediately. I will give them their new mandate and they'll deploy immediately after."

Takayoshi nodded and relayed the order.

Outside, the synchronized footfalls of RMPs pounded ominously against the frozen earth, their unnervingly precise rhythm echoing through the air, pulling curious onlookers from their tents as if drawn by an unseen force. Inside the shadowy command tent, the President leaned forward, his hands clasped tightly, eyes fixed on the General with the intensity of a predator assessing its prey.

"Go ahead and gather the commanders, but I want to see Colonel Belhasa and Colonel Kuznetsov before briefing the others," he intoned quietly.

There was something in his tone, like a calm before the storm.

The battalion commanders stood outside the command tent, waiting to be summoned by General Takayoshi and President Saltzer. In silence, they scanned the camp, their eyes darting from the soldiers milling about expectantly to the frozen earth beneath their boots. The winter sun sat low in the sky, casting long shadows over the temporary base. What unsettled them more than the cold was the unmistakable presence of nearly half the base's RMP force, gathered off to the side in neat, intimidating rows. One unit stood just inside the command tent, lights flickering in rapid succession as it received private instructions from the President of the Confederated States of America—transmissions no human ear could decipher.

A few of the commanders shifted uneasily. Though they couldn't hear what was happening inside, the implication was clear: something critical was about to unfold.

When the RMP finished receiving its orders, it pivoted in perfect synchronicity and advanced toward the remaining units. Without a word, it began blinking a new sequence—an unspoken command relayed to the others. Moments later, General Takayoshi emerged from the tent, his expression unreadable, and called out, "Colonel Kuznetsov."

Elizaveta stepped forward with her usual icy poise, but even she faltered slightly as she disappeared into the tent. The rest exchanged tense glances, lips sealed, the air too thick with risk to entertain whispers. With their proximity to the tent and the RMPs nearby, a misinterpreted word could be fatal.

Still, curiosity got the better of them. As one, they leaned toward the tent, ears straining. But whatever was being said inside, it was hushed—deliberately so.

They startled when Elizaveta exited just minutes later, her face set in stone.

"That was a short conversation," Ethan muttered, only to fall silent as the General appeared again.

"Colonel Belhasa."

Zain met Elizaveta's eyes on his way in. She offered a tight shrug, but no insight. He didn't expect more—but some hint would have helped. He drew a steadying breath and stepped inside. The door flap sealed behind him like a vault.

The interior was dim, warm, and silent except for the soft hum of an electric heater. President Saltzer sat at the head of the table, flanked by General Takayoshi, who was more tense than he'd ever seen him. An RMP stood near the rear corner, utterly still but unmistakably alert.

Zain snapped to attention. "Sir."

"At ease, Colonel," Saltzer said, his voice smoother than Zain expected, but no less authoritative. A polite smile crept across his pale face, the kind meant to disarm. "Please, have a seat."

Zain obeyed, but tension radiated through his posture. No part of him relaxed.

"I wanted to personally discuss this matter with you before your next mission," the president began, folding his hands. "I understand this pertains to the past, but I feel it is important to assess the circumstances directly."

Zain already knew where this was going. His jaw flexed. This wasn't a courtesy. It was an audit.

He said nothing, waiting for the inevitable reprimand—or worse.

Your actions were driven by a series of calculated choices based on directives issued by those in command, Tom's voice echoed in his mind. *I am merely the facilitator of protocol; you, however, are the executor of your own free will.* A reminding thought he neither needed nor welcomed.

"At the onset of this mission, you were given a directive…" Saltzer paused, giving Zain space to remember—as if those memories had ever left. "I'm here on behalf of all world leaders, including your own president. We understand the task was not an easy one, but as a high-ranking officer entrusted with command, your visible hesitation has raised…concerns."

Not a word about the content of the directive itself. Not a whisper about his mother.

Zain cleared his throat. "Request permission to speak freely, sir."

Saltzer raised a brow, faintly amused. "Granted. Though be advised—this conversation is on record."

"Understood."

"Then proceed."

"If you were given the same order, sir—to kill someone you loved dearly just to prove loyalty—"

"My wife," Saltzer said, cutting him off. "It was decided I would execute my wife, as my parents are deceased. So, you see, Colonel, it wasn't just military commanders being tested. It's a cause we leaders believe in so strongly, we placed ourselves in your boots—metaphorically."

The silence that followed settled heavily on Zain. Even the RMP in the corner seemed to pause, as though calculating the fallout of what had just been said.

But Zain couldn't let it go. "Then you understand, sir. Following orders is expected of us—but being commanded to violate the deepest parts of ourselves is…something else entirely. I did what was ordered, yes, and it cost me more than I can say. But the fact that I obeyed should serve as proof of my commitment, even if I'll never reconcile the morality of it."

Saltzer's eyes hardened. His expression, once affable, now registered only the thinnest trace of patience. "We expect blind obedience," he said coldly. "Every command—past and future—serves a purpose. The reasoning is not always yours to understand."

Zain swallowed. The words left a burn in his throat.

"So, the question is…will you be able to fulfill your duties without hesitation moving forward," Saltzer continued, "or do I need to—"

"I'm good to go, sir," Zain snapped, cutting off whatever consequences had been about to verbalized.

Saltzer studied him for another moment, then gave a short nod. "Then bring in the others."

****

Twenty minutes later, the battalion leaders exited the tent. No one spoke at first.

Their boots crunched over frozen gravel as they moved away from the command tent, their expressions taut with disbelief.

"Is anyone else getting a sense of Déjà vu?" Zain asked.

"I have to admit," Hanjun said finally, voice low, "that's the second briefing I've ever attended that somehow told us everything and nothing."

"Does anyone have a clear understanding of what we're supposed to do once we arrive back on station?" Xiu added.

"No, that was a classic case of saying a lot while saying nothing at all," Zain muttered.

"He did say our personal RMPs would provide mission-specifics en route," Elizaveta pointed out, gesturing ahead.

Four of the Five personal RMPs were already approaching.

"I take it we're headed back to the airstrip?" Ethan asked.

"Your equipment has been readied and your troops are standing by," Elizaveta's RMP intoned, its tone dry and clipped, much like Elizaveta herself. Zain sighed. At least Tom wasn't like that. He glanced around, searching, wondering where Tom was—then spotted him standing alone, half-shadowed by one of the supply trucks. The RMP's posture was subtly off, its head tilted as if…waiting.

Odd.

As soon as Zain locked eyes, Tom turned and walked away without a word.

"What the hell…" Zain muttered and followed quickly, his boots crunching behind Tom's swift gait. They moved toward the edge of the base, out of earshot.

"Okay, Tom," Zain called. "What gives?"

Tom halted. "Melyndie is gone."

The words hit like a punch to the sternum. Zain stumbled to a stop. "What do you mean, 'gone'?"

"I cannot locate her."

He turned, breathing fast, thoughts spinning. "You did put her biosignature into your database, correct?"

"Affirmative."

"And I presume you've already scanned—"

"She is not anywhere within range of my radar."

Zain's voice turned hoarse. "The last time she vanished she was pulled only a few hundred feet away. Is it possible she just...dropped outside your scan radius?"

"Possible," Tom replied, "but given our orders to deploy immediately, I cannot delay to test that theory. Any significant pause would raise suspicion."

Zain clenched his fists. "Extend your range. Scan everything."

"And hope, if she did fall, it wasn't into the Greenland Sea," Tom replied, deadpan.

Zain's jaw twitched. Tom went still; it's visor blinking.

"I expanded my range to its furthest capability...again. She is not nearby," Tom went on, turning back toward the transport. "Even if I had detected her, we'd be unable to assist. You cannot leave the battalion, which is scheduled to pull out first. If she turns up after we depart, she'll likely be assigned to another battalion."

"Son of a bitch," Zain growled under his breath. "Maybe it's better if her people managed to pull her back to her own time. Maybe that's what happened."

Tom paused mid-step. "Either way," it said, it's voice low, almost reverent. "She's gone." The words landed like a eulogy.

Zain remained frozen for a long moment, the roar of truck engines firing up in the distance. He told himself this should be a relief—that the burden of hiding her secret had been lifted. No more half-truths. No more split loyalties.

And yet, all he felt was hollow.

She had been by his side in a world turning upside down—changed him in ways he hadn't fully understood. Now, only the echo of her absence remained

And in that echo, something in him stilled. Something needed, though he hadn't known it, had gone with her."

Return a Stranger

Year: 2401

Melyndie's eyes fluttered open to a ceiling of seamless white, the sterile scent of antiseptic sharp in her nose. Blurred figures hovered above—three outlines warped by the haze still clinging to her consciousness. She blinked slowly, each motion heavy and disjointed, trying to draw the shapes into clarity. The forms of Dr. Kishida-Guan, 41GB, and 71PQv coalesced slowly from the fog, but she found herself unable—or perhaps unwilling—to focus on them. A soft chime hummed in the background, the sound of a scan initiating.

She should have felt relief. This was home. Familiar. Controlled. Safe. But instead, a slow ache settled over her, unfamiliar and raw—a sensation that had no place in her previous life. It wasn't fear or confusion, but something far more elusive. A hollowness. A sense of absence.

Loneliness.

The word floated into her mind, soft and slow, like a memory from someone else's life. Was this what it meant to miss someone?

Her brow twitched. She shut her eyes again as the murmur of voices began to pierce the fog.

"—not the right time to question her," said a technician. His voice was level, almost indifferent, but there was a note of practiced concern behind it.

"She's awake," Dr. Kishida-Guan replied with unmistakable urgency. "We need a report—immediately."

"She may be conscious," the technician said, adjusting a handheld scanner over her chest, "but that doesn't mean she's ready. Let her stabilize. Her vitals are still fluctuating."

Dr. Kishida-Guan's expression tightened, but before he could argue, 71PQv interjected. "Instead of pressing her," he said, glancing toward the diagnostic screen, "perhaps we should review the chip delay. She went off-grid for too long. Our tracking system couldn't maintain a lock—and if we're sending her back again, that can't happen."

"Agreed," said 41GB, stepping closer. "We must identify what hindered our ability to retrieve her after detecting the chip's signal. Let her rest. In the meantime, now that she's back, we can focus on reviewing all of our data."

Dr. Kishida-Guan's jaw slackened, if only slightly. He gave a terse nod. "Very well," he murmured. "Monitor her vitals. And remove the monitoring unit from her arm—pull the data. I want to see if it matches the live stream we had during her first few weeks in the before time."

The others moved off, leaving Melyndie alone in the antiseptic quiet of the med bay. Her eyelids drifted open again, this time slowly, her gaze fixed on the smooth ceiling above her. Memory returned in fragments—Zain's voice, low and uncertain; the quiet tension in his eyes the day she vanished. His presence during every dangerous crossing, every whispered conversation about safety, about keeping her close.

Now, there was nothing. No rumbling jeep. No dust in her teeth. No sense of momentum or purpose.

Only the quiet hum of filtered air and the knowledge that she would likely never see him again.

The ache in her chest deepened.

Was he thinking of her now? Was there a version of pain like this in his world? She imagined his silhouette beneath that brilliant desert sun, now eclipsed from her reach. The grief was unfamiliar but sharp in its intrusion.

She lay motionless for what might have been hours, until the soft sound of footsteps signaled someone's return.

"Melyndie?" 41GB's voice was low, almost cautious.

She turned her head and met 41GB's gaze—steady, inquisitive, but vacant of true understanding. Whatever haunted Melyndie's eyes, whatever storm had followed her back from the past, could not be recognized by someone who had never truly felt. Melyndie tried to answer, but her throat betrayed her, the attempt at speech dissolving into silence.

41GB stepped closer and placed a gentle hand on her forearm, her voice steady but strangely detached. "I can't imagine all that you've been through," she said. "Once you're cleared, I'll assist you through the debriefing."

Melyndie studied her—this woman who, months ago, she might have seen as kind. But now, after experiencing a world full of unfiltered emotion, of anger and sorrow and joy in their rawest forms—41GB's tone sounded more like protocol than comfort. Like Tom in its earliest stage of learning.

Melyndie turned her face away and closed her eyes. If she kept them shut long enough, perhaps 41GB would leave. She couldn't bear to be seen—not by someone who would interpret her expression as a glitch in programming.

She heard the faint retreat of footsteps, the gentle hiss of the door closing behind her. Only then did a single tear escape, tracing a warm path down her temple before falling to the cot.

She had longed to return here—so often, she'd imagined the serenity of her old realm. The blinding white lights, the predictability. But what she hadn't anticipated was how dead it would feel now.

The thrill of hiding her identity, the long hours pressed between soldiers and desert heat, the soul-crushing fear of being discovered—it had all come to mean something. It had awakened her.

Now, she felt like a stranger in her own time.

The hours stretched on. Technicians drifted in and out, adjusting monitors and checking vitals, but she barely acknowledged them. Her mind spun with memory. Red dust kicking up beneath wheels. Towering buildings. Strange rations she'd secretly come to enjoy. The odd, beautiful moments: the camel's quiet grace, Omar's gentle persistence, the sudden burst of emerald as the Quetzal bird flared its wings. Each memory was a thread pulling at her heart, tugging her back through space and time.

Only now did she understand why people had once captured everything. Photographs. Videos. Not to remember—but to hold on to feelings that mattered.

And it did matter.

Although not all of her memories were pleasant, they were still hers—moments she would have never experienced if geneticists G9983 and G13654 hadn't dared to defy the holy ones and decide not to include emotional suppressants into her genetic code. An act that ultimately cost them their lives.

****

In the far corridor, inside the primary laboratory, Dr. Kishida-Guan stood with 41GB and 71PQv as technicians worked around them, calibrating the tracking interface in near silence. The walls were lined with glowing panels, each one pulsing with data from Melyndie's chip.

They hadn't asked whether she'd completed her mission.

240

They simply assumed she had. That she'd managed to collect what was needed in those early weeks and then spent the rest of her time surviving—running, hiding, adapting. The thought that she might have done more, that she might have been deliberate, strategic, never crossed their minds.

Then the maintenance bot entered—unhurried, mechanical. It rolled toward them and presented its delivery: the DNA retriever.

The room went still.

Dr. Kishida-Guan stepped forward at once and snatched the device from the bot's grip. The lab's ambient chatter dissolved into silence.

"Do you think…" 71PQv began, but his voice faltered.

"If these samples were collected eleven months ago," Kishida-Guan snapped, inspecting the casing with a scowl, "then we may already be too late." He didn't scan the contents—just turned the device over in his hand, expression hardening. "We never briefed her on viability timelines. She had no way of knowing whether to continue collecting samples or whether to stop after retrieving one. We don't even know if there are any samples here at all. She may have failed to collect anything."

41GB stepped forward slightly. "But there's still a chance, if she collected something, some material survived. Shouldn't we at least run a viability scan?"

"Fine," Kishida-Guan said through gritted teeth. "Run it. Log it. Just don't waste the team's time cataloging junk if that's what it turns out to be." Rather than toss the device, he placed it down on a side console with a sharp, impatient thud—as though it offended him simply by existing. "We've already wasted too much time," he growled, pacing. "This recall system was supposed to be foolproof, yet we couldn't lock her position for months. If the chip's range and response delay aren't corrected, we'll likely lose her again—possibly permanently."

"The unknown interference wasn't anticipated," 71PQv offered carefully. "Our baseline parameters didn't account for shifts in temporal resistance or signal bleed, if that's what it was. Perhaps more testing with the chip is needed under varied—"

Kishida-Guan stopped pacing. "We needed more testing before the first insertion," he snapped, eyes flashing. "You both made that point repeatedly—and I overrode it because we didn't have the luxury of delay. We still don't."

"But we also can't afford another leap plagued with issues," 41GB said, her voice lower, almost hesitant. "Aside from the trouble with the chip's signal and the potentially defective genetic samples…there's the impact on Melyndie. She's returned, yes—but the psychological and neurological strain is clearly substantial. She hasn't spoken a word."

Kishida-Guan's jaw twitched. "Because we're babying her," he said. "She's genetically superior. Enhanced. Built to withstand the strain. And yet here we are—tiptoeing around her like she might shatter."

41GB and 71PQv exchanged another glance. It was brief, but no longer entirely neutral. A flicker of something passed between them. Concern. Disagreement. Something not yet fully conscious, but undeniably there.

"She will be debriefed," Kishida-Guan continued, voice tight. "The moment she's able to speak, I want a full report. Memory degrades with time, and I won't risk losing firsthand data. Understood?"

Neither of them answered at first.

Then 71PQv nodded. "Understood."

"I'll work on recalibrating the chip's temporal harmonics," 41GB added, her voice quieter but pointed. "If we don't address the resonance gaps, we might never achieve a stable lock—regardless of how refined the locator becomes."

Kishida-Guan exhaled, the sound clipped and frayed. "Do what you need to do. Just get it done." He caught the brief looks exchanged between them and recalibrated his tone. "Within a *reasonable* timeframe," he amended, voice cooler now but no less insistent.

The room fell silent for a moment as Kishida-Guan turned away, but the air between them had changed. Tension settled over them with the quiet precision of a system warning light—not loud, not yet critical, but impossible to ignore.

Doubt in their superior had entered the room, and it wasn't leaving.

"Will you update the Chancellor?" 41GB asked, more softly now.

Kishida-Guan didn't even look up. "No. When we succeed, I'll tell him. There's no need to burden him with every failed attempt. He knows what we're trying to achieve and how important it is that we do so."

Again, that look between 41GB and 71PQv. Their growing doubt remained unspoken, but it was it was getting harder to keep it hidden.

They returned to their terminals, the air between them taut with unvoiced concern.

Just then, a medical technician stepped into the lab. His face was composed, but his pace urgent.

"Doctors," he said, voice flat but hurried. "Please come quickly. We've detected an anomalous reading in a75b99r84GE's data."

He didn't elaborate.

Kishida-Guan's gaze snapped to him—sharp, unblinking, already parsing implications faster than the technician could explain. The word hung there, taut with potential threat.

Anomalous.

That single term drew a silence so complete it felt manufactured.

Then, without a word, Kishida-Guan turned and strode for the corridor. 41GB and 71PQv followed close behind, their expressions unreadable but far from at ease.

No one spoke.

But all of them felt the tension radiating from Kishida-Guan.

To him, anything anomalous was a threat. And with humanity's survival on the line, even a fabricated asset wasn't beyond replacement.

Crosstalk

The holy ones trailed behind the medical technician as he led them from the laboratory to the medical bay. The corridors were silent save for the faint thrum of electricity pulsing through the walls, a hum that seemed louder with each step. As they entered, the stark light of the bay bathed everything in clinical sterility.

Melyndie sat in a chair, her back rigid, an anxious expression pulling tight at her features. Several technicians bustled around her neck area, their movements swift and focused, but tinged with uncertainty. She kept her eyes forward, wide with concern, flinching occasionally at the cold touch of instruments. A scanner had been positioned just behind her, emitting soft pulses and low tones. The technicians' hurried murmurs filled the room like insect chirps at night—intermittent and dissonant.

Dr. Kishida-Guan approached silently but with a visible urgency that contrasted sharply with the stillness of the sterile chamber. His coat swayed with each step as he circled behind Melyndie, staring at the scanner for several minutes, unreadable. At last, he turned to address one of the nearby technicians. "Explain," he demanded, his voice cutting through the low hum of equipment and whispered consultations.

The technician, a young man identified as JN234A17, turned toward him with a tablet in hand. "We're uncertain what it is precisely; however, after much discussion, we've determined that it appears to be some form of device, not dissimilar to the tracking device, though slightly larger in size, that we embedded in a75b99r—"

"What exactly is the origin of this anomaly? How did it get there?" Dr. Kishida-Guan demanded, his voice a terse whip crack in the sterile room, barely concealing his vexation over the lack of tangible data being relayed.

"We've yet to ascertain that," JN234A17 responded, his gaze anchored to the luminous screen of his tablet as he relentlessly reviewed the enigmatic contraption's readings.

"Is it active?" the doctor asked as his gaze moved to the technician's tablet screen.

"We're picking up nominal readings, which is why our initial scans did not pick it up. Likely it was rendered dormant, in standby mode, when a75b99r84GE was returned from the before time."

Dr. Kishida-Guan navigated around Melyndie, positioning himself squarely before her, his eyes boring into hers.

"How did you manage to get a foreign object lodged above your cervical region?" His question was laced with a strange undertone of blame that triggered an instinctive defensive reflex within Melyndie. She stiffened, her body going ramrod straight, as if her spine were bracing against an invisible strike. Her expression morphed—first bewildered, then terror-stricken, and finally settling into a posture of stubborn defiance.

"I have no idea," she retorted.

"How could you be oblivious? It would require surgical intervention for its insertion—" he started.

"Not necessarily so," JN234A17 interjected smoothly. "Given its biomechanical attributes, it could have been injected through any medium—"

"Hold on! Did you say 'injected'?" Melyndie quizzed, her expression clearing from the fog of confusion.

"Indeed," affirmed the technician with a nod.

"The inoculation…" Melyndie's voice trailed off into a whispering murmur.

Dr. Kishida-Guan frowned, glaring at Melyndie; his face tightening with suspicion. "Explain."

Melyndie gathered her resolve, her voice gaining strength as the haze of realizations converged into a coherent strand of thought. "When I first arrived, it was at the onset of a global pandemic; a deadly virus spreading across the world. The government mandated that everyone must receive a vaccine to combat the threat. No one was exempt from it. Zain and Tom—"

"Who?" 41GB interrupted.

"Is that really important right now? We can go over all of the details later during a debriefing. Let her finish explaining how this relates to the anomaly." Dr. Kishida-Guan interjected firmly. "Go on."

"I discussed with Zain and Tom the potential consequences of not getting vaccinated and our concerns about doing so. Ultimately, we agreed that since those refusing the vaccine were to be terminated, and since we didn't know when I would be pulled back, it was best to comply with the general orders. That is the only time any foreign substance was introduced into my system—that I am aware of."

Dr. Kishida-Guan looked at both 41GB and 71PQv, his expression signaling his acknowledgement that there were many problems that needed to be addressed once this inquiry was concluded. It was as if it was the first time he fully acknowledged all of the issues plaguing their project and he fell into an eerie silence, his gaze pinned on Melyndie.

"It appears there are a lot of things we need to sort out… and to discuss… before Melyndie attempts another leap," 41GB added quietly.

Dr. Kishida-Guan nodded solemnly, his gaze now fixated on the floor as though processing each piece of information as a separate puzzle to be tackled. "Very well," he murmured finally, more to himself than to anyone in the room. "This vaccine—or what could have been disguised as one—might have been engineered not only to combat an outbreak but perhaps also to serve another purpose. JN234A17, remove the device from Melyndie—"

"Doctor, due to the location, the proximity to the spinal cord, removal will require more skill than that of a medical technician."

The doctor squinted in thought, then continued, "Very well. 71PQv, please notify our personal surgeon that we will need his services; to prepare for a surgical procedure." He turned away from his colleagues to continue his discussion with JN234A17. "Could this device, when activated, be the reason that we had difficulty locating and latching onto Melyndie's transport signal?"

"Highly probable," JN234A17 replied, tapping on the tablet to retrieve the data from the last attempt to locate and pull Melyndie back from the before time. "Even at its current low level of signal output, it is acting in conflict with the chip. So, yes, it could very well have interfered with the tracking and retrieval algorithms in our implanted device, effectively cloaking her, blinding her, from our systems."

"Deliberate?" 71PQv queried. He rubbed his chin thoughtfully, the implications of such a scenario unfolding in his mind like a dark flower. "This could represent a security breach of unforeseen proportions."

"I believe you are getting ahead of yourself," 41GB interjected. "After all, the inoculation that Melyndie mentioned was in response to a worldwide pandemic happening at that time. It is highly unlikely that someone would use that as an opportunity to inject a tracking device into Melyndie. That would require beforehand knowledge of who she is and from whence she came. Highly improbable."

"Okay, I can concede that, especially as Melyndie did state that all citizens were injected with this device; however, it does not hold to the provided explanation of combating a worldwide virus as it is biotechnological, not formulated for dispersing an antidote for illness," 71PQv insisted.

"Indeed, still before we jump to any conclusions, we'll have JN234A17 conduct thorough examinations on the device just to be certain it poses no threat. And, since the device was likely the cause of the initial inability to retrieve Melyndie from the before time," Dr. Kishida-Guan continued, "then I do not see any cause for alarm in the processes taken prior to the first time run."

And just like that, gone was the reticence and uncertainty in his mind. His tone filled with an almost childlike glee which caused concern to rise again in his colleagues—for they knew that he would be ready to transport Melyndie back to the before time the minute she was cleared, post-surgery.

41GB, in particular, a voice of reason, expressed her apprehension. "Doctor, it's best that we ensure that we've addressed all potential issues, as discussed, before we consider sending her back through time again. We cannot presume that the interference from this foreign device is the sole reason for our inability to track and retrieve her."

"We will have time to review all data and run necessary diagnostics," Dr. Kishida-Guan assured, "since she will be undergoing surgery and will have at least a week of recovery time."

Throughout the entirety of the conversation, Melyndie remained a mute statue, her usually eloquent tongue held captive by turmoil. A tempestuous whirlwind of thoughts and fears raged in her mind, each one more chaotic than the last. They all revolved around one thing—that foreign device nestled within her neck.

Had it somehow journeyed from its original injection site to affix itself to her cervical spine? The thought sent shivers down her back, each one sharper than the last. Was its true function genuinely for protection against disease as she had been told? Or was there an ulterior motive hidden beneath its benign facade? 71PQv had suggested that it could not possibly have been for the intended purpose as it was biotechnological. The implications spiraled, each darker than the one before.

Was Zain privy to the true purpose of the inoculation? Could Tom have known something and not revealed that knowledge to either her or Zain? These questions gnawed at her insides, festering into a paranoia that eclipsed everything else. It wasn't just about her own safety anymore; it was the creeping suspicion that maybe those she held as her closest allies in the before time weren't who she thought them to be.

Worse still was the chilling realization that the entire human population had been required to receive the inoculation. If the device was more than it seemed, then danger loomed not just over her—but over the entire world.

Melyndie's mind wandered back to the day of the inoculation. The long lines of worried faces. The sharp hiss of the jet injector. The firm but gentle smile of the nurse. Had it all been a prelude to something far more sinister? She tried desperately to peer back into Zain's dark, searching gaze, to find some clue she'd missed. But all she could recall was the weight of his worry, mirroring her own.

Dr. Kishida-Guan shifted his gaze back to Melyndie, a slight narrowing of his eyes indicating his focus on her. He observed as a range of emotions passed over her face in a flurry, and then called out to her. "Melyndie?"

She flinched, as if she had been physically struck.

"The surgeon has arrived, so we're going to make our way to the surgical ward. Are you strong enough now to walk?"

Melyndie nodded, her body stiff and her mind racing. She was being pulled in a hundred different directions—fear intertwining with duty, confusion mingling with resolve. As the medical team mobilized around her, preparing for the surgery that would hopefully remove the mysterious device, she couldn't shake the overwhelming sense of foreboding that clung to her like a second skin.

The room they entered was stark, bathed in the cold glow of clinical lights. The air smelled sharply of antiseptic, mingling oddly with a faint metallic scent that she couldn't quite place. As she lay down on the surgical table, straps gently securing her, Melyndie's heart pounded fiercely against her ribcage.

The surgeon, a man with sharp features and steady hands named Dr. Henley, greeted her with a small nod as he prepared his instruments. "We'll have you back on your feet in no time," he promised, his voice calm and precise—measured, like someone accustomed to controlling outcomes.

Melyndie gave a faint nod in return, but her eyes never left the overhead lights. She was silent, still—but inside, questions screamed.

She didn't ask if the device could be removed safely. She didn't ask what it truly was.

She only wondered if she'd walk away the same—or walk away at all.

The final day at the landing site felt heavier than the rest—weighted by the kind of silence that settles before a storm. Zain stood near the edge of the tarmac, his hands behind his back, eyes locked on the active radar tower that still swept its gaze across the sky in slow, measured arcs.

Two days had passed since they'd returned to Dubai, and still he found himself watching that tower like it might suddenly flicker and give her back.

But nothing came. No signal. No ripple in the air. Just the hollow sweep of machinery doing its job while the world stood still.

Zain exhaled slowly, jaw tight, as the weight of not knowing settled deeper into his bones. Somewhere out there, she was either alive…or gone.

He squinted toward the horizon, as if some shape might emerge from the heat shimmer. Melyndie's absence felt like a physical displacement—like something had been cut out of the world and left him staring at the hole.

"Merely gazing at the coordinates won't summon her back into existence," Tom proposed, its footsteps silent as it moved to align itself next to Zain on the tarmac. The expanse of desert terrain stretched out before them, a stark reminder of their solitude.

Zain didn't answer right away. He folded his arms tightly across his chest, shoulders braced against the weight of everything he couldn't control.

"I'm aware. It's just…I can't shake off the fear that, if she did hit the earth, she might have landed in a crevasse…or fell into the Greenland Sea even—as you suggested. She doesn't possess our type of resilience and adaptability, and without any means of transmitting a distress signal..." His voice faded into the sweltering, oppressive air, his chest rising and falling heavily as he wrestled with his mounting anxiety.

"The ambiguity surrounding her current situation is indeed unsettling," Tom responded, its voice devoid of any emotional inflection—a constant monotone hum against the ambient noises surrounding them. "However, we must resist dwelling on her potential plight when our mission objectives remain unfulfilled."

Zain turned slightly toward his RMP, watching it from the corner of his eye. There were days he wished it could feel what he felt—just to divide the burden.

"I presume you deactivated your audio and visual surveillance systems prior to initiating this discussion about Melyndie?"

"Affirmative."

"That's appreciated. The last thing I need is for those at command questioning my commitment even more than they're already doing."

"I have concluded that it would be advantageous for my 'technical malfunctions' to persist until such time they become suspicious enough to issue a recall order for maintenance. It is fortunate that the need to disconnect has become less frequent."

Zain raised an eyebrow at that but didn't comment. The machine was evolving, and he wasn't sure if that comforted or unnerved him.

"I appreciate your willingness to stand with me on this, Tom. Now, what exactly does phase two entail? The briefing with President Saltzer and General Takayoshi was notably scant in its specifics. Something I'm beginning to think is deliberate."

"I have been ordered to give this briefing to you at the same time as the battalion. Unfortunately, I do not think you will be happy with what needs to be done next."

Zain stared straight ahead, the muscles in his jaw twitching. "Well, that doesn't sound promising. Are there instructions on how to handle any resistance from the soldiers? Actually, never mind, I can probably guess. I certainly don't want those fears solidified."

"They will be eliminated," Tom interjected, even though it seemed like Zain already knew the answer and didn't want to hear it.

Zain's reaction was immediate. "Thanks for taking the hint," he snapped, but Tom ignored him and just continued speaking.

"I do not have all of the details, but I believe that the RMPs that were sent ahead are meant to serve two purposes: the mandate, and to prevent human interference."

Zain exhaled sharply through his nose. "Okay, this is sounding worse by the minute."

"I can assure you that the sound will not improve."

He glanced at his RMP, almost amused—almost. "Are you trying to be funny again?" But he didn't wait for an answer. His focus had shifted. "Do we have a time set for the briefing?"

"There is no set time. The briefing will take place as soon as all military personnel have completed their evening meal," replied his RMP.

Zain looked around at the men sitting on the tarmac, their laughter and banter filling the air as they consumed their MREs. The scene unfolded like a photograph from another life—one filled with normalcy and camaraderie. But it was a lie.

He knew it would all collapse as soon as the truth came out.

Despite their current jovial mood, he knew that once they were aware of the mission's details, the atmosphere would shift drastically. It was an assumption, maybe—but his gut told him otherwise. Something in Tom's clipped phrasing had set him on edge.

Half hour later, as the orange glow of the setting sun bled into the horizon and cast long shadows over the assembled troops, Zain stood before them, a bland expression on his weathered face. The air had cooled, but tension prickled at the back of his neck like a warning, causing it to sweat.

"At ease, everyone. RMP Tom will be going over phase two mission parameters shortly. I just want to remind everyone, before it begins, that you are soldiers and I expect you to continue to perform your duties with dignity and honor. Is that clear?"

Voices rang out in a resounding chorus, echoing across the cooling asphalt as they responded in unison: "Sir, yes sir!"

"Excellent. I'll hand over this briefing to Tom," Zain announced, taking a step off to the side and clasping his hands behind his back. He turned slightly toward his RMP, careful not to fully face the battalion in case any emotions showed through. He made a conscious effort to keep his face neutral, no matter what information the RMP was about to share.

Unlike with the onset of phase one, Tom did not merely play a pre-recorded mission briefing from General Takayoshi. Instead, it stood still for a moment, processing, almost…composing. Then its voice rose, clear and amplified, projected through the few remaining RMP units scattered across the site, so that all thousand soldiers could hear.

"Three days, five hours—"

"Tom, while I appreciate your precision to detail, I think it would be okay to provide estimations. For expediencies sake." Zain interjected.

"Approximately eighty-five hours ago," Tom immediately amended, turning to look at Zain as if seeking approval. Zain grinned and nodded.

It was the last grin that would adorn his face for months to come.

"A complement of robotic military personnel departed Iceland ahead of the human soldiers. Our mission—"

"I apologize for interrupting again," Zain spoke in a hushed tone only meant for his RMP to hear. "But can you clarify the mission of the RMPs that left ahead of us?"

Tom's head tilted slightly. There was a pause—longer than usual. Then its speakers clicked off. "I do not have authorization to disclose that information." Its eyes dimmed briefly before adding, "The information in my database was altered just before the briefing; modified as need-to-know."

A pulse of frustration spiked behind Zain's eyes. He closed them for a moment, steadying his breath. Controlled. Measured. Then he gestured for Tom to continue.

Tom turned back to the soldiers and reactivated its speaker system.

"We will follow behind the RMP using a map in my database, and assist with cleanup and collection. Our departure is scheduled for zero four hundred tomorrow. Thank you for your attention. At ease."

The silence that followed wasn't confusion. It was dread trying to take root.

"That's all? That's the entire briefing?" Zain couldn't hide the disbelief in his voice, which did not go unnoticed by Tom.

"I too am surprised by the limited amount of information that has been provided to me about phase two."

Zain watched his RMP more closely now, noting the faint hesitation in its timing, the careful tone mimicking incredulity. It was mirroring him—calculating the correct emotional response to communicate more…human.

If Zain hadn't been so on edge, he might have found it fascinating. But right now, it only deepened the feeling that something had shifted beneath their feet, leaving him, again, on shaky ground. "How quickly can we catch up to the advanced RMP units?" he asked suddenly, voice taut.

"If we take a detour…" it began, eyes flashing as it calculated, "…and mark a waypoint for our intended arrival based on their current speed and…" It trailed off again, running scenarios in real time. After a minute, it looked back at Zain. "If we leave within the hour and travel without stopping, we can reach the RMPs' next destination in three days."

Zain didn't hesitate. "Gather supplies."

He turned, scanning the crowd for someone he could trust— someone who wouldn't flinch when things inevitably broke down. But before he took a single step, he stopped again.

He spun back toward his RMP, who was already packing a duffel with MREs.

"Tom, wait!" he called, crossing back toward him in three fast strides. "If we leave, how will the battalion know what is expected of them? They are also unaware of where to go since the map is only stored in your database."

"There is nothing in my directives prohibiting me from sharing this information with another RMP. Or would you prefer that I stay behind—"

"No, it's you and me, all the way." As soon as the words left his mouth, Zain took a step back in surprise. In the year since he'd been assigned this machine, he hadn't realized how deeply it had embedded itself into his life—not just as a tool, but as a presence.

He cleared his throat loudly and then continued, "I may need your assistance. Just find an RMP to relay the orders and directions to. I'll find someone to assume temporary command of the battalion."

"Zain," Tom said as Zain turned again to walk away. "Thank you for your trust in me."

Unstoppable

For seventy-two grueling hours, Zain drove his jeep to its limits, testing the endurance of both man and machine. The air inside the cabin grew stale and acrid with recycled breath, the kind of air that bred headaches and hallucinations. By the second day, his thoughts had become fragmented and coarse, broken up by the drone of tires against shifting sand. He'd surrendered himself—figuratively, though at times it felt literal—to Tom's cold, competent control. Without the machine's meticulous oversight, Zain wasn't sure he'd have made it another mile.

They reached the next checkpoint just behind the robotic military personnel units. The RMPs were already there, stationed like sentient statues on the horizon—waiting.

Tom adjusted his grip on the mounted rail, preparing to move forward, but Zain halted him with a firm command. "Hold up! As much as it rankles me to admit it," he confessed through gritted teeth, "we need a clear understanding of what we're up against. If these RMPs are anything like you used to be...they won't just spill their objective because I politely request them to." He paused for breath before adding, "And if they've been dispatched ahead of us to prevent human interference, as you suggested, they might not take kindly to my sudden arrival demanding explanations, even if I am the commanding officer of this battalion."

No sooner had he finished laying out his thoughts than they retreated discreetly back from the scene. From this safe distance, they watched as the RMPs spread out in tactical formation. Their visual sensors flickered rapidly like strobe lights in the darkening desert dusk.

The silence seemed to stretch on forever, but it was only minutes as the RMP seemed to share their commands inaudibly; the only sign of activity, the blinking of lights in the visors. The lights went from blinking to a steady glow and then the peace in the night was shattered.

The hair on Zain's arms and at the nape of his neck prickled ominously as shrill screams pierced the air. Not one or two—but dozens, erupting in a dissonant chorus that punched the air from Zain's lungs. The shrieks twisted, fragmented, and were swallowed just as quickly as they'd come, replaced by a silence far more horrifying than the sound that preceded it.

Not silence, Zain realized—*absence*.

An eerie, dreadful calm followed—as if the night itself were holding its breath. The RMPs, unhurried and unflinching, fell back into formation and disappeared over the next rise like nothing at all had happened.

For a moment, Zain couldn't move. His fingers curled involuntarily against the jeep's doorframe. His lungs refused to draw air. He stared at the hollow space the RMPs left behind, struggling against the part of himself that demanded he turn away, retreat.

Instead, he made his decision in a heartbeat.

"Give me the next set of coordinates!" he barked, jumping into the jeep as Tom moved to the rear, simultaneously feeding the data into the nav system. The moment he heard Tom click into place, he slammed the jeep into gear, the engine revving into a feral howl as the vehicle shot forward, devouring the terrain in frenzied bounds.

The wheels churned sand and stone, sending vibrations through his bones.

"If you don't ease off on that throttle," Tom warned, voice cutting clean through the storm, "you won't live to reach our destination." It paused, then added, "I may arrive damaged, but I will survive. I have run the numbers and we'll beat the RMPs even if we cut our current speed in half."

Zain's jaw clenched. He gripped the wheel until his knuckles bled white. But eventually—reluctantly—he eased off.

The speed dropped, but the tension didn't.

They thundered across the desert beneath a star-splintered sky. The heavens stretched vast and uncaring above them, every star fixed in its gaze like a thousand silent witnesses. Cold beauty above. Dread below.

He stole a glance at Tom in the rearview mirror. The machine hadn't moved. But Zain could sense that it felt what he felt—this wasn't just another mission. Zain refocused on the unforgiving desert landscape, his mind racing as fast as their jeep.

The connection between him and Tom had grown stronger with each passing mile; no longer just commander and robotic subordinate, but comrades in arms bound by shared adversity and poorly understood directives.

After driving for an intense hour, they approached the outskirts of the next city. The only indication of its existence was sparse lighting and towering structures silhouetted against the moonlit sky. Zain found the silence deeply unsettling and couldn't shake the thought that the RMPs had already passed through, but Tom assured him they arrived first. Glancing at his dashboard, he saw it was a little after three a.m.—a relief to know most people were likely asleep, which explained the haunting quietness.

"We've arrived," Tom stated softly, breaking Zain's contemplation. Zain's shoulders hunched as they rolled to a halt.

Zain took a long moment to scan the ghosted skyline. "The RMPs?"

Tom responded, scanning with unflinching precision. "Arrival estimated in ten minutes."

Zain nodded, tension winding tighter inside him. "Let's find a spot in the foyer of one of these apartment buildings."

With a nod of agreement from Tom, Zain steered the jeep into a narrow alleyway adjacent to the building. The shadows cast by the looming structure swallowed them, effectively camouflaging their presence.

Tom led the way as they entered through a seldom-used rear entrance that creaked ominously upon being disturbed.

Once inside, the dimly lit corridor stretched before them, lined with doors on either side. Zain felt the weight of his decision pressing down on him—every choice hereafter could mean life or death, not just for them but potentially for others as well. He followed Tom to an interior vantage point near the glass entryway where they could maintain a clear line of sight on both the street and the approaching RMPs.

They waited.

The minutes ticked by at an excruciating pace, each second stretching into what felt like an eternity as they waited in silence. Zain's fingers twitched restlessly at his side, while Tom remained eerily motionless, its sensors continuously scanning the environment.

Suddenly, Tom stood straighter. "Motion detected," it whispered with an almost imperceptible pitch change that Zain had learned to recognize as its version of tension. "RMPs approaching from the northeast, as anticipated."

Zain peered through the glass door at the approaching formation. Even behind cover, he could feel the raw power emanating from the robotic troop. It reminded him, uncomfortably, of predators closing in on prey. "Are you able to tap into one of the units from here? Find out precisely what their mandate is? I'm assuming, of course, that they have been given orders contrary to your own."

"Affirmative, the first link between all RMPs was broken and individual instructions were given to each unit. However, any attempts to access their data would be detected and reported."

"Damn, we need to know what these units were ordered to do and why they were sent ahead of their human counterparts."

"That is why we are here now," Tom answered. "Do you no longer believe that we can uncover their mission through this method?"

Before Zain could respond, the RMPs, situated at city's edge, began to fan out—just as they had before. Zain's stomach dropped.

He braced himself as the visors lit in unison—cold and synchronized—knowing, with chilling certainty, that people were about to die.

As the visors flickered into life, casting their synthetic glow against the surrounding buildings, Zain felt the world tilt—just slightly, almost imperceptibly. The light clung to the windows and asphalt like frost, silent and invasive. The street below was motionless, as if the city itself had forgotten how to breathe.

Then came the stillness.

It wasn't the peace of sleep or the hush of a windless night. It was the dense, charged quiet of something about to rupture. Seconds stretched, distorted by fear. Zain leaned forward instinctively, his breath shallow, his body braced, his fingers curling against the cold sill of the entryway. Even Tom, unmoving and impassive, seemed locked in that breathless suspension.

The tranquility shattered as a piercing scream ripped through the stillness, cleaving the air like a butcher knife. It was raw, shrill, unmistakably human—a cry that resonated with primal fear and desperation. Before the echo of the first had faded, another followed, equally intense yet distinct in its anguish. Then came a third, more frantic than the last. Soon, they multiplied into dozens— each one overlapping and blending into a cacophony of terror that filled every corner of the night. The air vibrated with their urgency; each scream a plea for help that seemed to claw at the very fabric of existence.

Each one punctured Zain's chest like a needle. One shriek, sharper than the rest, erupted directly from the apartment closest to them. Without hesitation, Zain spun and bolted. The hallway blurred around him as he sprinted toward the door, heart pounding so hard it felt like it might bruise his ribs.

He didn't pause. His boot hit the panel with a crack, and the door crashed open.

What met him inside stopped him cold.

A woman crouched on the aged wooden floor; her arms wrapped protectively around a child who couldn't have been older than six. The boy's small fingers gripped a shard of twisted metal with a desperate ferocity, raking it across his own neck. Crimson rivulets streamed down his spine, tracing chaotic paths before pooling in dark, glistening puddles on the uneven floorboards. His hands moved with an unnerving intensity, tearing into his flesh with a strength that seemed otherworldly for someone so young. Just beyond them, an elderly woman lay collapsed beside a worn-out armchair. Her eyes stared lifelessly at the ceiling, vacant and unseeing, as if frozen in time.

The mother was frantically trying to stop her son's hands, her screams blending with the child's cries in a harrowing duet of pain and panic.

Zain paused, his heart screaming in his chest, an echo of the terror before him. He glanced around quickly, desperately seeking something, anything, that could be used to distract or pacify the boy.

"Tom!" he yelled over his shoulder. "Help her!"

Tom, still at the doorway, moved quickly now—a swift, deliberate motion that belied its earlier stillness.

Zain gaze darted around the room until it landed on a small, battered teddy bear near the end of the couch. It was grimy and one-eyed, but he grabbed it, hoping it might just draw the child's attention from his determined self-inflicted harm. He raced over and knelt by the boy, holding the bear where he could see it.

"Look! See what I've got?" Zain's voice was gentle but slightly raised, trying to be heard over the mother's continued sobs and the boy's wails as he now fought against the grip that Tom had on his wrists. He kicked, landing blow after blow against his mother's chest.

"It looks like he's trying to excise something from his neck," Tom said, unshaken. "I'll see what I can do to help him. It will be difficult, but you must try to restrain him…if you can. I must analyze his neck and attempt to remove whatever foreign object is causing his distress."

Zain hurled the bear aside with force and wrenched the boy from his mother's lap, enveloping him in a suffocating grip with his powerful, muscled arms. The mother, overwhelmed by exhaustion and shock, collapsed backward, her eyes wide and frozen, as if seeing Zain and Tom for the first time.

The mother's voice cracked with desperation as she pleaded, "Help him, please, help him—." Her eyes were wide with terror, her hands trembling uncontrollably as she reached out toward her son. The world around her seemed to blur and spin, a nightmare unfolding in slow motion. Her heart pounded violently against her chest, each beat echoing the panic that seized her. She could hardly breathe as fear gripped every fiber of her being, leaving her paralyzed yet frantic for someone to save him from this unimaginable horror.

Zain clutched the boy, feeling every tremor, every panicked breath. The child's strength shocked him. He flailed, screamed, bit— his eyes wild, unseeing, locked on something inside himself.

"I must scan his neck. You need to hold him—"

"I'm trying my damndest!" Zain snapped, his voice quivering not with mere frustration, but raw, visceral fear. His grip tightened with desperation, the child's blood a slick, unsettling warmth against his palms. In a frantic move, he forcefully pinned the boy against his chest, pressing him close, and wrenched his chin downward with a brutal determination, allowing Tom an unimpeded view of the vulnerable expanse of his neck.

Tom's sensors shifted to a deep indigo, emitting a low hum from its structure. "A biological implant is present," it stated, observing through the self-inflicted wound. "The implant is either malfunctioning or has been activated externally. Removal is not feasible. I will proceed with attempting deactivation."

A slender, shiny tool appeared in Tom's grip, its metallic sheen reflecting the dim light as it moved with unwavering precision toward the child's neck. The boy's eyes grew wider, and he opened his mouth to let out a scream—a piercing, heart-rending cry that seemed to fracture the air around them, making the glass shiver.

Then there was nothing but the sound of silence.

The boy's small frame went slack, his arms dropping lifelessly to his sides as if the strings holding them had snapped. His chest stopped its gentle rhythm of rising and falling, leaving behind a haunting stillness.

Zain, suddenly conscious of the rhythm of his own breathing, released a shaky exhale and gently lowered the boy onto the cold, hard ground. The mother lunged forward with desperate urgency, gathering her son into her arms as if trying to shield him from an unseen danger. She cradled him tightly, her body rocking back and forth while she buried her face in his hair, tears freely flowing as she clung to the fading warmth of his small frame.

"That poor boy," Zain murmured softly, his voice barely audible over the mother's cries. "Thank you for deactivating it, Tom."

Tom's response was almost lost in the weighty silence that followed—low and filled with regret. "I do not believe that I succeeded in doing so."

Zain's gaze snapped back to the child with a jolt of fear. The mother's sobs transformed into a raw, guttural sound—a primal wail torn from deep within as her son's head lolled backward, lifeless and pallid against her shoulder. A violent twist knotted Zain's stomach as he watched helplessly.

"The child…he is no longer with us," Tom said in a flat, mechanical tone that seemed to echo off the walls like a haunting refrain. "His tiny heart likely could not endure the shock." Each word dropped heavily into the room like stones thrown into still water—heavy and irrevocable, leaving ripples of grief in their wake.

Zain sat rooted to the spot, his eyes fixed on the lifeless child before him. The sight of crimson smeared across his arms and hands sent a shiver through his spine, and he felt an icy numbness creeping in.

He swallowed hard, trying to muster the strength to stand up, to do something—anything—that might undo the terrible finality of the moment. But he knew that no amount of regret or action could bring back the small, innocent life that had been lost so senselessly.

Zain looked over at Tom, his gaze fraught with accusation and sorrow. "You said you'd help him," he murmured, the words thick with grief.

Tom's sensors dimmed slightly, a sign of concession. "I tried," came the quiet reply.

The silence that followed was suffused with an unbearable weight, the atmosphere dense with unspoken blame and anguish. The mother continued to hold her son, her body shaking uncontrollably with each sob that tore through her. Zain watched her, feeling a profound helplessness imbue his limbs with leaden weariness.

Slowly, he reached over and placed a hand on the mother's arm. "Is there...anything I can do?" His voice was barely a whisper, drowned out by the sound of relentless mourning.

She did not look up, her world reduced to the small, still form in her arms. Finally, she spoke, her voice ragged and raw from crying, "You can tell me what happened to my boy."

Zain clenched his jaw at her demand, finding himself at a loss for words.

He stood up slowly, and turned to face Tom, "You have to help me understand what happened here."

"I must conduct a deeper analysis on the implant," Tom responded. "To do so, you must extricate the child from its mother's grasp."

Zain eyes narrowed. "Purpose?"

"It may yield insight into its origin and intent."

Zain swallowed hard, his throat constricting like a vise, then stepped forward into the stifling atmosphere that felt as if it were suffocating him with its oppressive heat and weight. He knelt beside the woman, who remained protectively curled around her son, her frail form acting as a living shield against the world. His hand trembled as he placed it gently on her quivering shoulder, the sensation like touching delicate, fragile glass that might shatter at any moment.

"I need your son," he whispered, his voice barely audible over the pounding of his own heart. "We need to figure out what happened."

For a long time, she didn't stir, wrapped in a cocoon of silent despair. Then, slowly, her tear-streaked face turned towards him, a portrait of anguish and resignation.

"He was gravely ill," she whispered, her voice a fragile thread of sound. "I knew I would lose him eventually…but not like this. Never like this."

Zain struggled to keep his voice from breaking, the weight of her grief pressing upon him. "Could his illness have contributed?"

Before she could respond, Tom interjected, his voice cutting through the tension. "I do not believe the illness is related."

Zain's gaze drifted to the old woman, her death a quiet, almost serene departure, yet no less chilling in its finality. He turned back to the mother, watching her grief deepen with each word. "Was your mother also ill? When did she…?"

"Oh, dear God." Her eyes fell upon the lifeless body, and her face crumpled under a fresh wave of grief, as though her heart might not bear the weight of another loss. "She was…sick," she rasped, each word a struggle against the tide of sorrow.

Zain nodded solemnly, then turned to Tom, determination etched in his features. "Scan the older woman. If she has a chip…extract that instead. We're not prying this child from his mother."

"Understood." Tom scanned the woman's neck with mechanical efficiency. 'Object detected. Proceeding with extraction." It moved delicately, with a kind of grace that felt surreal in the face of such loss. As Zain watched, his stomach turned. He couldn't tell if it was horror or rage—or both.

From outside the apartment came more sounds. Screams. Wails. It was a cacophony of terror unfolding everywhere. Zain clenched his eyes shut, desperately trying to shut out the relentless onslaught.

Tom pivoted slowly, the small device clutched delicately between its two metal fingers, its surface glinting under the harsh fluorescent lights. Its mechanical voice broke the tense silence. "We should return to the jeep," it stated with an air of urgency. "This is not the place for analysis." The words hung in the air as they exchanged a knowing glance, understanding that lingering here would be unwise.

Zain glanced down at the mother, lost in her grief.

"There is nothing that can be done for her…for any of them," Tom interjected. "We cannot stop what is happening, until I know what is happening. We must go."

Zain closed his eyes and nodded. He wanted to stay but knew they had to leave.

They moved in silence, their footsteps echoing softly against the cold concrete floor as they retraced their path through the dimly lit corridors.

Once settled inside the jeep, Zain shattered the silence that had cloaked them. His voice was sharp with determination. "The timing of the inoculations and these implants…it's no coincidence." As he spoke, his gaze shifted to Tom, filled with both concern and conviction, hinting at deeper implications behind his straightforward statement.

"I cannot give you an answer, at this time, that would satisfy," Tom replied. "But if you wish me to speculate…"

Zain's mouth curled, humorless. "Go ahead."

"This device seems to be biomechanical. To reach its location at the cervical spine, it must have traveled through the bloodstream and then attached itself there. Its design is unlike anything I've encountered before, but appears to have a direct purpose. I believe it is intended to be activated to eliminate specific targets."

"That's quite a guess."

"Insufficient data precludes certainty," Tom said. "But I do not believe I am far off the mark."

"No," Zain said softly. "I don't believe you are either."

They sat in silence.

Then Zain added, "The real question is why."

Tom tilted its head. "My guess would be to kill."

Zain's eyes narrowed, "Okay, smart ass, but I think the real question is who's behind it and what do they have to gain?"

"The potential reasons are manifold and complex. Suggestions on how to proceed?"

Zain's voice was low, brittle. "You said we can't stop them."

"If we attempt to intervene, we will be terminated."

"People are dying…" Zain's thought trailed up as he fired up the jeep. "Plot a course back to the battalion," Zain said, eyes locked on the road ahead. "I have a feeling that this is just the beginning. If we don't figure out what's happening—before Phase Two ends— there may not be anyone left to save."

Three days later, under the scorching desert sun, Zain's keen eyes picked up the dust clouds of his battalion. They were advancing like a relentless tide between cities decimated by death left in the wake of the RMPs. The vehicles, their gunmetal gray surfaces glinting in the harsh sunlight, maintained a steady march that echoed with discipline and precision.

Zain's hand instinctively reached for his radio, worn and scratched from countless operations. He keyed in a familiar frequency and spoke into it, "Major David Reese, respond."

A moment passed before Zain's radio came alive with static before settling into a clear signal. A voice replied gruffly on the other end, "Major Reese here. Is that you, Colonel Belhasa?"

"Affirmative," Zain responded tersely, his gaze still fixed on the distant battalion. "I'm approaching your position from the Southwest."

A tense silence hung in the air before Major Reese's voice crackled back to life, "Got you on my radar now, Colonel. I'll give our boys a heads-up not to mistake you for target practice."

"Much obliged, Major." Zain ended his transmission with a curt sign-off: "Belhasa out."

From behind him, through the open canopy, came Tom's voice; it was calm but laced with an underlying urgency. "Zain," it called from his position at the rear of their rugged jeep. "I must speak with you."

Zain eased off the accelerator slightly to dampen the howling wind whistling past them as they cut through the desert landscape. He turned his body slightly without taking his eyes off of their path ahead and asked: "Can we keep moving, or do you need me to stop?"

"Keep going," Tom replied.

"Will do. What's on your mind?"

Tom began carefully: "I think we need to tread lightly here." Its tone was serious as it continued: "While I have considerable freedom in terms of my Adaptive AI protocols, my operational parameters are strictly regulated by command and control. If anyone should detect that I am acting outside of orders, I could be recalled for reprogramming, dismantled for internal diagnostics…any number of things over which I have no say."

Zain nodded, understanding the stakes. "Same here. If command decides I'm a liability, they won't hesitate to relieve me of duty, strip me of my rank, and even court-martial me. So, if I'm reading you correctly, you're saying we need to investigate discreetly without raising alarms."

Tom confirmed with a simple: "Affirmative. That would appear to be in our best interest. Especially since there seems to be a persistent cloud of suspicion hanging above our heads."

"So, no going into any situation, guns blazing." Zain quipped dryly, adding: "This mission is going to be a tightrope walk. Especially if we unearth something that doesn't sit well with the higher-ups."

Tom responded in his typical analytical manner: "Is there not a human adage, 'hope for the best but prepare for the worst'?"

"Yeah," Zain replied grimly as he accelerated their jeep back up to speed, "but in this case, I suspect we'll be doing more preparing than hoping."

A flicker of curiosity sparked in Zain's eyes, a contrast to the stoic expression he usually wore. They were nearing the battalion, but his gaze was drawn to the imposing silhouettes of large machinery scattered amongst the troops. He turned towards Tom, seeking an explanation for this unexpected sight. "Where did those come from?"

"I do not possess enough information to provide a satisfactory response," came his succinct reply.

Without wasting another moment, Zain swiftly snatched up the radio. His fingers danced over the buttons with practiced ease as he keyed in Major Reese's frequency and called out into the void, "Major Reese, please respond."

The crackle of static filled their ears before it was replaced by Major Reese's steady voice. "Major Reese here, Colonel. I'm assuming that you want me to signal my location."

Zain shook his head even though he knew Reese couldn't see him. "Not required, Major. We can meet up to transfer command when we reach our next destination." His gaze wandered back towards the massive machinery looming ominously against the setting sun. "Speaking of which, how far out do you have us?"

"We should reach the city limits in forty-five minutes," came Reese's prompt reply over waves of static interference. "Is that all, Colonel?"

"No," Zain responded firmly. "When did the large excavating equipment arrive? And what in God's name is it being used for?"

"The equipment arrived on a transport plane less than half hour after you departed base of operations," explained Reese through bursts of static and white noise filling their connection. "As to what they're for, I prefer to brief you in person, Colonel."

Zain nodded, his features hardening into a determined mask as he responded with a concise: "Understood. Belhasa out." Zain tossed the radio back onto the seat next to him and drew in a deep breath. The next forty-five minutes were going to be interminable.

It only took ten minutes for Zain to catch up and pull alongside the advancing battalion. For the next thirty-five minutes, he focused on keeping his thoughts in check, reminding himself to not make assumptions too quickly.

The battalion slowed to a crawl as they reached their destination on the outskirts of their target location. Zain continued to drive until he reached the lead vehicle carrying Major Reese. As soon as his jeep stopped, Major Reese hopped out, the settled dust swirling around his boots. He cut a commanding figure, his uniform clean despite the desert's attempts to tarnish it. Without waiting for formalities, he strode over to Zain, extending a firm handshake which was quickly reciprocated.

"Welcome back, Colonel," Reese greeted with a slight nod. "I'm glad you made it back in one piece." He held back from mentioning that he had no idea where the Colonel had rushed off to a week ago and had been worried about his safety during the radio silence.

"Likewise, Major," Zain replied, glancing over at the large equipment that had just come to a stop. "Can you fill me in on what's been happening?"

"Of course, sir. But given our tight schedule, might I suggest we get the soldiers started first? The sooner they begin their tasks, the quicker we can move on."

Zain wanted to object, but he couldn't justify delaying the mission any longer. He allowed the major to take his final moments in command and watched as he signaled for the men to unload and start their duties. Then, he motioned for Zain to clear a path. "Shall we load up in your jeep and move it off to the side, sir? We're too close to the equipment."

Without responding, Zain climbed into his vehicle and waited for the major to join him. He glanced back to yell for Tom to attach but saw that it hadn't moved from its spot, which was unusual since it usually detached as soon as the vehicle stopped.

Tom's uncharacteristic stillness raised a flicker of concern in Zain's mind, so he called out, "Tom, you still with me?"

Tom abruptly came to life, as if shaken from a deep contemplation. "Affirmative, Colonel," it replied, oddly formal.

Zain's brow arched, but he figured he could only address one concern at a time, "Good to hear. Hang on, we're going to move out of the way of the troops." With a firm grip, Zain shifted the rugged jeep into drive, pulling it away from the frenzied hubbub of activity. The dust kicked up by the tires hung in the air like a veil, obscuring the grim reality of their situation momentarily. As soon as he found an isolated spot and parked again, he swiveled in his seat to face his RMP.

"Tom—" Zain began, but before he could finish, his RMP's voice cut through the silence.

"Audio and visual disengaged."

A soft sigh of relief escaped Zain's lips. "Thank you, Tom. He then pivoted to address the major. His gaze was hard but not unkind as he asked, "What have you been using the construction gear for?"

An almost bitter laugh escaped from the major's lips. "Not for construction, that's for certain," he scoffed. The sarcasm lacing his words was as palpable as the tension in the air. "They're for burying the casualties," he continued somberly. "Although we aren't certain just what caused such a massive number of deaths. It can't be from that infernal disease plaguing our world right now…right? After all, weren't those inoculations supposed to shield us? And they certainly weren't those who dared defy military orders during that time since those people were executed immediately. Even more confusing is how the upper echelon knew in advance of the death toll. Otherwise, how would they have known to dispatch the backhoes…" His words trailed off into silence and his gaze dropped to his hands—roughened by years of service and stained with dirt and sweat. "Quite frankly, Colonel," he finally admitted in hushed tones, "I'm at a loss to explain this catastrophic death toll."

Zain watched him pensively before replying dryly, "Didn't sound like it to me."

The major's gaze snapped back to Zain, a hint of desperation in his eyes. "Are you saying that you didn't know anything about this either, Colonel?"

Zain met his gaze evenly, "I wouldn't be sitting here quizzing you if I did," he replied, then turned his attention back to his RMP. "Tom?"

"That's a negative, Colonel," came the assertive response from the machine.

Zain nodded slightly, absorbing the implications of their grim tasks ahead. He shot a questioning gaze towards Tom, but the RMP appeared not to notice. He took a moment to compose his thoughts before speaking again. "Major, it's clear that there are higher powers at play here—powers that prefer to keep us in the dark." His voice was calm but carried an undertone of frustration. "Our best course of action is to comply but stay vigilant. Meanwhile, I expect you to fulfill your duties as if all of this makes sense."

Reese nodded in agreement, the weight of the situation settling deeper onto his shoulders. "Yes, Colonel," he said solemnly. "Oh, and one more thing I failed to mention…"

Zain sighed when the major's voice trailed off, "Collecting your thoughts, Major? Or your wits?"

"A bit of both, to be honest, sir."

"Alright, spit it out. It can't possibly be grimmer than the inexplicable sea of bodies we're meant to be burying from one city to the next."

"Indeed, sir. We've received directives to…well…order all capable individuals—which, essentially means every living soul left—to gear up for duty."

Zain's head swiveled as if he was grappling with comprehending the words just delivered to him. It wasn't as shattering as the sight of dead bodies strewn across cities, but it was equally perplexing. "Pressing civilians into service? What on earth for?"

"I'm afraid I don't know, sir. Just like with the other, the details haven't been disclosed to me…and evidently, not to you either."

Once more, Zain turned his gaze towards his RMP, "Tom?"

"That's a negative, Colonel," Tom reiterated.

Zain's eyes were drawn back to the barren landscape where shadowy figures of workers moved like specters in the ever-rising temperatures—digging graves that would soon cradle an untold number of bodies. The scene was unsettlingly surreal—a harsh divergence from the usual bureaucratic explanations and protocols.

He then swung back around to face Reese. "Major, I believe it's prudent that this discussion remains between us. Our soldiers are aware of their assigned tasks, and since we're in the dark, it's a high probability they are also. I think it's best if they remain uninformed.

The last thing we need is panic or wild rumors spreading faster than wildfire.”

“Understood, sir,” Reese responded crisply.

“If that’s all, major. You’re free to return to your duties.”

As soon as the major walked away, Zain climbed out of the jeep and headed toward the yawning pit. The machinery groaned nearby, but something else was drawing his attention now—faint shapes scattered along the ridge ahead. Civilians. Survivors. He hadn’t registered them at first—just shadows against the horizon. But now, as he drew closer, he saw that many weren’t just watching.

They were mourning.

A woman collapsed to her knees just beyond the temporary cordon, hands clawing the dirt as she rocked a child wrapped tightly in a worn blanket. Her mouth opened, and a sound tore from her that cleaved the silence. It wasn’t a cry—it was a rupture. A sound dredged from the bottom of a soul.

She wasn’t alone.

Dozens more had gathered. Men standing slack-jawed, clutching bundles. Mothers who held nothing at all—arms empty, eyes vacant. Some wept openly, inconsolably. Others stared like statues at the churning haulers, at the soldiers unloading the dead as though it were just another task on a daily roster. Among them, a teenage boy stood rigid, fists trembling at his sides, his shoulders rising in rhythm with suppressed sobs that never quite reached his throat.

The noise of grief was jagged and aimless—wailing, whispering, dry heaves. No unity. No comfort. Just raw, fractured agony.

Zain’s stomach turned.

He stopped a few paces from the pit; breath lodged in his chest. His vision swam as the hauler's bucket lifted, and then—like refuse—the bodies slid down the trench wall. Bodies, big and small. Some still curled as if sleeping. And this wasn't the only pit. There were dozens more scattered around the city limits, and just as many mourners had gathered to say goodbye to their loved ones.

A soldier's hand reflexively twitched toward her weapon belt as one of the corpses shifted in the fall, seemly still alive. Zain almost shouted—*it's dead, don't shoot*—but held back. Realizing that the soldier was responding in a knee-jerk reaction and after a moment, hands visibly shaking, she returned the sidearm to its holster.

The sight of it all struck Zain like a ton of bricks. He couldn't feel his legs, though he knew they were threatening to buckle beneath him. His hand found the edge of the hauler for balance, gripping it so hard the metal bit into his palm. Sweat dripped from his temple, and yet he was freezing.

This isn't war, he thought. *This isn't anything I was trained for.*

Tom's quiet steps approached from behind, but Zain didn't turn. He didn't want the machine to read his expression, not yet. Not until he was able to compose himself…if only a little.

"I…" Zain began, then stopped. His throat tightened painfully. He needed to say something, anything—*just to not be here.*

He cleared his throat, still facing the pit. "So, what was with all the formality in front of the major?" His voice was hoarse, brittle, the words pulled like splinters.

"I do not think it is in our best interest to advertise our relationship."

Zain gave a hollow laugh, then wiped his face with the back of his sleeve and finally turned to Tom. "Yeah. Yeah, I get that."

Tom tilted its head. "Are you well, Zain?"

"No," Zain said quietly, "but I will be."

He looked back one final time at the mourners. A woman had slumped sideways, sobbing into the dirt. No one came to move her. No one dared interrupt.

Zain took a step back, then another.

"Come on," he said, voice firming as he turned fully toward Tom. "Let's walk," he muttered. "Just need a minute to remember I'm still a soldier."

Tom walked beside him in silence for several steps, the servos in its joints whirring softly against the desert quiet. Then, almost gently, it said: "If I were human…I do not think I would want to remember that."

Zain didn't respond right away. He just kept walking, jaw set, eyes fixed on the horizon. The scent of dust and grief still lingered in the air behind them, but he didn't dare look back.

After a long silence, he exhaled and asked, voice low and ragged, "You think this was the plan all along?"

Tom turned its head slightly. "Please clarify."

"The deaths. Phase two."

Tom was quiet for a beat before answering. "From a purely analytical standpoint, the observable operations—systematic and multiphasic—suggest that whomever is orchestrating this may have anticipated large-scale casualties…or caused them."

The implication hung heavy in the air between man and machine. "Caused them," Zain echoed, feeling the weight of the statement. His mind flashed through previous briefings, marked more by what was unsaid than what was disclosed. "I don't think I need to ask whether we'd find chips in these corpses necks."

"I have no doubt that they all have chips," Tom confirmed. "Just as certain as I am that you do also, as well as every living individual on the planet."

Zain froze, momentarily petrified that his death could be imminent. Tom, sensing his fear, spoke words of comfort, "If you were going to be affected, you would have been when we were watching that boy fighting for his life in Julfar."

The tension slowly left from Zain's body and he turned to face Tom, "deactivate my chip. Now! And get it out of my body."

Tom didn't answer right away. Its head tilted slightly, as if calculating the best possible response. But Zain wasn't waiting. His gaze darted to a discarded shovel lying in the dirt—dropped by a soldier too shaken to finish his task.

Zain snatched it up and hurled it with all his strength at a nearby transport truck. The clang of metal against reinforced steel rang out like an explosion.

Dust flew. Soldiers nearby flinched.

"I said get it out!" he shouted, voice cracking. "I don't care how. I don't care if it kills me." His chest heaved. Rage rolled off him in waves, but underneath it—raw, unmistakable—was terror. Not fear of death. Fear of *control*. Of having a kill switch buried inside him all this time, like a lamb tagged for slaughter.

He stared at the pit, jaw clenched so tightly it ached. The bodies weren't just casualties—they were *targets*. Taken without warning, without cause. Lives cut short by something buried beneath their skin.

"They didn't even know it was coming," he rasped. "Didn't stand a chance."

His throat tightened, the question clawing its way out. "Were their deaths sudden, or did they fight it…with everything they had—like that boy in Julfar? So small. So young. But God, he fought so hard." The image hit him again—those eyes, wide with panic, his tiny limbs thrashing against death as it closed in. Zain had watched it happen. Helpless. Paralyzed. "Was it like that for all of them?"

He didn't want an answer. Not really. Not if it meant picturing thousands—millions—dying the same way, suffocating on their last breath, helpless to stop death coming for them.

His hands shook. He dug his nails into his palms to stop them. "We followed orders. Trusted the chain of command. And now…" He glanced back toward the grieving families, then reached up slowly, fingers brushing the back of his neck—where the chip sat buried beneath his skin. "The only difference between the living and the dead…our chips haven't been activated…yet."

Tom stepped forward, arm half-raised in a gesture that mimicked concern. "Colonel—"

Zain turned on it. "Don't you dare try to reason with me. Not right now. I've buried friends. I've buried family. But this—this is something else. This is *calculated genocide.*"

His voice fractured on the last word.

For a long moment, neither moved. The desert seemed to hold its breath.

Zain's voice dropped to a whisper, barely audible over the dry wind. "I want it out. Get it out, Tom."

Tom's tone was steady, almost gentle. "I will do everything in my power."

Zain closed his eyes, jaw tight, shoulders trembling as Tom silently scanned the back of his neck, sensors clicking softly in the stillness.

For a long moment, neither spoke.

Then, Zain opened his eyes—not calm, not composed, but changed.

"Just get it out," he growled. "And I swear—if I live through this, I'll make them choke on every life they thought they could erase."

The Spark

The night was settling in now, pulling shadows from under the earth—much like the secrets they were unearthing.

As Zain turned and walked slowly back toward his jeep, the edges of the sky bruised into violet and rust, his thoughts remained fixed on the trench behind him. A trench now filled—*stacked*—with the bodies of those executed without cause. Executed without warning. It wasn't warfare. It was quiet, sanctioned slaughter.

He moved on instinct, boots crunching over the packed dirt. His chest felt too tight. Every breath scraped like it was trying to drag truth up from somewhere deep. The civilians pressed into service. The new directives. The mechanical indifference of the RMPs. All of it screamed of something darker still unfolding.

He climbed into the jeep but didn't start it. Just sat there, his hand brushing the edge of the bandage at the back of his neck. The skin still itched. It would for a while. He remembered Tom's hesitation—the machine had paused, scanning, recalculating risk.

If an RMP decides to scan you to ensure you are chipped, the resulting outcome could be devastating—to us both.

But Zain had pressed him. Had told Tom that living with the threat of the chip was no different than being murdered for *obedience*. Better to be hunted for rebellion than silently erased while standing in line.

The surgery had been done in silence. Zain hadn't cried out. He'd only stared at the mass grave as the chip was extracted.

Now, the silence wrapped around him like the night itself. He rested his head against the seat, eyes closing—not from sleep, but from the sheer weight of knowing too much and being able to say nothing.

Tom didn't speak. It simply idled nearby, its systems humming, breaking the stillness of the night.

An hour passed.

Somewhere behind him, the crunch of boots against loose gravel approached—deliberate, reluctant. Zain didn't open his eyes. He didn't need to.

"Colonel," came Major Reese's voice, tired and frayed.

Zain sat up. The weariness returned to his eyes as he studied Reese—who stopped a few feet from the jeep, hesitating like a man about to touch a live wire.

"All buried," Reese said quietly. "But…um…I…"

Zain's eyes darkened. His words snapped before Reese could finish: "We're all weary, Major, so if you've something else to say spit it out."

Reese stiffened. "It's nothing, sir. Do you want to pull out immediately?"

"Have the soldiers ready to depart at sunrise," Zain said, voice as steady as steel. "Make sure everyone eats…and rests."

Tension visibly drained from Reese's frame. "That'll come as a relief to everyone, sir. We've been running on fumes for the past seven days."

Zain blinked, his expression hardening, his already thinning patience on the verge of snapping, like a frayed rope. "Do I want to know why?"

Reese's posture straightened, but his voice faltered. "Instructions came down from high command when we received our heavy equipment shipment," he said hesitantly. He glanced toward the desert's edge, expression tight. "We were told to stay hot on the RMPs' trail to prevent…well…with this scorching desert heat, the work will become even more unbearable when bodies start decomposing—"

"That's sufficient information, Major," Zain cut in sharply, lifting a hand to stop him.

There was a long pause, thick with unspoken tension.

"I don't care what orders came down," Zain added quietly, but with finality. "We don't keep pushing men past their limits to serve commands with no moral compass. They rest tonight. Understood?"

Reese drew in a slow breath and gave a grateful nod, as if released from a silent burden. "Yes, sir."

"You're dismissed, Major."

Zain turned in his seat and looked toward Tom, still stationed like a sentinel beside his door. Their eyes met, and Zain gave a slight nod.

A soft flicker passed through Tom's interface. The hum of its systems shifted slightly as its auditory and visual monitoring disengaged.

Zain finally exhaled. "Tom," he muttered. "I'm nearing my breaking point with all this subterfuge." His hand clenched the steering wheel. "The mounting death toll…the cryptic orders. We bury them, and then what? March on and pretend we don't know what's happening?"

Tom did not respond at once. It processed the moment like a machine built for precision—but the silence that followed felt… human. After a moment, he said, "May I propose something, Zain?"

Zain gave a dry, humorless laugh and rubbed his eyes. "That's exactly what I'm hoping for."

Another silence, heavier this time.

"Maybe the moment has arrived," Tom said, "for us to take a stand."

The statement lingered in the heavy stillness of the night, wrapping itself around him like the desert air—thick, dry…uncomfortable.

Zain didn't answer immediately. He looked away, jaw tight, mind racing through a thousand contingencies he didn't yet have the clarity to define. He wasn't a man prone to dramatics, but this wasn't strategy—it was survival. And worse…it was morality. Somewhere between the deaths and the graves, his orders had lost meaning.

"We can't keep marching to someone else's drumbeat, blindly following orders that haven't a shred of reason," he said finally, the words issuing on a growl of hostility towards the unseen adversary. "We can't stand idly by while innocent lives continue to be taken."

His hands clenched tightly on the steering wheel, grip white-knuckled and unrelenting. "I'm ready," he said, the words cold and deliberate. "To take this as far as we need to."

Tom's sensors pulsed faintly, processing. "I propose we leverage our assigned mission parameters to subtly alter our course of action," it began, voice low and precise. "We divert from the explicit instructions while maintaining an appearance of compliance. We begin by gathering more intelligence discreetly and establish a network of trust among those we deem trustworthy."

Zain leaned back slowly, his eyes narrowing as he weighed the proposal. It wasn't mutiny—not openly. Not yet. But it was dangerous, a slippery slope. A single misstep and they'd both vanish into the same kind of grave the soldiers had just finished filling.

Still…doing nothing was no longer an option.

After a long silence, broken only by the wind scratching across the jeep's frame, Zain nodded once. "Where do you suggest we find these unlikely allies? Certainly, you aren't suggesting that we try to coerce members of this battalion into committing treason."

Tom's interface dimmed, then brightened again—a flicker of calculated irritation. "Not coercion, Colonel. Persuasion. We cautiously identify those who are already questioning the orders—those who feel the dissonance between their duty and their conscience. We offer them a cause that aligns closer with what they believe to be right. We can also recruit civilians, more of whom will likely bear malice against what is being effectuated against them and their families." It paused. "Is that not when you began to question your loyalty to service, Zain?"

The words hit hard.

Zain turned away, his shoulders tensing. The heat of the day was gone, but sweat still beaded along his brow. His voice, when it came, was low. Raw. "Yes," he admitted. "Had they not ordered me to execute..." The rest of the sentence dissolved into silence.

Tom didn't push. Instead, it pivoted. "It only takes a spark to start a fire in someone, Zain." The words hung there, suspended in the dark. "Isn't that what Melyndie told you?"

The name stopped Zain cold. The mention of Melyndie made his heart thud painfully behind his ribs. "Something like that," he murmured.

The memory emerged unbidden.

"Can dissent be cultivated?" she asked finally.

"I think that's a given. It develops over time—through pain, injustice, exposure to people who see the world differently. Like a flame is kindled and fanned into fire."

"And sometimes all it takes is a spark from someone else's fire to start your own."

"Exactly."

He didn't speak for several moments. Then, finally: "So, we act as the spark for others," he said softly, almost to himself.

Tom's head turned minutely. "And the window to do so is rapidly closing as more people die each day."

"We may be unable to save them all," Zain said.

"No," Tom replied. "But we can potentially save many."

Zain let that truth sink in. He had once believed saving *some* wasn't enough. Now, he realized it was the only way forward.

"I must admit, Tom," he said quietly, "this…this act of perfidiousness is not something I ever expected…"

"From a cybernetic being?" Tom finished.

"Even from one with an advanced integrated adaptive AI system," Zain added.

"Perhaps it is something that I learned from being in your company this past year," Tom quipped.

Zain snorted, surprised by the brief flicker of warmth that pierced the surrounding dread.

A silence followed—not strained, but solid. A kind of understanding had settled between them. Not trust, exactly. Something deeper. Camaraderie forged not through design, but survival.

He leaned forward again, resting his arms on the steering wheel, hands clasped tight. The desert no longer felt quiet. It felt watchful.

"If we're committed to this…if we're really going to do this," he said, voice barely above a whisper, "then we need to be incredibly careful about how we proceed. Our actions must be methodical. Guarded. We can't afford blind rebellion. Mistakes could cost lives—ours included."

Tom's lights flickered once in acknowledgment. "I understand, Zain. We must also bear in mind that trust will be our greatest asset—and our biggest liability."

Zain nodded grimly. "And information—our weapon and our shield."

A silence, deep and resonant, settled between them—not empty, but brimming with everything unspoken. Beyond the jeep, the desert stretched outward like a wound that refused to heal. And somewhere beyond the reach of their headlights, the fires of rebellion began to smolder.

PHASE THREE

"The only way to deal with an unfree world is to become so absolutely free that your very existence is an act of rebellion."

Albert Camus

The river ran red at dawn.

Melyndie stood at its edge, the current carrying away ash, splinters, and fragments of lives torn apart. Behind her, the town lay in silence, its walls cracked, its streets abandoned. Too many had fallen. Too many were still missing.

She wrapped her jacket tighter about her, but it did not ward off the chill that came from within. Zain's words still rang in her ears—warnings of betrayal, of shadowy figures that walked among them. She had wanted to dismiss them. Now, she wasn't so sure she could.

On the far bank, figures emerged from the mist. Not soldiers. Not villagers. Something other. They moved with a confidence that chilled her blood, as if they already owned the land beneath their feet.

"Melyndie!" A voice called from the ruins, desperate, insistent. She turned, torn between the call of loyalty and the threat rising across the water.

The world had fractured, and every choice would splinter it further.

And in that breathless pause before action, she knew—some battles would be fought not with guns, but with trust.

Author Bio

Barbara is the author of 29 books across multiple genres, formerly published under Barbara Woster, B.J. Woster, and B. Woster. An educator with a Masters in Early Childhood Education, she crafts layered, character-driven stories that invite readers deep into their worlds. Barbara shares her life with her two cats, Kookie and Ellie, and treasures the love and support of her four daughters, who remain central to her life and are her inspiration. Her works continue to explore imagination, humanity, and the ties that bind us. Learn more at **BarbaraPelhamAuthor.com**.

Titles, written prior to 2025, as last name 'Woster'

CRIME THRILLERS (B.J. Woster):
36 Hours (psychological crime thriller / a Detective Hardwick novel)
Killing Faith (international crime)
Edge of Insanity (paranormal crime)
Seeker of Justice (psychological crime thriller / a Detective Hardwick novel)

ROMANTIC Thriller/Comedy/Drama (Barbara Woster):
Desires of a Deceiver
Fate's Intervention
Only One
Whispers of the Heart
Love Through Time
Dreamer of Destiny
Victim of Love

SCIENCE FICTION (Barbara Pelham):
3-book series:
Melyndie: a75b99r84GE (book one)
Zain: The Before Time (book two)
Melyndie & Zain: Shadows of Dissension (book three)

EARLY READER/MIDDLE GRADE (B. Woster):
Ehtaria: a land of their own
I Am Proud of Who I Am: I hope you are too (15-book series)
The Purple Christmas Tree

NONFICTION (Barbara Woster):
Parenting in the 21st Century: a horror story

All titles @ BarbaraPelhamAuthor.com